WIN, PLACE, OR DIE!

The screams were Human, to be sure, and they were screams of panic. And to Alexander's eyes, the cause of those screams was a moving nightmare.

The creature was wolflike, but yet not. Human, but not. It was as if the two had been blended together in one unholy mating. It rode astride a beast that was twice the size of a horse, but wilder and fiercer.

There were a half dozen of the creatures mounted on their nightmare steeds, and he could hear their voices as if they were laughing in triumph. Each was armed with a lance, and one carried a Human female under its arm. It was from her the screams came.

Alexander flexed his bow, and in an easy, fluid motion he nocked an arrow and let fly.

Already a second arrow was nocked, aimed, and away. The creatures slowed their attack and turned to face their unseen tormentor.

"I think, Parmenion," Alexander said, "you'd better ready your pike and prepare to receive cavalry."

By William R. Forstchen
Published by Ballantine Books:

The Ice Prophet Trilogy:
    ICE PROPHET
    THE FLAME UPON THE ICE
    A DARKNESS UPON THE ICE

INTO THE SEA OF STARS

The Gamester Wars:
    Book One: THE ALEXANDRIAN RING

Book One of
The Gamester Wars

The Alexandrian Ring

William R. Forstchen

A Del Rey Book

BALLANTINE BOOKS • NEW YORK

FOR OWEN LOCK
TRUSTED EDITOR, ADVISOR, AND FRIEND

Bring me a map and let me see how much is left to conquer all the world.

—MARLOWE

CHAPTER 1

CORBIN GABLONA LEANED OVER THE DINNER TABLE, sweeping the precious dinnerware onto the floor. "Here was the Carthaginian position."

He picked up half a dozen diamond-studded spice shakers with his large, beefy hands and laid them out in a line. Knowing that he was the center of attention, Corbin smiled happily at the ten Humans and half-dozen Gavarnians who sat around the dinner table.

"These are the feared Numidian horsemen." Several of the Family heads nodded in appreciation. Corbin then picked up a decanter of Malady Ambrosia and waved it in the air.

"This, why, this here is Hannibal." He laughed softly, so that his one hundred and sixty kilos shook like a wave-tossed jellyfish. With a dramatic flourish he placed the decanter in the center of the line, facing the upturned wine glasses that represented the Roman infantry.

"Now, what can we use for that Roman general—what was his name?"

"Scipio Africanus, you mean."

Gablona looked up at the speaker. "Ah, my dear Bukha Taug. I'm impressed that a Gavarnian would have known such an obscure fact."

Bukha smiled from the other side of the table, even though a Gavarnian smile usually signaled that someone was being considered for dinner. "Why, Corbin, even a Gavnar, and particularly a Gavnar of Koh status, is expected to know something of alien history. But, my good friend, your Hannibal was second rate, truly second rate."

Two Gavarnians came up to Bukha's side as if in support of their friend. All three of them smiled. Their forward canines glistened in the candlelight. The nap of their pelts stood on end.

"So you think Hannibal was second rate?" Zola Faldon interjected in his high rasping whine, ready, as always, when facing a "Gaf," to defend any Human, right or wrong.

"So you think Hannibal was second rate?" Bukha replied in a fair imitation of Faldon's whine, which was the more comical coming from a heavily furred creature two and a half meters tall. His fearful appearance was offset by his being the worst dresser of a species noted for being among the least stylish in creation. Bukha was wearing one of his more conservative outfits—a polyester jumpsuit of electric blue, accented by hot yellow stripes.

"You might not like my voice," Zola snapped back, "but by all of space, I wish you Gavarnians could do something about your damn musk. This place stinks like a kennel."

"You Humans don't smell any better. No wonder your ancestors and mine hated each other on sight."

"Ah, now those must have been the days..." one of the Humans replied, and there was a general murmur of agreement around the table.

"We could settle our own differences then." Another Human sighed wistfully.

"No damned Overseers," a Gavarnian growled from

the other end of the table, while he poured a drink for the Human sitting next to him.

"Yeah, those damned holier-than-thou Overseers," shouted the sole Xsarn, who was stretched out on a couch in the far corner, six tentacles wrapped around a covered feeding trough that none of the others dared look into. The Xsarn pulled its feeding tube from the trough and waved it in anger. However, as such displays usually resulted in a Xsarn's regurgitating its most recent meal, the diners shouted for it to stop.

"Come now, gentlemen, my fellow Kohs," Corbin interjected as he produced a bottle of brandy and a box of cigars from the sideboard and passed them around the table. "Let's be realistic. By the greatest of coincidences all three of our species discovered the transspace jump point into the Large Magellanic region at nearly the same time. Why, it was the greatest planet-grab in history, and the devil take the hindmost. It was fabulous—but somewhat bloody, I daresay."

"Ah, those truly were the days," the Xsarn replied.

"Easy for us to say today," said Sigma Azermatti, the oldest and richest of the Humans present. "It was also one of the biggest bloodlettings ever. We scrambled for the few places the First Travelers hadn't already mined and stripped. Why, we slaughtered each other by the tens of millions, and you're *nostalgic* about it? You Xsarns are crazy."

"The death of the one is meaningless," the Xsarn replied, attempting to sound superior.

"If we tried to kill you now," one of the Gavarnians interjected, "you'd drop that meaningless line, and damn fast."

"Gentlemen, no violence please!" the Xsarn shouted. "After all, we in the Magellanic Cloud are civilized now."

"Precisely my point," Sigma responded. "We're civilized beings now. The fighting in this region of space shattered trade and isolated hundreds of millions on planets that could support agrarian economies but lacked the sig-

nificant natural resources for higher tech levels. It was rare
to find a planet in this Cloud that the First Travelers had
not completely exploited hundreds of thousands of years
ago; with the collapse of trade support due to the war, this
entire region reverted. I thank the heavens the Overseers
came through here when they did and forced our forefa-
thers to come to peace. Otherwise all of us would be living
like our barbarian cousins on the majority of planets in the
Clouds, rather than sitting here aboard Corbin's yacht."

"Does this mean," Corbin interjected quietly, "that
you've converted to the Overseers' nauseating preachi-
ness and will no longer join us in an occasional wager or
game?"

"No, of course not," Sigma replied quickly. "But I am
saying that 'the good old days' weren't so good. The
Overseers were quite simple and direct—they abhorred
violence so they put a stop to all technological forms of
mass destruction."

"Holier-than-thou pious bastards," the Xsarn interjected.

"Bastardy is impossible for you Xsarns—you're
asexual," Bukha replied with a smile.

"Come now, gentlemen," Sigma continued, "their
high ideals have kept the peace in space for nearly two
millennia. They're even gaining control over some of our
interspecies fighting on the primitive worlds. By keeping
such fights local and forbidding our involvement in any
way, they keep us from escalating local conflicts into in-
terplanetary wars like the last one, which nearly destroyed us all. Gentlemen, if it wasn't for the peace
imposed by the Overseers, we wouldn't be sitting here
drinking brandy together, I can assure you.

"If they pulled out of this corner of space tomorrow,
we'd be back at each other's throats before a standard
year passed." No one responded, and Sigma looked
around the table triumphantly.

"You know that nineteenth-century earthside is my
specialty," one of the Gavarnians responded, "and I

daresay Sigma does have a point. We're like the nobility of Europe during that time. We speak each other's languages, we drop by for visits with each other and share the refined things that civilization has to offer. If those poor fools had had the Overseers to keep the peace, they might've been able to save their civilization from the twentieth-century wars. We, at least, do have them, no matter how much we dislike their paternalism."

"Thank heavens at least for the games," Bukha interjected. "They've yet to catch us doing that, at least, or else we'd all go crazy for a little action."

"Xsarnfood, those damned Overseers are Xsarnfood," a Gavarnian muttered, then nodded in the direction of the insectoid in the corner. "Apologies, my old friend, but you know what I mean."

"No bother, no bother at all," the Xsarn replied. "But, gentlemen, I don't see why you view this excellent dinner of mine with such loathing. Why, the stuff you Humans produce is like a rare vintage to us—especially when you've been eating spicy food. And as for Gavarnian—"

"Shut up!" the others roared together. The Xsarn dropped its head, realizing that a discussion of Xsarnian cuisine was not appreciated by the present company, even though they were its producers.

"I must say," a short, red-pelted Gavarnian next to Corbin replied, "I much prefer sharing brandy and cigars like gentlemen to ripping each other's guts out."

"Good chap, good for you!" Zola interjected. They all nodded their heads and congratulated one another on being so gentlemanly about such things.

"All right, Corbin," Gragth said at last. "I've enjoyed the socializing, but you didn't drag me fifty light-years just to look at my hairy face and hear me toast my siblings and curse the Overseers. What is it then? Are you organizing a game, because if so, by the memory of my brothers departed, we need one! It's been a little too peaceable of late."

"A game—did I hear someone say a game?" Zola

called in reply. An expectant hush fell over the room as all eyes turned on Corbin. The Xsarn stopped its meal, grabbed a scented towel, and wiped off its feeding tube to join its companions around the table.

Corbin sat back and gestured. Those around him fell silent. With a dramatic flourish he lit his cigar, took a long pull, and then exhaled the smoke in a shimmering blue ring.

He pointed up to the ring and smiled at his own wit for starting his proposal in such a novel way. "Remind you of anything, gentlemen?"

"You mean the smoke?" Zola asked.

"No, not the smoke, I mean the shape of the smoke." Silence reigned for a moment.

"You refer then to the Kolbard, the ring-world of the First Travelers?"

"Very good, Azermatti Koh," Corbin replied, and he placed a slightly sarcastic emphasis on the word "Koh," an honorific used only by Family heads controlling more than a hundred worlds or planetary consortiums. "You, of course, have seen before the others. Yes, I am referring to the Kolbard."

"And what in hell is the Kolbard?" Yeshna Veder, who was second only to Bukha in the Gavarnian hierarchy, asked in his soft silken voice.

"I can understand your not knowing," Bukha interjected to spare his friend a sarcastic reply from Corbin. "It's on the other side of the Cloud from you. In fact, it's nearly three thousand light-years in, toward the home galaxy and several degrees off the plane of approach. No resources worth exploiting."

"Thank you, Bukha. I couldn't have said it better myself," Corbin replied as Bukha came around the table to sit next to him. Bukha nodded to Corbin as if prompting him to say something.

"Ah, yes, maybe I should point out that . . . well, you see, Bukha and I got together on this little idea a couple of years ago, or was it longer than that, my good friend?"

"No, quite right. Make it about two years standard. But rather than hear it from me, perhaps there is somebody waiting here who can explain all this better than I."

With a dramatic flourish Corbin pushed at the paging disc on his wrist. The doorway at the far end of the room opened to reveal a short, rotund Human and a tall, slender Gavarnian. The Human's hair was gray and thinning, combed forward in a vain attempt at covering the balding top. He might have been slender once, but that was long past. His stomach bulged and he had the ruddy complexion of someone accustomed to taking his entertainment in liquid form. But intelligence gleamed in his eyes.

The Gavarnian next to him was obviously of an advanced age, since his pelt was going to white. But his dark, almond-shaped eyes mirrored a sharp, eager mind. His suit was a subdued combination of orange and gray stripes; for his race, a being of impeccable taste.

"Aldin Larice and Zergh Tumar," Zola shouted with glee. "Then it's going to be a game after all!"

Aldin smiled and nodded in Zola's direction. "I thought that after losing three hundred–odd worlds to Corbin in your last bet you'd curse the day you saw me again."

The others laughed good-naturedly at Aldin's comment—the way beings have laughed throughout the ages when an expert in their favorite sport makes a joke, even when the joke is on them. Aldin was a vasba, a professional battle and simulation arranger, and considered by many to be the best in the entire Cloud.

Aldin smiled in his tight-lipped way, reached over, and, without asking permission, poured himself a half snifter of brandy, knocking most of it back in one gulp.

There, *that's* better, he thought, trying to calm himself. Good stuff, that Ralindin Brandy, far better than the stuff he could afford. He wanted to let the tension build a bit more, but didn't dare push it too far. The men admired him for his grasp of Terran military history stretching all the way back to its legendary origins on Earth, but they were still the most powerful men, Gavarnians, and Xsarn in the Magellanic Cloud, and as such were not beings to be trifled with. Accidents for enemies, real or imagined, were not unknown—even in the days of the Overseers.

Aldin placed the snifter to one side and smiled. "Most honored Koh Gragth, in your estimate, who in the history of the origin planet of my species was perhaps the greatest general?"

Gragth of the Esag Consortium flashed a wide, frightful grimace. Snifter in hand, he rose from his chair and looked across at Aldin.

"My personal favorite was Saladin," he replied smoothly. "Now *there* was a Human who understood how a Gavarnian makes war. I could also mention Ali al-Gadah, but his little campaign wound up destroying half of your planet; and besides, his own country was radioactive and heavily cratered by the time it was over. But of all my favorites of Earth history, the greatest general would have to be Alexander. We Gavarnians admire him not only for the way he made war but for his own reckless courage, as well. He was the stuff of legends, as if touched by the gods. And know that even today many of us, including myself, believe that the Unseen Light does single out some beings for great things, for so it was once said by Kubar Taug. I think you humans call it the Great Man Theory of history, where it is postulated that occasionally a truly great man of exceptional worth is born, his destiny—to rule."

Aldin looked around at the table and quickly took over the conversation, for he could see where half a dozen others were about to advance their own favorite theories regarding who was best, along with the various pros and cons of the great man theory. "Thank you, Koh Gragth, for such a well-phrased analysis. I am gratified that you mention Alexander, for he is the subject that I wish to discuss."

"Then you plan to make a simulator of Alexander for our gaming pleasure—is that it?" Zola interjected enthusiastically.

"Not exactly."

"Then why are you here?" the Xsarn asked. "You are the best procurer of primitive battles in this region of space, otherwise Corbin wouldn't have locked you up with that lifelong exclusive contract. Now Corbin mentioned the Kolbard—have you found something there? Come on and explain yourself, Aldin—I care not for riddles."

Aldin smiled; he had their undivided attention. "Gentlemen, would you be at all interested in betting on Alexander the Great?"

"A computer simulation of Alexander?" Azermatti inquired.

"No, most noble Koh, I mean Alexander the Great for real."

"Just what in the name of my most beloved food are you talking about?" the Xsarn asked excitedly.

"For half of my lifetime we've known the location of old Earth," Aldin replied. "And the location of Lhaza, the Gavarnian home planet, has been known for several generations. Therefore, at the request of Corbin and Bukha, my colleague Zergh and I have been out exploring time."

Sigma was already nodding eagerly. The old fox has guessed what's coming, Aldin thought. He gave a nod of recognition to the eldest Koh.

"But what good is that?" Zola asked. "We've found half a dozen nexuses of time distortion, to be sure, but none is near enough any place of interest. They're just like space-portal jump points, ninety-nine percent of them are off in some half-ass corner that isn't any good. Lucky for all of us that we found the dimensional jump from our galaxy to the Cloud, otherwise we'd all still be back there."

"Damn it, Zola," Bukha replied heatedly, "it was we Gavarnians who found that jump point first, and you Humans just sneaked in behind us."

The Humans all started to roar back at Bukha; the issue of who arrived in the Cloud first was still a source of contention. Only when the Xsarn threatened to add its shockingly fetid breath to the shouting did they finally calm down and return their attention to Aldin, who, wearing a patient look of disinterest, sat through the storm with his friend Zergh.

"If we could continue, gentlemen, I would like to state that Zola was right about time jump points. The vast majority of them are useless. You can only go through for a brief period and the effect is local. The hardest trick has simply been to learn how to control the points so that you can get a fix on the exact moment you wish to enter. After all, what the hell good is there in jumping through time if you can't decide where you want to go?"

"You've found a time nexus in near-Earth space, and you've learned how to control it!" Azermatti said.

Aldin nodded in acknowledgment.

The Family heads broke into a wild flurry of excited conversation, and Aldin caught Corbin's eye. The rotund Koh was beaming with satisfaction. Corbin had spent nearly a billion katars and Bukha another billion on the research, and they were about to cosponsor the greatest gambling event in the history of gaming.

Corbin stood up and extended his hands. "Gentlemen, gentlemen, *please*! Bukha and I have a little announcement: we wish to propose a game, a betting arrangement unlike any in history. Gentlemen, would you please lend your attention to my master vasba, and he'll explain the gaming scenario. And remember, gentlemen, we aren't talking about a simulation, we are talking about a game unlike any in the history of games."

Aldin bowed in acknowledgment to Corbin and the rest fell silent again, eager to hear the new wrinkle to their oldest, longest-lived passion—military history combined with gambling. A century past, Corbin's father had doubled his holdings in one day by wiping out the Demano Family in a bet centered on a simulation of Crécy that they had managed to arrange between two tribes on a primitive world. Thus had started the rise of the mighty Gablona fortune.

The legendary battles of Earth held the Humans' particular fancy. Earth was no more, having been destroyed in the war between the Humans and Gavarnians—and thus their nostalgia for it was even greater. With the outlawing of warfare by the Overseers, nostalgia over the pageantry of ancient times held sway among the Cloud's ruling classes. On many of the primitive planets, as well, memories of humanity's distant heritage were still kept alive across millennia and light-years beyond imagining. The same was true for the Gavarnians and Xsarns, who had lost their home planets in the war, as well. The ruling classes in the Magellanic Cloud came to know their worlds of origin's battles and strategies the way other ruling classes once demonstrated refinement by their knowledge of horses or operatic arias. And in such a society a master vasba, though technically still of the lower classes, was a man who could sit and share a drink with aficionados who held the most exalted positions.

"Gentlemen, the wager will be on the real Alexander the Great, brought across five millennia to fight again."

"But my dear vasba," Sigma interrupted, "if memory serves, the legendary Alexander died in 323 B.C. from malaria or poison, and our records show that he did not have any long, unexplained absence. Now, to the best of my knowledge, the theory of the indestructibility of the past has been fairly well proven. How do you expect to retrieve him, since you cannot alter the past?"

"A most excellent question, Azermatti Koh. However, you should look again at your Arrian. For it was written that Alexander retained his lifelike appearance for many days after his death. And—here is the interesting point— his body was left alone in a sealed room for some time while his generals argued about the succession.

"Now, gentlemen, I propose that he was, for several days, in a deep coma after the doctors of his time had already pronounced him dead. Therefore I shall take my vessel through the time nexus then transport down to the chamber where his body lies in state. It will be a simple matter to take his body measurements and then leave a replication in his place. The people of his time will never know the difference, and the theory of the indestructibility of the past will not be challenged in any way. History records that his body was taken to Egypt. I belive that the body was indeed someone other than Alexander."

"This is absolutely remarkable!" Zola cried. "You mean to bring back the real Alexander for a game?"

Aldin nodded.

"But for what game, and where?" Gragth responded. "Now I do confess that such an event would interest me, but at the risk of sounding ethnocentric, I must state that, as a Gavarnian, I do feel a little left out."

"Ah, the best question of all," Corbin said, as if waiting for the Gavarnian protest.

"How so?" the Gragth replied.

"I think I could ask any Human here who was the best of the Gavarnians, and the response would be the same."

Corbin looked at his fellow Humans and, as usual, it was Zola who responded first.

"Now, there might be some room for debate here," he said with a professorial tone, "but I think we'd agree it would have to be the Great Uniter of all the Gavarnian races, Kubar Taug, who disappeared after the battle of Oaertam. He went up to the mountain of prayer with his standard-bearer and never returned. I daresay that he just might have taken a trip longer than any the ancient Gavarnians could ever have imagined."

It was Gragth who grasped it first. "You mean to say that you've not only found a time nexus near Earth, but one near our home, as well?"

"It is true," Zergh said, finally breaking his silence. "I was there. It is possible that soon we shall all see the Great Unifier, Kubar Taug. Neither Corbin nor I could visit the time frame of our proposed generals, since it appears that crossing a nexus once sets up a pattern of disturbance that does not settle for years. But we are confident that both Kubar and Alexander can be taken and, in fact, we plan to do so within the month."

"I had mentioned the Kolbard somewhat earlier," Corbin continued, in spite of the excited conversations going on around him, "and through a little research we've discovered several interesting facts. The ring, as you most likely know, is several million kilometers in diameter and nearly five thousand in width. Much to my surprise, it is a fertile location for our little wagers, for it appears the Overseers are not even aware of it. Certainly none of their patrols has ever ventured by for a visit."

"To know what the unknowables do, that is a new form of power, and mysterious to us all," Yeshna interjected.

"Let's just say I prefer my sources stay anonymous for right now," Corbin replied. "Nearly two and a half standard millennia ago Humans, Gavarnians, and Xsarns settled that unique world created by the First Travelers. But since it was artificial, there were no raw materials. The naturally formed worlds all have something by way of ores and minerals, but this realm has nothing to help a tech-level rise. Currently half a hundred conflicts go on around the ring's periphery. The fools have no real skill in such things, and as a result, the best of the fights are nasty but inconclusive. Metal is scarce and therefore highly valued.

"On one of the smaller continents an ugly little war is going on between Gavarnians and Humans. It's been waged inconclusively ever since the Great War, which nearly shattered all interspace commerce and cut off thousands upon thousands of settled worlds. It really isn't even a war, just an endless series of raids, usually by the Gafs— excuse me, Gavarnians—against a completely degenerate Human population in desperate need of a leader. The cultures are unique, as well; the Gavarnians are a fair approximation of the twelfth dynasty, the time of Kubar himself, while the Human side is similar to Novgorodian Rus. Alexander is known to them, a part of their legends of the Old-World Gods. That conflict will provide fertile ground for the two beings to forge new empires.

"I might also add that, as a test of the Great Man Theory of History, it would be interesting to observe two individuals who must start with nothing and rise up again to positions of power."

"Fascinating!" Sigma exclaimed. "A true test of the theory at last."

"And, of course," Zola interjected, "we'd be doing the poor sods down there a service by ending the war for one or the other, rather than let it drag on forever."

Most of them were not sure if Zola's comment was sarcasm or not, but they all nodded dutifully and muttered polite platitudes about helping out the less fortunate creatures in their universe. Having thus reassured themselves about the moral implications of the game, they turned back to Aldin.

"Therefore, gentlemen," Aldin continued, realizing that Corbin had finished his little monologue, "I propose that we send Alexander and Kubar there. The people of the region are aware of their historical past; both species view their heros as beings from the legendary golden age of the past."

As he finished, the would-be bettors were so excited that they immediately shouted agreement and demanded to be included. Corbin and Bukha smiled at each other; as organizers of the event, they were entitled to five percent of all winnings. From the enthusiasm visible, before the betting was done they would likely collect five percent of everything the other families owned.

"Of course, there has to be a game controller to insure honesty and fair play," Sigma interjected.

"Ah, yes, but of course," Corbin replied, reminded of an inconvenience he wished had been overlooked. "Since its national pride, shall we say, is not involved, might I suggest our good friend the Xsarn?"

The Xsarn rose up as if to give a speech, but remembering its manners among non-Xsarns, it simply nodded an affirmative rather than subject its companions to an extended sampling of its breath.

"It should receive the standard one percent, as well," Sigma stated.

"Outside our five, of course," Bukha replied.

"That's not the standard way," Sigma interjected.

"But our expenses in organizing the game and doing the time research were beyond imagining."

"Oh, I can just imagine," Sigma replied sarcastically.

"But to show we understand and do appreciate what you and Bukha are doing for us, shall we say a quarter-percent each from the two of you, the other half-percent to be assessed against the bettors."

A mumbled chorus of agreements rose on that point, as well.

"May all Overseers kiss our hairy behinds, for a game is on!" Gragth shouted and raised his glass in a toast.

"Actually, sounds rather appealing to me," the Xsarn replied as it slipped its feeding tube into a half-empty brandy bottle.

Corbin gazed around the room as his fellow Kohs drained their drinks and cried out with delight at the prospect of the most exciting game that had ever been offered.

The royalty fees alone would make him rich, and his stature in the history of gaming would be forever untouchable. Of course, he'd make a killing in the game, as well. The betting would follow chauvinistic lines, Gavarnian and Human betting according to race, but Corbin had another angle, and before the game was over, he'd have the bettors cleaned out, especially Sigma. He nodded toward his hated rival while finishing his brandy.

"So, they brought it all," Aldin said to his companion as they walked back through the corridors of Corbin's yacht in a frustrating attempt to find their suite. Corbin loved mazes; some of the corridors in his new gaming yacht had been designed to amuse him.

"Left here," Zergh muttered.

"No, it's right."

Zergh, shrugging his massive shoulders, decided not to argue, and followed his old friend until Aldin finally gave up.

"There is one thing though," Zergh whispered cautiously despite his jammer. A good vasba always wore a jammer; a gaming bettor would go to any length for inside data. Bugging the food was not unknown.

"What's got you worried now?"

"All of them, every last one of those rich bastards. This will be the biggest game in history. I know you Humans are habitual liars and cheats, and I suspect the Koh will do anything, including murder, to win the fortunes that will be wagered on this one. Aldin, I said in the beginning this project was a little too big, it will bring out the worst in you Humans."

"Oh, thanks for the compliment," Aldin replied evenly as he stopped in confusion at a ten-way three-dimensional corridor intersection. He finally decided to take a hard right.

"There's one question you've yet to answer for me," Zergh said softly, looking around suspiciously. "That fat slob Corbin cheated you blind on your commission for the last game. That's nothing but Xsarnfood when he claimed the winnings you invested were lost in a freighter accident. His royalty statements are the longest lies in history. As his exclusive vasba, you're supposed to receive ten percent of all *his* game earnings after expenses. You've made him billions but what have you got to show for it? Thirty years of service to that bastard, and when payment time comes something has always gone wrong, or those lying thieves called accountants have doctored the books. And then like a damn fool you still take the contract for this Alexander venture that he offered you."

"It looked interesting," Aldin replied quietly.

"Interesting. Listen, my friend, maybe it's because I'm a Gaf, and we have this thing about pride and honor. But by my three brothers, if on top of all of that someone had seduced my only niece and heir, and then turned her into a brazen court mistress, well, I'd—"

"I would prefer you don't talk about it. I'm a vasba, a game procurer, and the Alexander contract will be the biggest event in the history of gaming. So please don't trouble me with prudish Gaf honor. Tia's nineteen years old, it's her life. The money, well, I was foolish to trust him, and that's that."

Aldin stopped at the next intersection and looked around. "I think I've been here before," he whispered.

"Only the third time. Now follow me for a change. Do you actually think you can trust him, this time, to deliver your ten-percent cut of his fees for arranging the game? I know my Bukha is good for it, but you know about the honor of Gafs."

"Considering my current credit rating and how my creditors rearrange one's appearance when not paid, I can only hope that Corbin's good for it," Aldin said wearily.

It was always the same, Aldin thought, with Kohs such as Corbin, who were the new breed of wealth coming up. In his own father's time, a gentleman was a gentleman. But Corbin was one of the new rich, like Yeshna of the Pi to Infinity Consortium. They were the damned new breed of money before everything, without sense of honor, family breeding, or scruples. To them a vasba was amusing to be around, but was still a servant in the family court.

"Anyhow," Aldin said wearily, "I made the mistake of marrying one of the Gablona cousins; you can imagine what my alimony payments are like."

Now that had been the craziest move of his life. He had been young, trying to rise above his station. She had married him because, for a while, it had been fashionable for women to marry "tradesmen." The fashion passed and the divorce had followed and Corbin took insane delight in reminding him of "dearest Edwiena" at every opportunity, pointing out to him her latest indiscretion.

"So, my good friend," Aldin said, trying to force a smile, "love the Gablona dynasty or not, I need a job."

Turning the next corner, the two came up to a blank wall.

"I can't stand that man's idea of fun!" Zergh shouted in exasperation.

"If Corbin plays this game as I think he will, that will be an understatement," Aldin replied coldly.

CHAPTER 2

"REALLY, ALDIN, I CAN'T SEE WHY YOU MUST SNAP YOUR commands at me. After all, do remember my station!"

Exasperated, Aldin turned and looked at his niece. "Listen, Tia, just because you are Corbin's mistress doesn't mean that I've got to speak to you in a tone of reverence. You were my apprentice long before Corbin laid hands on you. I know he wanted you on this trip just to make sure his investment in Alexander was not tampered with, but I am still running the show."

Tired of the eight-hour running argument, Tia figured the last statement simply wasn't worth responding to. She made a third check on the deep-range scanning system, reconfirming the adjustments to their nexus jump. They were still blaming each other for the "little miscalculation," as Tia put it, that had caused them to appear a thousand years off in time and thus lay the groundwork for a radical departure in a nomadic tribe's religious philosophy. Thinking about that caused her anger to boil up again.

"And another thing, Uncle," Tia snapped, "remember you yourself said that the past cannot be altered. Therefore it must have been preordained that you appeared on top of the mountain in front of that old guy. Don't blame me for it—just count yourself lucky I snapped you back up here."

"Just shut up. It's lucky for me I remembered the story so I didn't foul things up." Aldin was feeling guilty about that one. He had debated whether to land a couple of days later to try to clear everything up, but that just might make matters worse. He regretted, as well, that he hadn't tried to omit a line from the stone tablets, perhaps the one on adultery...

"Are you sure that the date is right this time and that we're orbiting at the proper position?"

"Care to check my instruments?" Tia asked in a hurt tone, as if she had just been accused of lying or wishing to cause yet another little mix-up.

Aldin got up and leaned over Tia's chair to double-check the data. All instruments indicated that they were in geosynch above Babylon on the morning the histories claimed Alexander died. The calculations were relatively easy since the records indicated Alexander's passing as eight days before the summer solstice of 323 B.C. and twelve years after a major lunar eclipse in Anatolia. With that information punched in, the ship's navigational system simply had to calculate the date in relation to the relative positions of the Earth, the Moon, and their angle to the sun.

He hoped that Zergh would have the same success. Lhaza had no moons and the astronomical records for the twelfth Gavarnian dynasty were far from complete. There was no way of communicating with him since they were in different time periods a thousand light-years apart.

Satisfied with the nav reports, Aldin left Tia to her job and went back to check on their passenger.

Opening the doors to the medical bay, Aldin took one

last look at Wiyger Luciana, a former plastacement contractor for the Gablona Family. Aldin had met him on several occasions to discuss minor bets, and lost on all of them. A rumor was floating among the Family retainers that Wiyger had built a substandard foundation for Corbin's palace on the ice world called Vol. Of course, Corbin and Luciana, Inc., had publicly agreed that the collapse of the palace was due to a freak summer storm, an unfortunate occurrence for the three hundred Family retainers who froze to death.

Aldin looked closely at the corpse. He hoped that the build and height were relatively close to those of Alexander. Once he and Tia had obtained the data, it would be fed into the medicomp, which would alter the body and deliver a full replication within twelve hours. Then the retrieval would simply be a matter of switching the bodies.

To pull it off, Aldin thought, and here came the difficult part. Arranging primitive combats and computing odds was his business, but he was about to enter Alexander's palace to steal the body while the successors were already coming to blows in the same building.

He was terrified. He had been tempted for weeks just to bolt on the whole arrangement, but Wiyger was an instructive object lesson for anyone who wished to cross a Koh. He had tried to talk Corbin out of it, but that had been useless.

"After all," Corbin had replied smoothly, "you did sign the contract."

"But I thought that you'd hire someone else to actually snatch Alexander."

"What, and run up even greater expenses? Your contract stated that you were to design and implement the project, so start implementing and stop whining."

"But I'm a vasba!" Aldin ventured bravely. "I simply arrange the game and calculate the bets."

"Go back to your contract and read the fine print,"

Corbin said. "If memory serves, section Y, paragraph three."

"Couldn't we renegotiate?"

Aldin turned away from the corpse and returned to the forward cabin. "Better get on your traveling robes."

"Couldn't you make them of something other than wool? It chafes my skin."

"I'll chafe your skin—the skin on your butt with the bottom of my boot."

"If my Corbin heard you address me like that . . ."

"I know, I know. But Corbin isn't here, and since he asked me to train you as a gaming consultant, train you I will. Now, is your speech implant working?"

"*Agricola puerum amat.*"

"That's the farmer loves the boy, and you're speaking Latin. Remember, just think that you want Greek and it will automatically slip into your neural processes and have you thinking and speaking in the appropriate language. Within a couple of minutes the synapse link will merge into the language and you won't even notice the difference from your normal speech. The damn thing's worth a hundred thousand katars, so for heaven's sake, don't get clunked on the head and smash it up. Otherwise it comes out of my expenses. All right, try it again."

"I bear greetings and gifts from the philosophos Aristotle to the king. Trained in the mysteries of the Delphi, I have been sent to my lord Alexander in his hour of need—"

"Fairly good. Let's just hope the accent is correct, that's one thing I'm afraid we can't know till we land. Remember, if their Greek sounds strange, just explain to them that we're originally from a trade post near the Pillars of Hercules. The implant will quickly register the difference and automatically alter your speech process."

"It will all still be Greek to me," Tia replied. She jumped beyond the range of Aldin's kick.

* * *

"Are you set, Tia?" Aldin could see that even the usually unflappable Tia was nervous at the prospect of transjumping down to ancient Earth. The youngster had a touch of the hypochondriac about her, and in spite of the vaccinations Tia was absolutely terrified of bubonic plague and the common cold.

"Just remember, if you get a runny nose, use your sleeve."

"I jolted up on a megavac, just in case."

"Let's hope your megavac is proof against a Macedonian sword." And before Tia could cry an objection, Aldin punched the stone on his belt buckle, activating the relay to the ship's transporter system. He experienced a momentary blackout as his molecular structure disintegrated.

It was the hour before sunrise and already the eastern sky was washed by the early light of a purple-blue dawn. Beneath the walls of Babylon his consciousness returned in a moment of disorienting blindness and pain that was typical of a beam jump.

Instinctively he felt his body, making sure that everything was still present. The beam jump had been perfected a millennium earlier, but like many another traveler he still had his doubts, fearing that one day he'd come through with a body part missing or attached to the incorrect region.

Raising his head, he made a quick recon of the area. As near as he could estimate, the ship's computer had dumped them precisely on location, in a small ravine near a minor gate, where an infrared scan had indicated that no one was about.

"Tia?"

"Over here."

In the early-morning shadow, Aldin could barely make out his niece. He should have darkened the jump-room to aid his night vision, but it was too late to worry about that.

A faint cool breeze stirred the reeds along the canal bank, the canes rustling and sighing with a gentle hypnotic swirl. Good, Aldin thought. There *should* be a special feel to the time when a legend is breathing his last. The moment should have a magic, a gentle stirring within that awakens an awareness of some deeper link with destiny. Aldin tried to reach out and feel that moment even as the morning breeze wafted across the open fields, carrying with it the first stirrings of a city about to awake. Enthralled, Aldin climbed to the edge of the ravine, his eyes adjusted to the light, and looked out to the walls that girdled Babylon for a score of miles.

"The Xsarns would love it here," Tia whispered. "Take a whiff of that breeze."

"Ah, shut up! You sure know how to kill a moment."

"I mean, *smell* it! Damn, I never thought a place could stink this bad."

"Come on, let's walk to the gate," he said, the romance of the moment having evaporated. "It should be opening soon." Even as they stepped out onto the road, the world around them seemed to stir with life. The greatest king in history might be dying, but for the multitude it was a day that still had to be lived. Dung- and reed-fired meals were being prepared along the roadside as hundreds of travelers, who had arrived beneath the walls after the closing of the gates, prepared to enter the greatest city of the once-mighty Persian empire.

In preparation for a day of trading beyond the gates, merchants were soon setting up their stalls along the side of the road, and their shrill cries filled the air.

"What a cacophony. You'd think these people would at least have the dignity to wait for dawn before getting started," Tia complained.

"Think of speaking in *Greek*," Aldin whispered in reply. "Remember, the language implant will work properly only if you think *Greek*. Start doing it now and it should be an unconscious act within minutes. These Greeks and Macedonians are rather snobbish about their language—speak anything else and you lose face with them. Remember that."

"I'll try," Tia replied, her response, in Greek, shaky but passable.

Aldin felt for a moment that bringing her along might have been a mistake, but if worse came to worst it would be good to have someone to cover his back. Hoodwinking the Macedonian successors to Alexander might look easy on paper, but it would be quite another thing to pull off. Even as they practiced their Greek in whispers, the gate of the city was before them, and the guard, a Macedonian by his uniform, did not seem in the best of moods as he shouted curses at the waiting line of people.

Aldin quickly surveyed the scene and as he did so a single horn sounded in the distance. In an instant it was picked up by another and yet another. Stepping back from the brooding height of the city walls, Aldin could see columns of smoke rising from the top of the ziggurats within. The ascending swirling clouds were tinged with fiery red, reflection of the first light of dawn, which now broke across the open plains and marshes to the east.

The crowd around the gate grew silent for a moment, some of them going to their knees and bowing to the east, while others extended their hands to the heavens and cried out their greetings to the dawn. And the gates that stood twelve meters tall swung back, as if guided by the hands of giants unseen.

"Let's go," Aldin whispered, and he started forward, joining in with the pushing, jostling mob.

"Do you know where we're going?" Tia asked.

"No."

And without another word Aldin walked up to the Macedonian guard, a soldier well past his prime. The guard duty was likely a bone thrown to the old soldier who could no longer keep up. As Aldin drew closer he saw that the man was missing part of his nose. An ugly scar had been gouged upward from the missing part to an empty right-eye socket. Whatever the man had tangled with, it had taken a good part of him away with it.

Aldin's heart was pounding. For his entire life ancient soldiery had been a question of academic speculation and a source of data for gaming. He was about to speak to a man who might have served with Alexander from the beginning, who might have stood in the phalanx at Guagamela, or charged with his leader across the Granicus. This was a man who had truly *been* there.

"Excuse me. Ah, I'm bearing a—a greeting from . . ."

"Step aside there, you're blocking the road," the guard shouted in a barely recognizable dialect.

Tia hurried to Aldin's side. "Let me take care of it," she whispered.

Tia minced up to the guard, whose bulk made it appear as if a Bathsheba were approaching a Goliath. "Who is your hegemon?" she barked.

The guard stared coldly at Tia.

"*You*, yes, I'm speaking to *you*. *Who* is your hegemon?"

"Aristophane. Why?"

"Then I would suggest, soldier, that you get him. My companion Cleitius and I are envoys from the famed Aristotle, sent with a gift for the king."

The guard looked closely at Tia and his military bearing started to slip. "But my lord Alexander, he's dying. With the others I marched past him but yesterday, and I saw. He is dying."

"Do you know of Aristotle?"

"He whocedon. He was the teacher of my lord."

"Then you know he had many special powers. We might be able to help our king if you do not delay us. But if you do cause delay, I would not want to be you when the truth is learned."

The guard looked to his companion who was listening

to the conversation, and there was a quick nod of agreement.

"Follow me," the guard said eagerly, and he pushed a way for them through the shouting dust-covered crowds shoving through the city gate.

Tia gave Aldin a quick wink and a self-satisfied nod, but when she glimpsed Aldin's expression of extreme distress, she quickly imitated him.

Once they had passed through the massive bronze gates, the guard turned into a squat, mud-brick barracks hall. Following his lead, Aldin stepped in after him, where he was assailed by the smell of unwashed bodies, dung fires, cooking food, and leather. It was a rich heady smell that made him slightly dizzy.

The guard stopped before a bunk where a short barrellike soldier lay stretched out on a rope-weave bed.

"All right, just what the hell is it now, Parmenion? You're the most shiftless son of a mutilated dog that has ever cursed my presence. Besides, you stink like an Egyptian sewer." The man groaned as he opened his eyes and looked at the guard.

In a nervous and excited voice Parmenion started to explain. Aldin tried to follow the conversation but it was held at such a rapid clip that it was difficult to run with. He hoped that his implant would analyze the data and learn to function in the proper dialect and faster.

As Parmenion spoke, the noise in the room died down and Aldin noticed that the other men were staring at him.

In short order the three were back out on the street with Parmenion leading the way down the main avenue, which approached an area of the city devoted to the myriad of cults and religions that prevailed in the Persian Empire at that time.

A feeling of anxiety seemed almost palpable, and the shrines were crowded. For the Persians were old hands at that sort of thing. The death of a king and civil war were synonymous, and most expected that the streets would run with blood as soon as the bronzed warrior from the west breathed his last.

Aldin noticed, as well, that more than one cast a hostile gaze upon him. For a moment he feared that his origins must somehow show. Parmenion somehow sensed his anxiety.

"'Tis nothing personal, you see. They expect that we'll be at each other's throats, and some of their throats might get in the way, if you get my meaning, if the worst should happen and the great king goes to his fathers."

Aldin noticed a genuine note of pain in Parmenion's voice. So the legends are not legends, Aldin thought, the men must truly love him. The Greek or Macedonian soldiers that he passed *did* have a dazed and distant look to them.

They crossed a great square that was strangely empty, and Aldin sensed that they must be approaching the palace. A low wall in front of them was pierced by a single gate and, approaching, he could hear wild shouts of confusion from the other side.

A heavy guard was posted at the gate, but one of the men, recognizing Parmenion, waved them through.

In the courtyard beyond, men ran to and fro shouting wildly, some walked in shock with unseeing eyes. Others, weeping in anguish, were shaking their fists at the heavens. Some stood in groups and gazed suspiciously at any who drew close.

"I fear it might be too late." Parmenion groaned. "Too late." And as a heavily armed soldier raced past him, he called out a sad greeting. "Ho, Antonilius, how goes it within?" He gestured toward the Persian palace that occupied the far end of the courtyard.

"He speaks not. He slips away," the man cried and ran on.

"Quickly," Aldin cried. "Perhaps we can still help."

He pulled Tia closer. "As soon as they think he's dead, the arguing will start, there'll be mass confusion. We'll never get in if they think there's no need for a physician. I'll divert their attention. You hold the scanner in your palm like a medallion and point it at him. The computer will gather the data and do the rest."

"What's that?" Parmenion asked, his voice edged with suspicion.

"Nothing of importance to one such as you," Tia snapped.

"Now, now," Aldin replied, playing the opposite role, "don't berate the guard—caution is his job. I was merely reminding my friend to pray with her sacred medallion, presented to her by the oracle of Siwah. For our king is beloved of the oracle, and perhaps the medallion will help."

The conversation was cut short as they arrived at the main entrance to the palace. Parmenion stood in confusion a moment, dismayed that no guard was posted. "This cannot be allowed. Something is terribly wrong, terribly wrong." He shrugged then led the way in.

Grabbing hold of the first man who looked like he held some authority, Parmenion pointed out the two travelers and gave a hurried account.

"I don't give a good damn," the officer cried. "He's gone, he's gone so it doesn't matter."

Aldin stepped forward and grabbed the officer, who was edging into hysteria. "You know of my master." And as if to lend authority, Aldin pulled out a sheaf of "letters of introduction." "We are physicians, and even when others despair, we may still be of help. Lead us to his apartments, and you may yet save your king."

The officer hesitated, but even as he debated what to do, loud arguing and the clashing of weapons echoed in the next room. "Follow me," he said at last, and pushed his way past a knot of shouting, bawling men.

"In here." He pointed to an open doorway that seemed to lead into an audience chamber. It was packed with men.

Surely this can't be the room, Aldin thought, it's chaos in there. But he pushed his way into the crowd.

Parmenion hurried to Aldin's side and helped him to

shoulder his way through the crush. All order and discipline have simply disintegrated, Aldin thought. The most powerful man in the ancient world dies and within minutes his empire and the order he has created are sucked into the darkness with him.

Suddenly the way was blocked, and Parmenion started to explain their story again.

"They don't look like physicians to me," someone cried, and the crowd, which seemed on the point of becoming a mob, turned its attention to the confrontation between the fat guard and a bantam-size officer.

"In fact, they seem more like troublemakers than messengers. I can't believe you'd be so stupid as to let them in here," the officer shouted.

The crowd that surrounded them stepped back a couple of paces. The officer's hand already rested on the hilt of a sword. "I think they should be thoroughly searched before being allowed to approach the presence."

Damn it, Aldin thought, this could take hours, and we're so close! Over the head of the officer he saw the thin veil that must mark the separation between the bedchamber and anteroom.

"Who are you?" The voice was low and gruff.

Aldin turned and faced another soldier, one who had the look of the desert and a lifetime's hard campaigning etched into his features.

"Messengers of goodwill from Aristotle," Aldin quickly replied.

"My lord has not had converse with Aristotle since the betrayal by the philosophos' nephew. Why should that old conjurer wish to send messengers now?"

"We were to bring this gift as a renewed offering of friendship." And Aldin reached into his pouch and produced a gem-studded pendant. It was a cheap trinket back home, but gold and emeralds still impressed Macedonians. At least, that had been Aldin's reasoning.

The man said nothing, but took the pendant and held

it absently in his hand while continuing to scrutinize Aldin and Tia. So much for theory.

"We hastened here," Aldin continued, "abandoning our retinue when we heard that the great king was sick. The good soldier by our side escorted us from the great gate to the palace." And he pointed to Parmenion, who was standing stiffly by their side.

"That fat wreckage a *soldier*?" A smile almost crossed his face.

"I was at Granicus, and Guagamela, my lord Ptolemy." Parmenion's voice revealed the insult that he felt.

Ptolemy nodded in reply and turned away.

"We have studied medicine under Aristotle; perhaps there is still some way we can help."

"He is gone," Ptolemy said sadly, and as if in response to his words the lamentations in the room increased in volume.

"If he is truly gone, then we cannot hurt him. There have been times when men have been thought to be gone and yet are not. At least let us look and try. Surely we cannot harm."

Ptolemy hesitated for a moment, and then turned to a young aide standing beside him. He leaned over, whispered something to him, and then strode from the room.

Ptolemy, Aldin thought, and he looked in wonder as the man disappeared into the press. He wanted to shout to the man that he would found a three-hundred-year dynasty in Egypt, but Tia was already pushing him forward. The crowd parted before them and the light curtain was pulled back.

"And what of his half brother?" someone in the background shouted. "He should be the rightful heir."

"He's a half-wit," came the heated reply.

"You're the half-wit, by Zeus, and I still pledge myself to the brother."

"And what of the unborn child? Heh, what do you say of that?" screamed another.

Aldin suddenly heard the unmistakable sound of swords being drawn.

The military historian in him was fascinated, the man terrified, but another task remained, so Aldin turned away even as the men poured out of the room and the sound of fighting erupted in a corridor beyond.

He approached the silken curtain and hesitated. To Aldin's time, the man beyond it was dust for five thousand years but if the scam worked, soon he would be a living, walking presence in a realm beyond imagining.

Aldin pulled back the curtain.

He was more beautiful, in a rugged masculine way, than Aldin had imagined. It was as if a Hellenic Greek statue had been given the texture and coloration of life. The form of Alexander had influenced a century of sculpture. Many had thought those sculptures to be idealized. Aldin saw that in fact they had never done justice.

A muffled sob distracted Aldin. He looked behind him. Parmenion's face was bathed in tears.

What sort of man was he, Aldin wondered, that could bring an aged veteran to display such emotion?

Aldin drew closer. He had imagined Alexander to be bigger; only a giant could bestride fifty centuries. This man was small, even for his own age, but his body was perfect in its proportions. His reddish blond hair was damp with fevered sweat and hung in loose, tangled knots.

His features were drawn—his eyes sunken.

Aldin looked around the chamber. A slender young man sat on the floor in the corner. "Bagoas?" Aldin asked.

The young man nodded in reply.

It was Alexander's eunuch lover, and Aldin stared at him for a moment, fascinated at such a strange love that had survived in the history of a man who most believed had conquered only through bloodshed.

"He is gone to his father," Bagoas whispered.

"But still I must check," Aldin replied. He walked up to the side of Alexander's bed and nodded to Tia.

She unshielded the medallion and pointed it at Alexander. "I know a girl whose name is Jewel," Tia said in common speech.

Aldin looked at her and rolled his eyes. The phrases would be gibberish to Parmenion and Bagoas, and as such would seem like an appropriate incantation. But still, the girl should have some respect!

"And this here girl did love to screw!"

"Tia!"

But she was away, full tilt now, reciting a stream of obscene limericks.

Aldin tried to ignore her as he unraveled the bioscan system from his traveler's pouch. There were no external signs of respiration and the body was extremely pale, but there was no cyanosis and in the stultifying heat decomposition should have started within several hours of death. Aldin produced a small mirror and held it before Alexander's mouth and nostrils. And then in a quick single motion he let his other hand slip behind Alexander's neck, where he pushed a flesh-colored scan/med dose unit between Alexander's shoulder blades.

The skin was disturbingly cool to the touch. If Alexander hadn't languished in a deep coma after his apparent death, the whole trip would be a waste. Facing Corbin with the news would be no great pleasure.

The pickup unit in his ear clicked on as the scan med dose unit activated and broadcast data to Aldin and the ship's computer.

"Heart rate, thirteen per minute," a small voice whispered. "Pressure sixty over thirty-five."

Aldin struggled not to show his exultation. He was right!

Tia looked at Aldin. He gave a subtle nod, then forced himself to show a look of anguished pain.

"Brain scan nominal on all counts, projected damage threshold within seventeen hours. Pleurisy, pneumonia, and major aberration in pancreatic function—initial diagnosis. Termination line within seventy-two hours."

Parmenion had drawn closer, trying to contain his grief. But there was a curious look in his eyes, as well, as he looked at Aldin and then back to Tia.

"Did I hear you say something?" Parmenion asked.

"Ah . . . no."

Parmenion looked at him with a curious expression. Aldin returned his gaze and forced himself to look distraught. "It is as I feared, he is gone."

"Unless otherwise overridden," the computerized voice whispered, "will administer stabilization medication as programmed."

Aldin ran his finger across the medallion signaling his assent to the ship's computer. The comalike state would be maintained while medication prevented further deterioration. As he did so, his other hand brushed against the adobe wall, and he applied a pinhead monitor unit that could observe the room, so they could check out the area before jumping back in with the replacement body.

Tia gave him a quick nod. The scan was finished. All they had to do was step into a side room, get pulled out by the ship, then reinsert later with the reformed body.

"There's nothing more we can do here," Aldin whispered sadly, trying to force a tear to his eye. "My friend and I will leave now."

"Just a moment." Ptolemy's aide stood in the corner of the audience chamber. "Did you say you were from Aristotle?"

"Yes."

"Strange, ever since our late lamented Alexander executed his nephew, we haven't heard a word from him. And suddenly on the day he dies, you show up on our doorstep. Some of the men in that hallway believe there is a plot afoot, that *poison* might have been at play here. I understand that Master Aristotle is quite knowledgeable in such areas."

Aldin shrugged his shoulders. "I would not know of

such things. I am merely a messenger from him to our late king, nothing more. I have his letter in my pouch if you wish to see it."

"Yes, but of course. My lord Ptolemy will inspect that later. For now, he insists that you remain here at the palace so that he can talk with you when time permits." As the aide spoke, the sounds of fighting erupted again.

He gave them a cold, sinister smile. "You, guard!" The aide pointed at Parmenion. "You know where to show them, and you are responsible."

The aide turned and strode out of the room.

Aldin suddenly felt a heavy hand resting on his shoulder and, turning, looked up into the scarred face of the Macedonian guard. "Now, sir, there's nothing to worry about."

"Of course not," Aldin replied gamely.

He knew all about the famed Macedonian hospitality. It was just the standard practice of torture that preceded questioning that had him worried.

CHAPTER 3

"WHAT DO YOU THINK THEY'LL DO?" TIA WHISPERED, forgetting to use Greek.

"Just shut up," Aldin hissed, and then nodded a smile toward the far corner of the room where Parmenion sat by the doorway, drawn sword resting on his knee.

All their belongings had been taken, including their medallions. Fortunately his belt with its concealed electronics had not been touched; the only other way to communicate with the ship was through the small transmit unit he had swallowed just before departure. He had no desire to wait until that key component rematerialized.

He had made the mistake of asking Parmenion the time, and that had aroused further suspicions, since the measurement of time in this era was a haphazard thing at best. However, from the gradual darkening in their room he guessed that it must be drawing toward evening, and he estimated that replication should soon be completed.

Even as he smiled at Parmenion there was a short burst from his audio pickup.

"Replacement ready to be transported. Awaiting your signal."

"So tell me, Parmenion," Aldin asked, rising to his feet, "I heard you say that you fought at Gaugamela."

Parmenion shifted and looked up at him with pride. "I was in the front rank, opposite the first chariot assault. Ah, now that was a sight."

Aldin only half listened, and he gave a subtle hand gesture to Tia, indicating that things were ready back aboard the ship. If the situation turned ugly, they could have themselves pulled back to the ship. To return, however, would be impossible, for the hue and the cry would be up for the two "sorcerers."

"...I saw this ugly black-bearded dog," Parmenion roared, still talking about Gaugamela, "he was coming straight at me with spear lowered. And then you know what I did?"

"I couldn't possibly guess," Aldin replied, and Parmenion continued on with his tale.

Aldin stretched and stepped closer to Parmenion as if engrossed in his tale. The arguing and occasional clashing of weapons outside had been going on with increasing frequency as the day progressed. All they had to do was to somehow put Parmenion out of action for a couple of minutes and then make a dash back to the room where Alexander lay in a coma. But how to do it?

"Guard, just what the hell are you prattling about?"

Parmenion shot up and stood rigid at attention. It was the bantam-size officer standing in the doorway.

He looked over at the two prisoners and advanced toward Aldin with an air of superior contempt. "I think you have a little problem, friend."

Aldin, sensing the man's mood, didn't reply.

"You see, a number of envoys have arrived today. Even now my lord Ptolemy has taken the time to meet with them. And you'd never imagine where they are from."

Aldin could only shake his head, not wishing to say anything that might enrage the captain.

"They're from Pella, where your so-called employer is supposed to reside. They traveled the same road you should have, and they claim no knowledge of an embassy from Aristotle, who, I might add, is just one step removed from arrested now that Alexander is gone."

Aldin simply smiled and shrugged his shoulders.

"And besides," the captain continued in a gloating manner, "those travelers carry a letter from Aristotle, as well, bearing his official signature and seal. Which does not, for some strange reason, match the signature on your letter at all."

Aldin shot a quick sidelong glance at Tia, who had visibly paled and was already looking quite guilty.

"So we have here an interesting situation." The officer advanced closer. "Perhaps you are part of a plot to kill our king and were sent to make sure that he was indeed dead and, if not, to administer another dose.

"Then again," he said with a smile, "you just might be two innocent fools who didn't know the game you were playing."

His left hand was resting on his sword hilt, and Aldin watched it carefully. But it was his right hand that shot out like lightning, caught Aldin in the solar plexus, and sent him crumpling to the floor, gasping for breath. Tia backed up against the wall, her eyes wide with terror.

"But I think you're guilty," the captain hissed. "And I'll take personal delight in helping to smash your body to a shapeless pulp until you finally talk. After that I'll pull your eyes out of their sockets.

"You, guard, my men will be here shortly to take these two to their questioning." With an ugly laugh he strode out of the room.

Aldin lay on the floor trying to regain his breath, and Tia came over to his side.

"Could you help me get him over to the cot?" Tia asked, looking imploringly at Parmenion.

"Get him there yourself," the guard growled.

"Please, he's an old man," Tia begged. "I tell you we're innocent. Do you think we would have rushed to Alexander's side after we had heard the news that he was dead if we intended harm? We would have stayed clear and been safe. I tell you we're innocent, and my friend here is hurt. Please help me."

Parmenion hesitated for a moment, and then with a mumbled curse he came over to Tia's side and started to bend over to pick Aldin up. In one swift movement her foot came up and caught Parmenion in such a way that he would be walking with difficulty for some time to come. His breath escaped in an agonized *woosh*, his one eye bulging out as he doubled over.

"Good going, girl," Aldin groaned, staggering to his feet.

Parmenion was still bent over, gasping, as Tia snatched up a small stool and raised it up high.

"Not too hard," Aldin said, actually feeling a touch of sympathy for their guard.

The stool caught Parmenion across the back of the head and he fell forward, his arms outstretched and grabbing for Aldin. He caught him on the belt.

"Xsarnfood!"

In horror, Aldin fumbled to release Parmenion's grip on his belt buckle, but the damage had already been done. The signal for the body transfer had been activated.

A dull shimmer suddenly appeared at Aldin's feet, right next to Parmenion's twitching body. Before Aldin had time to react, the shimmer turned into an even pulsing glow as the energy field formed. There was a faint outrushing of air, and then, with a faint *pop*, the field distorted and disappeared.

An exact replica of Alexander's body lay on the floor. Parmenion, who was still semiconscious, gave a gasping moan of horror and then his one eye rolled up as he passed out, either from fright or the blow to the head.

"Well, that throws the crap in the fire," Tia whispered.

"Damn good job that computer did," Aldin replied. "Damn good job. Can't tell the difference at all." He found the thought so amusing that he had to chuckle as he realized that if they pulled it off, a shady plastacement dealer would be the center of a shrine for centuries to come.

"Now what are we going to do?" Tia asked.

Without even trying to formulate a plan, Aldin grabbed hold of the cloak around Parmenion's shoulders, yanked it off, and wrapped it around the body.

"Parmenion's helmet, get it off," Aldin hissed. "And his belt, too!"

A minute later the door to the main corridor opened and a very frightened Tia peeked out, fearful that she'd get a spear in her face.

She looked back at Aldin.

"Why don't we just transport over to the room with Alexander?" Tia asked hopefully.

"Can't. The transport only locks on to living tissue and what we are wearing, nothing else. It can send a corpse down, but not back up. We'll have to haul it there ourselves."

"Please, Aldin, I beg you. Corbin will understand, I can work on him. Let's just get the hell out of here. If we get caught hauling this body around . . ."

"If you don't shut up, they'll catch us anyhow and we'll get crucified. Is it clear?"

"There's a group arguing down the end of the hall," she whispered.

"Fine, let's go."

Aldin kicked the door wide open and staggered out, the arm of the corpse slung over his shoulder.

"Help me, damn you, or by God's blood I'll yank that transceiver off you and leave you here."

Tia came to the other side of the body and grabbed it, helping Aldin to drag it out into the corridor.

"You're crazy!" Tia hissed.

"Stay calm, this palace is in an uproar. They'll never notice us. I read that for most of the night Alexander's room wasn't even guarded, so it'll be simple, now let's go."

Still trembling from the blow to his stomach, he soon broke out into a sweat as they dragged the corpse down the hallway and past the first group of arguing soldiers.

The Macedonian guards barely spared them a glance; men being dragged out from the brawling was a common sight. Aldin only hoped that no one insisted on pulling back the helmet and taking a look.

They turned the corridor and started up the stairs to the main audience chamber where Alexander lay unattended.

"Ho there, is that Certius?"

Aldin kept on moving, ignoring the shouted command.

"I say, there, is that Certius?" A heavyset officer stepped in front of them.

"No, sir," Aldin replied in a differing whine, keeping his head low as if in subservience, "this be Aristophane. Too much to drink in grief, that's all. And him still sick with the fever and all. I heard it's catching good, sir."

With a mumbled curse the officer stepped back and let them pass.

A file of soldiers marched past them, brief snatches of their conversation echoing in the dimly lit corridor.

"Machus claims he'll personally yank out the fat one's teeth, one by one."

"I don't care, just as long as I can have some fun with the girl first."

"Ah, we know what kind of fun you want, Tremenichas." The others laughed crudely as they shouldered their way past Aldin. Tia, in a near panic, tried to pick up the pace, but Aldin held her back, partially out of not wanting to draw attention, but also because he was out of breath.

In another minute they would know if the approach to the main room was clear, but in another minute the guards sent to pick them up would be raising the cry. It would be a close thing.

They came out on the last landing of the staircase and turned toward the audience chamber.

All was quiet as the three drew closer. In the shadows he could see a sentry and Aldin felt his heart sink.

"Stop and identify."

Aldin knew he didn't have the strength to overcome this man; he would have to rely on simple salesmanship.

"Ah, soldier, it breaks my heart to bring my brother here." He tried to raise the corpse up a little bit as if he wanted to show it to the sentry. "It breaks my heart indeed. We followed the king from the beginning. I can still remember the clear bright day when Philip brought him out into the courtyard, and we raised the shout for the newborn lad. And now he is dead."

Aldin felt himself getting so into the part that there was even a faint shudder in his voice.

"I couldn't serve him, I was short of wind, you see." He coughed slightly to add emphasis. "But my brother here"—again he nudged the corpse—"was in Hephaestion's brigade and fought from Issus to the Indus. So overcome was he that he near drank himself to death tonight. So I beg you, good sir, please let us in for just one moment so that we might gaze one last time and bid our farewell."

"I've got orders, the room is closed. I can imagine it's not too pleasant in there right now, what with all this damned heat."

Even as he spoke they could hear shouted cries in the distance. The alarm was being raised.

"Look here, it's all my brother has." Aldin dug his hand into Parmenion's pouch, hoping that there'd be something. He felt some cool metal and pulled out a handful of copper and a couple of silver coins. To a collector back in the Cloud they'd be worth a thousand katars, enough to buy him a month in the finest pleasure palaces of Quitar, but he couldn't quibble now.

"A gift from my brother, please take it."

The guard hesitated and looked to his companion in the shadows.

The man nodded his approval and the guard took the bribe.

"Go on in and make it quick. And see that your brother there doesn't make a mess."

Even as he spoke he and his companion walked past them to the head of the staircase to see what the commotion was all about.

The door pushed open, and the two dragged the body inside.

It was cooler in there, dark and eerie. The great chamber was empty and echoed to the padding of their sandals as they dragged the body across the room.

Aldin approached the dais and again he was taken by the beauty of the man whose body was illuminated by a single torch, which flickered fitfully at the head of the bed.

There was no time for formality now.

Aldin dropped the corpse by the side of the bed.

"Come on, let's go," he hissed, and motioned for Tia to grab hold of Alexander's feet.

"So help me, Aldin, if we get out of this, I'll never—" She hesitated for a second. "What the hell is that?"

"Someone's coming, now move it!"

Forgetting all ceremony and respect, Aldin pushed Alexander off the dais.

Rushing around to the plastacement contractor, Aldin yanked off the helmet, belt and cape, tossing the equipment onto Alexander. Then with a strength that surprised him, he lifted the replacement up and dropped it where Alexander had lain only seconds before.

"Drag him over by the window," Aldin commanded, even as he struggled with the sheet that had covered

Alexander and tried to arrange the corpse to look as if it had not been disturbed.

"Alarm. Body thieves. Alarm!"

A form suddenly leaped through the doorway, knocking Aldin off his feet. Aldin swung with desperate blows, pummeling his assailant on the shoulders and head.

"Help! Alarm!"

He could see Tia dragging Alexander away from him, moving toward the window.

"Not away from me, you idiot," Aldin screamed. "The beam, the beam, get next to me—*Yowlll*!" he cried out in anguish as his attacker's teeth sank into his leg.

Tia, at last comprehending, turned around and dragged Alexander back toward the struggling pair.

In the distance Aldin could hear more shouts, and the sound of running feet. The guard was closing in.

The hell with this guy on me, he thought, and when he saw that Tia was within range he hit the activation button on his buckle. There was a panic-filled moment when nothing happened and he thought all this punching, kicking, and other nonsense had broken something vital— then the distortion hit.

A faint popping *hiss* brought him to consciousness as the distortion shut down. Instinctively he checked his body to make sure that nothing important had been left behind.

"By the teeth of Zeus!"

"Damn it, Aldin, you brought that guard with us!"

Aldin could feel the grip around the lower half of his body relax and then go limp.

He kicked his way clear and stood up.

Parmenion was sprawled out, unconscious, and for a second Aldin wasn't sure whether he had simply passed out or the shock of transjumping had killed him.

"Now what the hell are you going to do?" Tia asked.

"Never mind him, it's Alexander I'm concerned about."

Aldin crouched over the unconscious form and touched him lightly on the throat, even as he realized that a pulse would not be noticeable. The body was cool to the touch and he felt a quick tug of fear.

"Help me," Aldin cried, and together they picked Alexander up and took him into the med-support room that had been previously occupied by the substitute body.

Aldin placed him on the now-empty table and hooked a direct monitor line to the patch he had attached earlier to Alexander's back.

He scanned the instrument's readout and breathed a sigh of relief.

"Initiate revival?" the computer queried.

"Affirmative, but keep the subject lightly sedated."

"By all the gods, I am ready" came a weak cry from the next room.

Fearful that the momentarily interrupted scuffle would resume, Aldin slid up to the open door leading into the transport chamber and peeked out.

Parmenion was on his hands and knees, his body shaking like a jellyfish.

"So you've decided to accompany your king to the next world?"

Aldin gave Tia a look of reproach but didn't stop her.

"Happily and without hesitation." Parmenion moaned.

"Then why did you assault the messengers of the gods?"

"Really, Tia, give him a break."

Parmenion snuck a quick peek at the two standing in the doorway, and with a loud moan he quickly averted his eyes.

"I—I was serving my king. I knew not that you were sent by the gods to take him to the next realm. And remember, noble ones, that it was I who led you to him, and I who helped when the bigger of you was hurt."

Aldin drew Tia back from the doorway.

"We should send him back," Tia whispered. "We pulled the switch and he was the only witness, but now he thinks we're gods. Let's give the poor man a drink and then send him back down to the spot that we jumped down to last night."

"He let two prisoners escape," Aldin replied. "They'll give him the punishment we would have received."

"Well, I guess it's your problem," Tia replied. "He was hanging on to you when you came through, so—"

Her comment was cut short by the high-pitched shriek of the ship's alarm, which was counterpointed by Parmenion's agonized wail of fear in response.

"Ship approaching," the intercom boomed, "ship approaching. Signal from unidentified vessel that we are to prepare for boarding."

"Who the hell?" And together they ran for the forward control room, nearly tripping over Parmenion, who was still prostrated on the floor.

"Ship design and probable origin," Aldin shouted as he leaped for the command chair.

"Unable to determine," the computer responded.

"Punch us out of here!" Aldin cried. "Take evasive action and run for the time nexus."

"Receiving message from approaching vessel, it is in galactic standard."

"Hook it in." Aldin groaned. "I think I know who it is."

"Unidentified vessel, bound out of Magellanic Cloud, currently Earth orbit. We have reason to believe you are involved in illegal process, procuring participants for gaming situation. This is an Overseer vessel; you are to cease any attempt at flight."

"Get us the hell out of here!" Aldin shouted.

They were slammed back into their seats as the ship's

pulse system engaged a fraction ahead of the inertia damping unit.

"Cease all movement." The voice was Doppler-shifted as they accelerated up and away.

"Damn all self-righteous Overseers," Aldin raged. "Bastards never mind their own business."

"Ship attempting to flee. Such action is a violation of Overseer Law. Cease action at once."

"Aldin, they might shoot to disable!" Tia cried.

The Overseers were dedicated to pacifism, but it was pacifism at the point of a gun, and Aldin knew she was right.

"Ship command, evasive maneuver radical."

"Acknowledge, evasive maneuver about to engage."

Even as they shifted, the first beam of blinding light arched across their path. The simple act of evasion could possibly throw them into a beam and kill them, and he knew that the Overseers hoped such a thought would prevent him from his course of action. And he hoped, as well, that they'd stop shooting rather than risk a kill on the "destiny of their souls," as they called it.

"You are undoubtedly engaged in an illegal action. If you cease your evasion and allow boarding, we will merely provide counseling."

Oh, heavens, Aldin thought, the last thing he needed was several hundred hours of moral lecturing about the folly of his ways by one of their damned missionaries, and six months in one of their damned peace reorientation centers.

"Eat Xsarnfood!" Aldin cried, and Tia cackled with delight at his reply.

"Approaching first distortion field to nexus," the ship advised after transmitting Aldin's gastronomical advice, which prompted another shot across their bow.

"Do you think we'll get away?" Tia asked. "I've heard about their counseling; I'll be damned if I'll take any of that crap."

In fact he half suspected that the Overseers would not

appreciate six months with her, either. The thought of surrendering just for the fun of it crossed his mind, but he pushed it aside; the commissions for the game far outweighed the pleasure of possibly discomfiting an Overseer.

"Go back and strap in Alexander, and make sure Parmenion is strapped in, as well. The turbulence will be rough at this speed."

"You're not gods!"

Turning, they saw Parmenion standing unsteadily in the doorway.

"Maybe not," Aldin shouted, remembering to switch back into Greek, "but by all the heavens, there's somebody chasing us who thinks he is. And if you give us any trouble we'll push you off this sky-wagon and let you fall into their hands. Now go help the girl with your king."

Parmenion hesitated for a second, and then with a shrug of his massive shoulders he followed Tia out of the room as she shoved her way past him with a mumbled curse.

"First nexus approach in ten seconds."

"Ship full stop," Aldin cried impulsively.

"Say what?" Tia cried, rushing back into the room.

"Just shut up. Maybe I've decided that life with them is better than life with you," Aldin yelled.

"Oh, yeah, well, Corbin will give you the same that Luciana got if you pull this on me."

"Shut up and see to Alexander!"

"Overseer ship decelerating," the computer chimed in.

Aldin noticed Parmenion's confusion over the computer voice, but an explanation would have to wait.

"Transmit, but provide usual voice distortion to avoid identification."

"Proceed."

"To Overseer ship, we surrender. Our primary drive unit is overheating. We accept your offer of counseling, but please get us off this ship, I think it's going to blow."

"We are glad that you have seen the folly of your ways," the Overseer pilot replied. "Switch on coordinate beacon and prepare to be placed aboard our ship."

"Ship nav, prepare for full acceleration," Aldin whispered.

"It will not be so bad, friends. You'll soon be enlightened to our higher ways."

"Oh, yeah, well, kiss my butt!" Aldin yelled. "Ship computer, hit it out of here."

In a blinding flash, they leaped away, leaving the Overseer vessel in their wake. Parmenion and Tia were knocked off their feet, and Aldin's vision blurred as they hit the edge of the field. Even as the pursuit ship started to accelerate, they crossed the first time nexus and disappeared.

"So long, suckers!" Aldin cried.

"So long, suckers?" Tia asked.

"Oh, yeah, I forgot you kids don't study your history of linguistics any more. It's an Earth term that means that you've taken someone for a fool.

"Well, let's get back to our passenger," Aldin said happily. "I hope that jump through didn't knock him off the table."

"The king!" It was Parmenion shouting from the next room.

Together Aldin and Tia rushed into the medical chamber. She stopped in the doorway with a gasp and Aldin nearly knocked her over.

"Am I in the realm of my fathers?"

He lay on the table, his eyes open, staring at them as if from some great distance beyond measure. Parmenion knelt by his side, tears of joy streaming down his face.

"I guess I better start explaining," Aldin whispered, his voice edged with awe and fear.

CHAPTER 4

"So I'm not dead?"

Aldin smiled softly and shook his head.

"Then if not dead, where am I? Have I been taken prisoner?"

Again Aldin smiled, trying to project his best bedside manner, which he knew couldn't be very reassuring.

"Majesty, they've snatched you for ransom," Parmenion blurted out. "They are in league with some evil god."

"If I'm in league with an evil god," Tia hissed, "rest assured I'll cut off a very important part of your body if you say another word."

Parmenion looked at her defiantly, started to open his mouth, and then, mumbling to himself, he turned away.

"Leave me alone with him, and I'll explain," Aldin said softly, still looking straight into those strange, mysterious eyes that seemed to hold an almost hypnotic power.

"Majesty!" Parmenion turned, ready to defend his king in spite of Tia's threat.

"It's all right," Alexander said weakly. "If they mean

my death, they can have it. But I think not, otherwise I would not have been brought back from the doorway. Go, soldier, I command it."

Parmenion bowed low and walked out of the room, but the tone of his mumbling was obvious to everyone, even Alexander.

"A good soldier," Alexander said softly, and a faint smile crossed his lips. "Now tell me, how?"

"Might I ask what you remember?" Aldin replied. "And then perhaps I can better explain."

Alexander stopped for a moment and his brow creased as if he were searching for some half-forgotten thought.

"It was as if I were falling." He sighed. "A slipping away into the darkness, to be embraced by the cool of a summer night.

"I could hear them all the time, like voices from beyond the pale. They cried that I was dead, and I tried to tell them not to lament. I heard them arguing, and then fighting."

He hesitated and looked at Aldin.

"They will die without me. The dream of unity will be lost. You must heal me so that I can return and lead them again."

"I can't."

"Then I am to die. Or am I already dead?"

"No, you'll live, Alexander. But return you, I cannot."

He could see the flicker of anger surface. He had said no to the most powerful man on Earth. The most powerful man on Earth, and Aldin realized that already that time was five millennia past, and all those to whom he had talked only hours before had returned to dust.

Alexander tried to sit up.

"I command..." he began, but fell back trembling with pain and exhaustion.

"You must believe me, O King." The words felt funny, but somehow Aldin felt no discomfort using the phrase with such a man. "If I could fulfill any wish of yours, I would. But to return is not possible. But do not lament, for destiny has given you the chance for a higher calling."

Alexander looked at him searchingly, suspicious of what he was hearing.

"And what worlds are there still for me to conquer?" Aldin whispered.

"What was that?" Alexander asked.

"Oh, just a quote attributed to you. Now you're still weak and should rest."

"But I must know why and how."

Aldin could only smile. He would have to ask him about Aristotle and the training he had received at the tutor's hands so that even now his mind was questing for answers.

"Computer med unit," Aldin said softly, "mild sedative, continue with standard medication and nutritional program."

"Acknowledged."

Alexander looked around, startled by the soft feminine voice of the computer. "Who was that?"

"Soon enough, soon enough. Now sleep."

Aldin could see the sedative taking effect, yet Alexander fought to hold consciousness, as if he feared to ever close his eyes again.

"But I must know," he whispered.

"You will." Even as Aldin spoke, his patient drifted away. Aldin sat by him watching the gentle rise and fall of his chest, his breath still rasping from the congestion of pneumonia. The medic servobot unit nudged Aldin aside and hooked an oxygen tube to Alexander and deftly inserted an I.V.

Aldin felt a sense of awe at what he had just accomplished. He had reached across the millennia and saved one of the greatest generals in history. He had expected to feel a slight condescending attitude to this man—after all, there was five thousand years of civilization separating them—but he was indeed a leader of legend. Aldin wondered suddenly if the Gavarnian leader Alexander was to meet would ever be able to match him. His thoughts turned to his fellow vasba Zergh, and he could not help but wonder if Zergh was feeling the same way he was at this moment.

"I am not sure I understand, Zergh."

Zergh stood up and stretched, his reddish-gray pelt expanding out and swaying gently as he rocked his body back and forth. "Nearly a day must have past, exalted one. You should rest, there is still time to talk."

"No, I wish to know all."

"You're still weak from the poison. Why not sleep and I'll return later."

"No." It was no longer a statement, it was a command.

With a sigh Zergh sat down and signaled for his assistant to bring another drink.

"I'll have one of those, as well."

"But, exalted, think of your health."

"I am thinking of my health." He barked a short gruff laugh, and Zergh had to shake his head in amazement. Either he had the endurance of ten or he was delirious and would soon pass out.

"You're thinking about how I can stay up like this for so long, aren't you?"

Again he displayed an ability to somehow read another's thoughts.

"I think I should be watchful of my thoughts around you, Kubar Taug, for you seem to be able to pull them out of the air."

Kubar laughed again. "If I could not feel such things, I would never have lived as long as I have, nor would I have conquered a world. A conqueror must know his enemies, but even more so, he must know the thoughts of his friends and how far he can trust them.

"Now you're starting to wonder about the poison and

why I drank from the cup offered by my spouse before I went to the mountain to meditate."

Zergh could only shake his head.

Kubar smiled. "Funny, that was only three days past. Three days and what you call four thousand years ago. And now I ride to another world, not as a dead man but as one still alive for yet another adventure."

He shook his head and his mane gently rustled behind him. "I should be grateful. Indeed I am honored by the place that history has given me. But did you ever think that I was simply tired of war and conquest?"

"But you conquered an entire world and united us," Zergh replied. "What greater thing can one aspire to?"

Kubar looked at him and smiled. "Returning to what I was just talking about, I will say that I did suspect that cup, but I drank anyhow."

"Why?"

"Tired, perhaps."

Zergh looked at him and didn't believe.

"Perhaps, as well, it was a test of loyalty. I guess you know I loved to do such things as a proof of my trust, and, well, that time I was wrong. But no, that is in a way a lie to myself. You see, I had just won my greatest triumph; the unification was complete, and I knew, as well, that the Council could hold it together after I was gone. So I thought on the words of Lagata, our greatest warrior-poet, when he said that it is good when one makes his mark upon his world, but it is better to know when to leave, so that the mark will shine the brighter."

Kubar fell silent for a moment as if lost in thought. Zergh wanted to say that somehow he had been right; that by "disappearing" when he did, he became the martyr to the unification and thus made it complete. For half a thousand lifetimes the legend had been told and retold how Kubar Taug had come to unify and when his task was completed he had returned to the Unseen Light. But he felt that such words, such praise, would be mere platitudes to one as great as Kubar.

Kubar looked up at Zergh again and smiled. "So tell me, what is it you call them?"

"Humans."

"Yes, Humans. But most of all tell me of this one they named Alexander."

"You've told me how, but you haven't told me the reasons why."

Startled, Aldin sat up from his bunk to find Alexander sitting by the foot of the bed, smiling at him with a distant, enigmatic smile.

"You should be resting, you're still not completely recovered."

"I suspect that my name has somehow survived across five millennia not because I was one given to rest. There is not enough time, Aldin. The gods gave us sleep to cheat us of our glory. To sleep is to be dead."

Aldin shook his head and, turning to the serving unit, he punched up a coffee and made a gesture of offering to Alexander.

It had amazed him how quickly this man had adapted himself to the technological shift, accepting the various shipboard computers and servobots with an eager curiosity. He had rebelled slightly at the language implant, expressing the Hellenic disdain for any other language but his own. But the practicality of it finally won him over. He accepted even the question of translight space travel with barely a shrug, thus laying to rest the concern of several Kohs that the shock of his surroundings would render him useless.

Perhaps the greatest source of interest for Aldin was teaching Alexander how to access the history library and then to watch as Alexander read the accounts of his own life. His rage at Plutarch's ridiculous fables about his drunkenness and debauchery had echoed through the ship for hours. And Aldin could little blame him, wondering how he himself would feel if his life's history had been so badly distorted, and then believed across hundreds of generations.

"So now your questions turn to the future."

"There is nothing else but the future, Aldin. Though I know you and these demigods of your time find me interesting, I doubt if you went through the trouble of this little transfer simply for your own amusement. And my guard has pointed out to me that we seem to have been chased by something that you were evidently rather fearful of."

Aldin felt as if the eyes were boring straight into him. It was a searching look for truth, and there was no getting around it, for this man would know when someone was lying.

"I've been sent to take you to another world where there is a war."

"I am flattered by the interest in me, but again why me, why not someone from your own time?"

"Because it is you, Alexander. If you could conjure Hector from the dust to fight by your side, would you not do it?"

Alexander smiled at the mention of his hero, and in spite of his attempt to appear aloof, it was obvious that he was honored by such a comparison.

"So you wish a Hector for your war, is that it?"

Aldin nodded slowly, and said, "I'm taking you to a realm like few others in the hundred thousand inhabited worlds of the cosmos. It is a place made by a most ancient race known only to us as the First Travelers. It is believed by some that they trod upon our Earth ten million years ago and played a part in the birth of man, and of the Gavarnians, as well."

"The Gavarnians?"

"In a moment, but let me explain the First Travelers. They had such power that they even built worlds for their own amusement, the way you would build a city. One such world they built in the shape of a ring—a ring so large that the land area of a hundred Earths would fill but a small part of it . . ."

Alexander was silent, intent, and listened to Aldin's every word.

"Twenty-five hundred years ago this world was found by men, and it was empty of intelligent life. The First Travelers seemed to have built it only to abandon their work and move on."

"Why?"

"We don't know. We have never seen them, even the Overseers . . ."

Aldin cut himself short, not wishing to get into that angle.

"Something you'd prefer I didn't know about?"

"Well, of all the things you need to know about, that is one of the least useful, shall we say."

"I shan't force you. Continue then."

"They simply built such things as the ring and then disappeared. As I was saying, those who settled this place lost contact with the other worlds while a great war was fought. Only recently have we found these people again, but their knowledge had slipped back to the most basic of things. How shall I say it, they were somewhat . . ."

"I think you mean primitive, as in my time."

"No insult intended," Aldin replied.

"Nor taken. I would be indeed vain if I thought that man's knowledge of the world stopped when I died. Of course there would be progress."

"So what we found," Aldin continued, "was a loosely knit civilization locked in a war with a race of aliens."

"Aliens?"

"Oh, I see, I think we forgot something in our earlier conversation. You remember that I mentioned the Gavarnians?"

"Yes."

"They have the intelligence of men, but they are not men."

"You mean they are another race of creatures?" Alexander paused for a moment, a look of wonder coming to him. "I had always hoped that beyond Bactria I would find such a thing, and now, at last."

Aldin shook his head and smiled. "On the level of combat that we are speaking of they are nearly impossible to defeat. They walk like men, and talk like men, but their appearance is more that of a wolf."

Alexander gave him a quizzical look, as if Aldin were stretching the truth. "On the level of combat? What do you mean?"

"Simply that war on this ring-world is no different than in your time. It is sword, spear, and bow."

"So none of your new machines or discoveries apply there? How is that, for men will always seek better ways to make war? My father and Dionysius of Syracuse learned this and used men of knowledge to build machines that could destroy. Why aren't your machines used in this fight?"

"Neither we nor the Gavarnians knew of this war until recently. And I might as well tell you that there is a third race, the Overseers, who have forbidden all war and thus prevent new machines from being brought into this conflict, even if we wanted to."

"Even if you wanted to?"

"Why shouldn't we? Our machines would only serve to provoke mass destruction. Far better to let them settle their differences in the manner of your time."

Alexander smiled as if he could sense the hidden meanings in Aldin's words. "A little more interesting, as well, isn't it?"

Aldin was silent.

"So that is why you reached out for me across the eons. You want me to take over this war and to fight it to a successful end."

"Precisely."

"But I am a stranger to them. Why should they accept me?"

"These people are not all that warlike, and they are disorganized. A man such as you will be able to find his way and soon prove himself."

"An interesting challenge. So, without title, name, or army I am to forge my own way."

Aldin shrugged his shoulders. "They do know of you, and in fact admire their ancient history. If you can convince them of who you are, so much the better."

"This sounds like the dream of a madman," Alexander said coldly.

"But what a challenge."

"Will you be with me?"

"Once I leave you upon the ring, the demigods whom we call Kohs forbid all contact with either you or the Gavarnians. That will be your challenge."

"The challenge is always safer, Aldin Larice, when it is not you who must face it."

"Then you refuse?"

"I didn't say that, but it is a difficult problem. I assume that little machine you put in me will help with the language, but what of the customs of these people?"

"We shall place you near a mountain tribe much like your own Macedons. They are in fact descendants of people north and east of Macedon. But the legends of your deeds are known to them."

"I still think you are crazy. I mean, why should I do this?"

"Well, there are the Gavarnians to consider, and Human honor to uphold. You see, even now a Gavarnian leader, as famed and honored as yourself, will be placed upon the other side. He will attempt to organize and lead his people against the men of this world. The men have the potential advantage of generalship such as yours; the Gavarnians, however, have the advantage of simple brute strength. It takes two, even three men to match one Gavarnian for strength."

Aldin was hoping that this point alone would lure him in, and he didn't have long to wait for a response.

"Tell me of this Gavarnian leader that I must face."

"Orbital matchup with Kolbard is complete, current position as indicated."

Aldin swiveled away from the command console and looked at the three standing behind him.

Tia attempted to look uninterested, but even someone as jaded as she was awed by what was before them.

Their orbital path ran along the periphery of the Kolbard. Two barrier walls serveral hundred kilometers high ran parallel on either edge of the ring, enclosing the region's atmosphere. As they edged close into the barrier, Aldin commanded the ship to pull in toward the mid-region of the arc. They skimmed the wall then slipped over it, and there below them was a world of shimmering blues and greens, as if they floated above a lush planet girded by a ribbon of light that arched up into infinity in either direction.

"Upon the back of a tortoise," Alexander muttered, "which rests upon the back of an elephant, which rides atop the back of a lion."

"What's that?" Tia asked.

"Oh, just how one of our teachers attempted to explain what the world rests upon . . ." His words trailed off as he shook his head in amazed bemusement.

With a low moan and a curse about evil wizardry, Parmenion turned away from the view.

"Soldier, I saw you stand at Guagamela against the Persian chariots, so why should something like this disturb you?"

"That I could understand, that I could fight. But this smacks of evil magic." He squinted at Aldin, as if he were about to sprout wings or breathe fire.

"There'll be a lot more for you to see," Aldin replied, then turned his attention back to Alexander.

"Are you ready to go down there?"

Alexander shrugged his shoulders and smiled. "Somehow I must view all of this as a bonus given to me by the gods. It is a chance to prove what I am, without my father to lay the groundwork. To build an empire from scratch, as he did, now *that* is a worthy challenge. I'm ready."

Aldin couldn't help but smile at the response. But Parmenion didn't seem to be happy at all.

"But what about me?"

"Why, you're staying here with us," Aldin replied.

"I can't leave him go down there by himself. I mean, it just isn't right. I'm his sworn guard."

Aldin had been afraid there would be a problem over this and he tried to reason.

"The Gavarnian is landing by himself. It wouldn't be fair to give Alexander an assistant."

"And you hid my sword, you dirty scum; why, if I had it in my hands right now I'd—"

"Enough." Alexander stepped forward, putting a restraining hand on Parmenion's shoulder. "It would be nice to have at least one countryman with me. Couldn't it be arranged?"

Aldin shrugged his shoulders and shooed them out of the room. He knew that Zergh's ship was already in place on the opposite barrier wall of the ring. Now that they were both positioned, a signal from Corbin would start the game.

He punched into the Gavarnian channel. "Aldin to Zergh, are you ready for drop-off?"

"This will be an easy bet to clean up on, Aldin," Zergh replied in his clear gruff voice. "Kubar is even better than I had imagined. Care to make a little side bet?"

"Ten thousand katars?" Aldin offered.

There was a moment of hesitation. "Done. Now, what do you want?"

"Just a minor wrinkle," Aldin said. "I inadvertently

picked up a guard. I'll present my full records to the Xsarn as verification. I was wondering if you had run into a similar problem and if so, perhaps we could arrange a companion for each."

"Thank the stars. I have a half-crazy spear carrier in the next room. I had to lock him up to keep him from killing me whenever I didn't show Kubar the proper respect."

"Agreed, then?"

"Agreed. Drop-off within the hour then. I'll notify Corbin that everything is ready."

Parmenion's initial enthusiasm was somewhat dampened as Tia explained in the simplest of terms how the beam system would work. He looked sideways at Alexander, trying to mask his fears.

Aldin came up to Alexander and extended his hand, which Alexander took in a firm, confident grip.

"May your gods watch over you and bring you glory."

"Ah, yes, glory." He smiled again. "An entire world. Let's just hope they agree with my methods."

Tia came in from the com center and nodded. The signal had just been given.

With a wave of his hand, Aldin turned aside and activated the beam. There was a shimmer and a *pop,* and the two were gone.

Aldin stood silent for a minute, feeling a tug of guilt that he had not been more honest with Alexander and explained the real motivation for bringing him to the Kolbard. But that was no longer his concern. It was time for him to get to Corbin's new gaming yacht, which was berthed atop one of the hundred-kilometer-high weather control towers. This action might take a year or more to manage and already the bets were pouring in.

CHAPTER 5

"SIRE, I'M AFRAID."

Alexander looked back at Parmenion and smiled. Aldin's ship was long since gone, and for hours they had been climbing up toward the high ridge of a line of hills. Parmenion was panting for breath as sweat dripped from his body, staining his tunic and leather armor.

Alexander stopped for a moment and took a deep breath, exhaling it with a sense of wonder. Ever since the arrow had torn his lung in a battle years before, breathing had been difficult. Aldin's miraculous machines had somehow made him whole again, and for that, at least, he was grateful.

"What do you fear, Parmenion?"

"Look to the sun, Alexander, it moves not. Therefore time moves not, and we are trapped here for eternity."

"Interesting logic; you sound like a Euclidian. But remember we are not walking upon our world but another, so fear not."

"Walking upon another world," Parmenion mumbled, "and he tells me to fear not."

Alexander looked up at the sun again. So strange—it was a sun, but different. The light was sharper, somehow more white, he thought. And he wrestled again with his own fear.

He was the companion of fear. They never knew, none of them ever knew nor would he ever tell them of the fear he had so often felt in his own heart. But of course, he could never tell, for that must be part of his legend: that Alexander was without fear, even here, on what that man had called the Kolbard—an eternity away from home.

And what of home? What of Roxana, or the unborn one that would be his heir? His mind raced over what he had overheard in the death chamber of the Babylonian palace, even as he felt his life slipping away.

He almost had to smile at the memory. They had been his wolves, his ravenous ones, to unleash upon any who stood in the path of his glory and his dream. And he had heard them turn upon each other. Out of the dim recess of coma he had listened as they fell one upon the other, even as wolves do when their leader should falter or die. Turn they would, and turn again, until the new leader was anointed.

But they were dust now, dust, their names linked only into the shadows of his glory, or so the fat one, the one whom he had first thought was a god-messenger, had told him.

Five thousand years ago. He shook his head, feeling overwhelmed by the thought. *Five thousand years*. He looked again to the sky as if somehow out there he would see his world and, by seeing it, regain balance and understanding of the whys and wherefores of what had happened to him.

Five thousand years and what the fat one, Aldin, said was 150,000 light-years away. Aldin tried to explain that, as well, but the number was meaningless to Alexander. He pushed the thought aside as was his custom. Whenever there was something that he could not understand, he would worry over the question, but if no answer came, he would push it away until such time or place as he could again devote himself to learning about the unknown.

But now, there was a far more immediate concern. A new adventure was beginning for him, and he thought about the unusual circumstances of it for a brief moment. What was the real reason for this Aldin to do what he did? Granted, curiosity about himself must have been a factor, but there was something else, and he felt it was not only to unite these people and lead them against an invader. For if Aldin and the demigods called Kohs had wished that, they would have landed him with great fanfare and pomp to awe the barbarians into doing his will. But instead they had landed him there as a thief in the night, almost as if Aldin had wished no one to see what was being done. But that was not his immediate concern, either.

He slowed his pace for a moment and surveyed the hills around him. The land was not unlike that of Bactria: high hills lightly forested and capped with snowclad peaks. The air was fresh, bracing, and clean as it had been in Bactria when compared to the hot, humid stench of Babylon. Directly before him was a mountain beyond all imagining, a towering behemoth that rose straight into the heavens until it seemed as if it would reach to the very sun. Aldin had explained that it was used as a port for the massive ships that sailed the heavens, and also as a tower to cool the air and thus balance the temperature, and that such mountains bulged like spikes on the outside of the ring, as well.

Such a thing was beyond Alexander's grasp, and he could only believe that these First Travelers whom Aldin said had made this place were in fact gods, or children of gods. Even as he gazed upon the tower in the shape of a mountain, he called it Olympus in his own mind. Aldin had told him that it was viewed as a holy place, and that a dozen or more villages surrounded it. What looked to be almost next to the mountain—but was in fact more than fifty leagues away—was a replica of the first mountain, and then four more beyond that. Aldin said that several hundred thousand people lived in the region of the first three towers, but beyond, to the far north rim of the ring, was desolation except for occasional hermits and brigands. The other three towers were in the region held by the creatures known as the Gavarnians. He looked in their direction for a moment, hoping to see the signs of their capital city on the ocean's coast, off to what in his own mind he called the west. But from such a distance all he could see was the shimmer of the ocean shadowed by a high floating bank of clouds that trailed from the three distant towers.

Hundreds of leagues away toward what Alexander decided was the east, the direction he was heading in, there appeared to be a purple wall that seemed to reach to the heavens. Aldin explained that such barriers were set at regular intervals, otherwise the winds generated across the vast expanse of open space could create weather far worse than anything encountered in the great plains of central Asia.

Again the realization of what had happened to him started to well up inside, but his disciplined mind forced the emotion away. If fear of the unknown or the dangerous had ever taken hold of him, he never would have taken an empire, nor could he build a new one on this world. Looking back over his shoulder to the west, he could see the same type of wall, but this one, running north and south, appeared to be far closer.

Since the world he was on curved up, rather than down, the horizon did not disappear. Parmenion was still terrified by that sight alone, but already he was growing used to it. He'd have to, he realized, otherwise he'd go mad.

Not good country for a phalanx, Alexander realized. It was rough and hilly, cut by narrow ravines and brooding heights of bare windswept rock. Aldin told him that the terrain of this region varied greatly, since the First Travelers had apparently taken delight in forming the land without logic, guided by a whimsy to place one thing next to another in wild confusion. A single day's march to the south would bring them into open plains of unbelievable richness, but that was held by whomever he was to lead his new people against.

And then another thought struck him with awe: he had merely conquered a world; these First Travelers had actually built a world.

"Sire, listen!" Parmenion was at his shoulder, whispering even as he pulled him toward a rocky outcropping that offered concealment.

Alexander cocked his head, turning it from side to side, listening, and then he heard it, dancing at the edge of recognition like a distant wave one was not sure was heard or imagined.

He looked at Parmenion for confirmation.

"Sounds like a scream," Parmenion whispered, "a Human scream."

Alexander shrugged his shoulders and started to uncase the bow that Aldin had given him. After a brief struggle he strung it and tested the pull. It was as good as a Scythian weapon, perhaps even better since it was made of a metal, most likely a highly tempered steel, he thought. And again he shook his head in wonder.

He pulled one of the arrows from the quiver and held it, testing the balance. It was light, so very light; the four-barbed head glinting wickedly in the multihued manner of a razor-sharp weapon. Such precision, Alexander thought, and such cost to make one of these in Macedon.

"Shall we?" Alexander inquired of his companion with a smile.

"Ah, sire, it's really none of our business."

"But it is, Parmenion. We have to meet these people sooner or later, so why not now? Eh, unsheath that sword, if it is not rusted in place, and come along."

He said it with a smile as if joking, and shamed, Parmenion fell in behind his king.

I never thought I would someday lead an army of one, Alexander thought, but there must be a start and why not here? And he realized, as well, that the more humble the origin, the greater the glory if he should survive.

Survive—already he was a legend as he had wished, so this adventure was merely an extra reward, as if the gods had decided to give him an even greater challenge. Perhaps that was it, the gods were challenging him further. He smiled at the thought.

If that were the case, he would not disappoint them.

The cries grew louder as Alexander approached the crest of the hill. Crouching low, he approached the ridgeline with caution, moving from boulder to boulder.

There was another cry. This one high-pitched and filled with panic. He suddenly realized that to come to battle like a thief was unbefitting one who was king. Standing erect, he strode forward, as if by his mere presence the disturbance on the other side of the hill would somehow cease.

"By the gods!" Parmenion gasped.

Alexander felt his old companion again, the tremor of fear—but this was a fear unlike anything he had ever faced before. He had feared his father, at least in the beginning, and there had been the fear of failure, but unlike those around him, there had never been the fear in battle. Now he felt it.

The screams were Human, to be sure, and they were screams of panic. And the cause of those screams was to his eyes a moving nightmare.

The creature was wolflike, but yet not. Human, but not. It was as if the two had been blended together into one unholy mating. It rode astride a beast that was twice the size of his Bucephalas. It was like a horse, but somehow fiercer and wilder.

There were a half dozen of the creatures mounted on their nightmare steeds, and he could hear their voices as if they were laughing in triumph. Each of them wielded a lance, and they rode forward in attack formation, spears lowered. One of them carried a Human under its arm, and it was from her that the screams came. He realized now that the screams were ones not of pain but of rage, as she shouted imprecations at the men who were running away. That made him realize for a second that he could indeed understand what she was saying, even thought it was not Greek, Persian, or any dialect he was used to. The implant of Aldin's worked even here and he could understand, as well, the fear in the voices of the men she was swearing at.

Before her captors nearly half a hundred men were running in panic, casting aside their flimsy spears to allow for a more speedy retreat. All this he saw in a glance, and he knew what he must do.

Alexander flexed his bow once more to test its balance and pull. He reached to the quiver strapped to his back and pulled out a shaft of gleaming metal. In an easy, fluid motion he nocked the arrow and pulled back, sighting on the beast who was bringing up the rear of the charge.

He knew this was the moment of the testing, and he knew, as well, that the moment he shot they would turn their wrath upon him.

The arrow snapped out—a sliver of lightning streaking on a fatal path. It caught the creature high in the back, punching straight through what appeared to be a corset of mail. With a loud piercing shriek he pitched forward, lifted from his seat by the impact. The horse sheared to one side, bearing its master out of the attack.

Already the second arrow was nocked, aimed, and away. This one hit a second creature lower in the back but had the same effect. And then the others were aware of him slowing their attack and turning to see where their unseen tormentor was located.

"I think, Parmenion, you'd better ready your pike and prepare to receive cavalry."

But his command was unnecessary as Parmenion had already sheathed his sword. He took the top section of his pike, inserted the socket into the second section of ash, and locked it in place. He stepped to Alexander's side, knelt down on one knee, and snapped the weapon to the present position, so that a charging horse, if foolish enough to press the attack, would impale itself on the long barb.

Parmenion was trembling with fear. He had withstood many a charge, but never one from a horse that stood twenty-five hands tall.

The third arrow winged out and missed its mark as the creature pulled his mount up short just as Alexander fired. The arrow disappeared into the rising cloud of dust.

"Sire, one of them has a bow," Parmenion shouted, and Alexander suddenly noticed the creature that had pulled up short. He was unslinging his bow even as he goaded his horse into the attack.

Another arrow snapped out. This one nearly lifted the creature out of his saddle, the bow falling from his hand.

The remaining three hesitated for a second, then the one carrying the Human female dropped his prisoner to the ground and, with a thundering roar, goaded his horse forward into a lumbering charge.

"Look, look how slow," Alexander shouted. "Impressive, but too slow. The elephants of Pontus were far worse."

The creature lowered his lance, pulled his shield up high for protection, and came forward, all the time howling with a high, piercing keen that set the hair on edge.

Alexander nocked an arrow and stepped forward several paces, stopping just short of the iron head on the end of Parmenion's pike.

"Sire, shoot," Parmenion shouted. "You can get off two or three before he hits!"

"I want to watch," Alexander said. "It's almost beautiful."

"The sight of our blood won't be beautiful, not in the slightest."

But Alexander ignored him, caught up in the remarkable display of the moment. Onward the creature came, now standing high in what Alexander took to be ropes that extended down from either side of the saddle. The horse was indeed impressive, but slow, not able to go much faster than a trot. The armor looked fairly good, but appeared to be nothing more than a leatherlike jerkin.

"Sire! Please shoot him!"

"Another moment."

The creature was closing, so that above the howling he could hear the puffing of the horse, the rattle of the accoutrements. And the creature, as if sensing what he faced, did not blanch, but rather stood higher in the saddle, displaying his defiance.

Alexander shook his head and then drew the bow. His opponent raised his shield up, protecting his side and face.

The bow snapped, and the howling stopped. A riderless horse trotted past Alexander. The beast came to a stop to one side as if it would now watch the outcome of the struggle.

Alexander looked to the other two, who were silent, watching. He strode forward for a dozen paces and cast his cloak aside so that his bronzed and silvered armor shone for the first time in the light of another world.

"I am Alexander, known as the Great, son of Philip, once ruler of half the known world."

He dropped his bow and unsheathed the sword that Aldin had given him. It felt light, well balanced, finer than any steel of the Aramaic sword makers. He was touched by the fact that Aldin had engraved the blade with his titles and the names of his greatest victories. Even across five thousand years they had remembered that. He looked at how the blade shone in the sunlight, and again his gaze turned heavenward.

He looked back again to the remaining two. One of them stood in his stirrups and held his lance aloft. His shouts drifted on the wind and Alexander realized that this creature was speaking to him, but the words held no meaning and he was disappointed that Aldin had not taken care of that, as well.

He assumed it was a challenge, and in response he started to walk down the hill, but even as he started to advance, the two turned their horses about and trotted away.

Reaching the crest of the opposite hill, they looked back again for a moment and then disappeared from view.

"Sire, a good shot that one, but what a devil it is."

Parmenion had advanced over to the body of the one that had charged. Alexander came over to join him. The arrow had driven clear through the shield, catching the creature in the throat. He still could not understand what it was that he had just fought, but he knew that bravery at least was one of its virtues. The creature must have known that he was going to die but still he came forward, rising up in his saddle to meet what Alexander was forced to deliver.

"If this is what we must face, then we have a formidable foe."

"And if those running cowards are what you must lead," Parmenion muttered, gesturing in the direction the men had fled, "then you really have your work cut out."

Alexander knelt down by the side of the creature. It was half again as tall as he was, covered from head to foot in a light matting of soft black hair. Again he had the feeling that he was looking at a Human, but it was a Human that was nearly half wolf. Picking up the still-warm hand, he examined the fingers, which were almost manlike except for the remarkably long thumb that sprang from the wrong side of the wrist.

He looked to the creature's face. The eyes were still open, oriental in appearance with a double folding. The ears were nearly on top of the creature's head, protruding from either side of a studded leather helmet. The armor was well made, but there was hardly any metal; it all appeared to be of leather. Alexander touched the creature's eyelids and closed them. Standing, he picked up its cape and laid it across the body.

"A worthy foe," Alexander said softly, and then looked back to his companion.

"Parmenion, I think it time that we go and meet our subjects."

Parmenion could only shake his head in wonder. This man, this one from the gods, had no doubt, no question; he knew that they were indeed already his subjects.

The horse stood to one side, eyeing the two of them with suspicion. Alexander slowly extended his hand to either side and, speaking softly, he started to approach the beast. The creature shied and stepped back.

"Parmenion, give me a cloak."

Alexander took the cloak that Parmenion snatched up from the body of his fallen foe and draped it around his body. He sifted around the horse in a wide circle so that the wind was at his back, and then started to advance.

The horse was still.

He approached the creature head on, reached up and stroked it lightly on the nose, all the while talking softly. After several minutes he started to work his way to the horse's flank, still stroking it lightly.

It was bigger than any horse he had ever seen, almost the size of a yearling elephant. The pommel of the saddle was well above eye level, and he could just barely grasp it with his hands. The horse shied slightly and nickered, but Alexander hung on, all the while speaking softly.

He took a deep breath and, with a quick graceful movement, pulled himself up then swung his leg up over the horse's back.

The creature started to buck and Alexander fought to stay on. He could barely straddle the animal with his

legs, so wide was the back, and he struggled for balance
as he reached for the reins.

"Sire, try putting your feet into those leather loops,"
Parmenion shouted.

Alexander looked down one side of the horse and saw
the loop Parmenion was shouting about. But they were
too low, and then he saw the strap that adjusted them.

The horse was still bucking even as Alexander
reached over and struggled with the strap, pulling the
loop up higher. He somehow knew that he was being
watched, and to fall off now would be a loss of whatever
mystique he had gained in the fight. The loop was high
enough, at last, and he slipped his left foot in. He
reached over to the other side and quickly hiked the second strap into place and seated his foot in the loop.

He placed his weight down on the ropes and felt a
sense of control. They were remarkable, and the utter
simplicity of the idea stunned him. Why hadn't he, or
one of his cavalry officers, thought of them? Grabbing
hold of the reins, he stood up in the stirrups, and with a sure
gentle hand he quickly brought the beast under control.

Then with a kick of the heels he urged the creature
into a run. After the horses of the Scythians and the
finest of Persian stock, the creature was disappointingly
slow, but he knew that a massed charge of a thousand
such beasts would strike terror even into the best of his
armies—the way the Elephants of Porus had once done.
He realized that this creature combined the best of both.
The terrifying mass of an elephant, but also the greater
agility and control of a horse, and could forage on its
own and not require a mountain of fodder every day.

He galloped up alongside of Parmenion and reined the
horse in.

"Come on, Parmenion, better to ride on Bucephalas
than to walk." There was the trace of a distant smile on
Alexander's lips.

"You still miss him, don't you?" Parmenion asked,
more like an elder brother than a lowly soldier. For like

many of his now-distant army, Parmenion could remember his king as a young boy, and could remember, as well, the boy's lifelong companion who had carried him on a hundred fields of strife, to finally die on the plains of the Indus. He could still remember, as well, their leader who by then was nearer to being a god than a man, resting the head of his companion on his lap and crying like a boy who had lost his first dog. His memory must have showed in his eyes, for Alexander nodded and turned away for a moment.

"His soul came back to serve me here in my hour of need," Alexander said softly. "Again I ride Bucephalas. Now climb up, you sentimental old fool. Let's follow those cowards and see where they hide."

Parmenion accepted his king's hand and scrambled up behind Alexander. He was frightened beyond words by the beast, but he refused to show his fear.

"Speaking of those cowards, did you see where the girl went to? At least she had the courage to curse them."

"No, sire, she disappeared in the confusion."

"Somehow I have a feeling she's still in the area, so keep a watch."

Together they trotted off, riding into the high hills in search of those who had run away.

"Do you smell that, Parmenion?"

"Not as bad as Babylon, sire, but still, what a stink."

They had been climbing into the high hills toward the massive mountain for what Alexander thought must have been several hours; it was impossible now to tell, for the shadows never changed, and always the same crystalline white orb hung motionless, directly overhead. To either horizon he could see the blue-green band extending upward like opposing horns, until they disappeared in the glaring light. To either side ran white barrier lines that Aldin said prevented the air from rushing away. He understood, but still he could not believe.

Even these high hills had been constructed and contoured by godlike hands. That, he realized, was the context he'd have to place this madness into. Otherwise he would indeed lose all perspective. This was the realm made by yet other gods, just as his gods, his sires, had shaped the world of Macedon and the vastness of Persia.

The path they were on narrowed down to a defile barely wide enough for two horses to pass through.

"If any unpleasantness is planned, it will be here," Alexander said softly.

Parmenion lowered his pike, while Alexander nocked an arrow. Even as he pulled the arrow out of the quiver, there was a faint rustle from the defile and then the blowing of a horn.

"Well, let's not come in skulking like thieves," he said, and spurred the horse forward.

There was no one at the defile, but there was evidence of a hasty retreat. Several lances and a number of shields lay scattered about.

"Ah, the dogs, they run again," Parmenion shouted.

"Could be a trick; always remember the Scythians."

They pushed forward, making yet another turn on the trail, and he pulled Bucephalas up short.

The trail ended a short distance ahead in a rude stone palisade that enclosed a small stockade. Looking around, Alexander realized he had wandered into a small valley of green fields and blooming orchards. The fields looked well tended; if anything, these people appeared to be good farmers. There was the faint scent of flowers, but the predominant smell was one of death. Upon the walls of the palisades hung several corpses in various states of decomposition.

"Just like home," Parmenion said with a chuckle.

There was a grunt of a reply from Alexander, and Parmenion could sense his displeasure at the sight. The man before him had ordered such ends for countless thousands and he couldn't understand this sudden disdain. As if sensing the emotion, Alexander turned in the saddle.

"There's another enemy. What fools to kill each other like—"

His words were cut short by a wild cacophony of horns that caused Bucephalas to shy away and snort with fear. As if in answer, a volley of arrows snapped out.

"Well, at least they have archery," Alexander shouted as he and Parmenion together raised their shields. The bolts scattered around them, none striking the two soldiers or their horse.

Alexander stood up in his stirrups and drew back on his bow. Aiming high, he released and the arrow sang upward, soaring far above the wall then disappearing from view.

There was a loud shout of amazement from the defenders, who still remained hidden, but their volleys stopped.

Alexander stood in his stirrups.

"I am Alexander," he cried, hoping that the implant was doing its work. The words formed in his mind and he spoke them knowing what they were, but still he couldn't be sure.

"I have been told of your suffering at the hands of these creatures called Gavarnians. I, Alexander, known as the Great, King of Macedon, Hegemon of all the Greeks, King of Kings of all the Persians and such lands to that of the Indus and the Eastern Sea, have been sent to you from the world you once called Earth."

"Ah, go on," came a derisive cry.

"I tell you I saw it," shouted another from the fortress. "He killed four of them, he did. You saw him shoot."

"The man's a crazy," replied the first. "Look at him out there."

"If you think he's a crazy," came a high voice from

behind Alexander, "then come out here and say it to him face to face."

Alexander turned and looked to where the voice had come from. It was the girl.

She strode forward, barely sparing him a second glance. She was clothed simply in a tunic that nearly reached her feet and was tied around the waist by a knotted cord. Her blond hair hung in two thick braids that fell across her high arching breasts. Her features were light—an oval face and high cheekbones, and a sharp look that expected a response of deference.

"At least he saved me," she shouted. "More than you fools could do."

"But, Neva, what can you expect? There were six of them."

"Open that gate, you damn fool."

"But, Neva. What about him?"

She looked back at Alexander as if noticing him for the first time.

"Most of them are idiots," she muttered, and then she looked back.

"He killed four of the Gafs," she shouted toward the fortress, "what do you think we should do? Let him in and honor him as he deserves."

"If we do that," came another voice that held a note of sarcasm as if speaking to a despised child, "and the Gafs find out, they'll really be after him and us. There's a price on him already, I daresay."

"Enough of this, damn it, now let us in!"

She turned back to Alexander and she smiled.

"If there's a price on you," Parmenion interjected, whispering to Alexander, "then how can we trust these cowards? They might kill us in our sleep."

"Because the leader of the town will swear your protection," Neva responded as if offended by Parmenion's suggestion, "and the word of a Ris will be honored."

"If there is a price on me," Alexander interjected, "know then that I bring conflict with me."

"But of course." Neva smiled. "You can train these people to fight against our neighbors, the Kievants."

"I thought your foes were the Gavarnians."

Neva pointed to the bodies hanging on the walls. "Those are Kievants. The Gafs pay us for each one brought in."

"I think you have your work cut out for you," Parmenion muttered.

"Bring me to your leader," Alexander said wearily. "I want to talk to him about Kievants, and Gafs."

"But you are talking to her right now; just don't tell my uncle—the fool still thinks he runs the place!" Neva replied with a smile, then she turned away.

"Now open those damned gates, you pinheads, or I'll personally come in there and cut off somebody's balls and feed what's left to the Gafs."

"Amazons," Parmenion mumbled. "Damn that Aldin Larice."

CHAPTER 6

"GENTLEMEN," ALDIN SAID, "THE PAYOFF FOR FIRST EN-counter betting is five point five to two in favor of Alexander."

Turning from the screen, Aldin stepped over to the room-length window that provided a panoramic view of the Kolbard beneath them. The view was stunning as he looked straight down to the floor of the ring a hundred kilometers below. The fertile lands held by the Gafs were to his left. It was a well-managed patchwork of green fields and woodlots, intersected by half a dozen rivers that flowed down to the vast inland sea. Reaching almost to the sea, and providing a natural boundary between the western end of the Gavarnian lands and the hills occupied by the Humans, was a shimmering open region. A million years of wind erosion had peeled off the topsoil to reveal the substructure of the Kolbard, creating a vast open desert of bare, polished metal.

To the right were the steep rolling hills and deep ravines occupied by the Humans. Almost straight down he could see the place where he had dropped Alexander off only hours before. A quick punch up on the keypad by his side brought to the screen a high magnification view from one of the hovering drones positioned to monitor the action. He watched Alexander for a moment, still amazed at what he had just managed to accomplish. Turning away from the screen, Aldin looked back at the Kohs in the control room.

Corbin's yacht, *Gamemaster*, was docked to the support bay constructed atop one of the cooling towers of the Kolbard. Except for the monitor and control equipment set into one wall, the rest of the room presented an image of an old, well-endowed hunting lodge, or gentleman's gaming club. The furniture was overstuffed leather, the walls were highly polished teak imported from one of the tropical plantation worlds. Even though the ship was less than a year old, it already had that old familiar masculine smell of expensive cigars, quality brandy, and leather. Of course, the entire vessel was the envy of the other Kohs, and Corbin gloried in this ability to upstage his business rivals.

The servobots quietly made their rounds serving drinks to the Kohs.

"Excellent, my good Aldin," Corbin said, his tone reflecting his pleasure at the auspicious start of the activities, "most excellent indeed. Alexander is everything I had imagined him to be."

"Imagined him to be, and even more," Zola interrupted as he appeared at Aldin's side. "It was foolish of me to bet against his initial contact. I shan't do that again."

"Human-to-Human contact is one thing," Bukha responded, still facing the tote board. "But let me assure you, the first organized encounter between Gavarnian and Human will be a straightforward and foregone conclusion. Alexander or no Alexander."

"But you saw it from the remote scan," Corbin replied evenly. "He lifted four of your much-vaunted Gavarnians out of their saddles without taking a scratch."

"You know," Zola said silkily, coming up to Bukha's side, "maybe your warriors are simply not up to snuff."

Bukha turned toward Zola and gave him a full toothy grin, with his fangs slightly bared.

Zola stepped back. "Well, no need to get barbaric about it."

"Not at all, not at all, just yawning. No hostility intended."

"Gentlemen, the first segment of betting has ended," Aldin interrupted. "You may settle your accounts through the main filing system. As is custom, our hosting Kohs Corbin Gablona and Bukha Taug shall provide feasting in celebration."

"Any word on Zergh and the delivery of Kubar Taug?" Sigma asked.

"Drop-off will occur shortly," Aldin replied. And there was a muffled round of excited conversations as the Kohs went over to the table that floated into the room, laden with the finest delicacies to be found anywhere in the Magellanic Cloud. Even the Xsarn was joining them, putting aside his regular diet for once, to eat what he considered to be uncooked food.

Looking over his shoulder, Kubar Taug saw that his squire was with him, bearing the Vota, the silver rod of office that he had designed for himself back across the millennia. But that was the past, lost to dust, across two thousand estas, what Zergh told him was measured now by the Human term of four thousand years. Dust, they were all dust. All his friends, the tens of thousands of his host, the grand and massive players in the drama of uniting a world—all gone to dust.

And his siblings, his three brothers who had died before him. Cliarn was dead just days past, or was it four thousand years? He turned away from his squire and closed his eyes. His three brothers, he thought, and the aching filled his soul as it did for all Gafs. For like all Gavarnians, he had come into the world at the same time with his three other brothers and a single sister. But the brothers had left before him, to wait in Binda, the Hall of Quiet Repose and Longing, waiting until the four were again united and thus could journey together to the Unseen Light.

Oh, my brothers, he thought sadly, how long have you waited for me. Have you sat in silence across the millennia watching as all others were united but still I would not come? Have you feared that I would never stand in the Portal of Light? Or did your spirits come with me through time, as well? Were they granted that reprieve, at least? Did Cliarn, whose dying eyes had looked into his but days ago, did he bring the two who had died so young?

"Cliarn, forgive me," he whispered, as he had said to himself ten thousand times while journeying across the heavens to this new world. This new world. Opening his eyes, he looked again upon the alien sun, which was blinding white, rather than the soft ruby glow of home. He averted his gaze and looked at the upward sweep as the horizon curved up and away to either side—twin horns of blue green with occasional streaks of brown.

Looking to what Zergh said was the equal of north, he could see three soaring mountains that seemed to loom nearly overhead, even though they were at least dozens of leagues away. Behind him there were three more, one coming straight out of the great sea. The city he was walking toward rested at the base of the mountain which already he called Valdinca, the Mountain of Spirits. When this thing, this quest was over, he would climb up Valdinca, if such a thing were possible, and see where the great sailing ships of the stars had once docked. Back home he had sailed the sky, and the memory filled him with joy, for it was during his reign that balloons first rose above his world, floating from the heat of fires and also from the breaking of water. He had won his greatest victory at Heda with that tactical surprise. Perhaps that would be the way to reach up to the mountaintops when this was over.

When this was over. He smiled to himself at that thought. How often, how very often he had thought that phrase "when this is over" during the darkest days of the fifth coalition, or in the exile of a hundred nights. How often he had dreamed of the beginning, when it had only been himself and his three glorious brothers of blood birth, united together.

But his brothers were ashes. And she was ashes, too, as were the children. All that, the price to conquer a world. He looked again at Paga, and Paga as always had the expression of worried concern for his lord.

He was a squire. Kubar had begged Paga to take the ranks that he truly deserved, but always his old childhood friend had refused, wishing only to serve him. It was Paga who had saved his life more than once when there had been only a score of them, hunted and despised—the hunting more a blood sport than war for the nobles he faced. It was more than half a lifetime ago when he had organized the first company of a hundred from his village to rebel against the established order of serfdom and overlord. Yes, Paga was the last of that glorious company.

There again the word glorious. When the campaign of twenty estas was ending at last, how often they had used that word. Glorious, that was the lie to give the bereaved. Somehow that one word made the burden more bearable for some as they united not only a people but a world into one class of free beings—a union that had to be paid for with a generation's worth of blood.

He looked again at the upward sweep of a world that his senses told him was somehow made backward, or out of a mirror where the horizons did not behave as they should. So for the passing of five hundred generations his name had been enshrined—how he had gone to the mountain Valdinca after the last battle and the death of Cliarn, and there disappeared, to join his ancestors.

He chuckled to himself. The disappearing had been the final act, the final cement that had united them under his semidivine legend—and here he was now, an age later, asked to do the same thing all over again by his most distant descendants who had swept out to the stars, as he had dreamed they would.

He smiled at Paga and motioned that they should kneel and wait. It would not be long, of that he could be sure, for Zergh had told him that they would be placed next to a much-frequented path that the patrols often rode upon. Patrols of an overlord—the mere thought of it made him shake his head in sadness. For though they glorified his name they had forgotten once again. In his name the dream had held until new worlds were gained, but there the old corruption had taken hold, and once again there were overlords and serfs, warrior class and downtrodden.

They revered him yet they forgot what he had stood for. The prophet Jesdha was right when he said that it was the curse of prophets to always look beyond what normal beings could see, and thus break their own hearts in the process. So he would have to start again, here on this new world that a fellow Gavarnian had taken him to aboard a floating ship of miracles. He pondered on that for a moment, and had the feeling that he had not been told everything, but he would let that matter pass until his task was over.

He sighed with the realization of what had to be done. Zergh had told him that the old conventions before the unifying had again taken hold. It was as if these descendants, fearing the future, had returned to the distant past. Therefore he would proclaim himself as in the old legends and then the proofs would have to be given—and for that he had to prepare.

With a ruffling of his silken robes, Kubar Taug knelt in the dust of the roadside and assumed the position of the first contemplation, and Paga, standard-bearer and weapons carrier, knelt with him. They did not have long to wait.

He heard a rhythmic noise in the distance. It sounded like the canter of a dispa, but he knew already that their two-legged beast of burden was not used on this world, but was replaced instead by a beast taken from the hairless ones, and bred to a larger size.

He closed his eyes, his breathing controlled, looking inward to the source, wherein he had first come to realize his calling to a higher destiny. The approaching riders drew nearer and clattered to a stop.

"You, gray one, you block the way of the feday, the messenger of the Taug."

Kubar was silent. So his own name had come to be the name given to a ruler, but he could not now react to the insult. He extended his hand in the subtlest of gestures for Paga to restrain himself.

"I say, you, gray one." The voice was impetuous, having been slighted by his lack of response. "I spare you for you are elder to me, but move aside or my breeding and station shall be forgotten, even though you wear the garb of an ancient."

Kubar remained motionless, his eyes closed.

He heard his challenger dismount, his armor creaking, his boots crunching on the hard gravel of the road.

"If you seek your end, gray one, if you wish to join your brothers, then I shall be forced to oblige."

He could hear the sword being drawn and with it the intaking of breath from Paga.

"I shall command you but once," Kubar said evenly, "for I am Kubar Taug, across the generations come yet again to unite you all as one." And as he spoke he rose up and faced the warrior who approached him with sword already drawn and poised to the third chord, the position known as the Macna, used for the killing of someone whose social class you were not sure of. So that old useless relic of etiquette had survived, as well, Kubar thought.

The warrior changed to the sixth chord of contempt and smiled. "You are a mad one and as such must lie and thus hold no class. Prepare to die."

As soon as the warrior had said the word lie, Paga started forward bellowing with rage, but he was already too late.

In one fluid motion, Kubar's sword snapped from its scabbard. Before the warrior's expression could even change from a smile to one of pain, his head rolled from its body. With a flick of his wrist Kubar snapped the blood from his blade and returned to the kneeling position, in the spreading pool of blood.

Paga faced the stunned companion of the dead messenger. "How far to the one you call your taug?"

"Half a dozen dimmings away, but his brother is less than a dimming ride from here."

A dimming? That was something the one called Zergh had neglected to explain. He only hoped that this dimming was not too long off.

"Go and announce to him," Paga shouted, "that Kubar Taug has crossed time to lead yet again!"

The messenger looked at Paga in disbelief.

"Go then, or you must face my sword as well."

"I've already seen enough from the hairless ones that is strange, so that one more strangeness to report is nothing," the messenger said, and he held up a bandaged arm as if this were a proof. "I shall bear that message."

Spurring his mount, he rode around the body of his companion and pressed on.

Paga felt a light touch on his shoulder, and he stirred from his meditation.

"I think I understand the term of the dimming," Kubar said thoughtfully.

Paga could see that his master's curiosity was aroused and came to his feet to stand by Kubar's side.

"Notice that it is darker, yet no cloud covers the sky.

I felt it some time ago, a slight cooling of the air. Do you notice?"

"It is darker," Paga said excitedly, and he looked again to the strange white sun, which still hovered directly overhead in the same position.

"Is it dying?" he cried suddenly, looking around and trying to control his fear.

Kubar chuckled softly. "Astronomy was not your interest, my warrior blood kin. I remember my observers of the night said that some stars did glow brighter and then dimmer. This world, this Kolbard, as Zergh put it, does not turn its face away from the sun above, but a form of night occurs nevertheless when the light of the sun dims."

Kubar looked back up the road toward where the messenger had disappeared.

"They said less than a dimming, therefore I must assume they shall return shortly. I hope we don't have to go through another such wasteful folly." As he spoke, he looked at the now-rigid body at his feet.

"I hope not, as well. I think that those for whom we wait are coming," Paga replied evenly, pointing down the road the messenger had taken. Secretly he feared that the warriors of this world would think the two of them mad and blood challenge would follow blood challenge until they were both dead.

It was still confusing that the horizon did not act as a horizon should, but Kubar could see where Paga was pointing to a serpentine line advancing toward them.

"I must contemplate before I act," Kubar said softly, and returned to the kneeling position.

"There are now two dead," Paga said evenly as he gazed at the second headless corpse, which had fallen on top of the first one, the fresh blood pooling into the gravel to mingle with the dried black stain from the earlier killing.

A murmur arose from the circle of warriors that surrounded them.

Kubar again sheathed his sword and looked straight at the leader of the party.

"I am Kubar Taug, and I lower myself to speak in answer but speak I must to explain. I am not mad. Only a madman would lie to those whom he wishes to serve with, at least it was so in my day. Or have the Gavarnians grown degenerate?"

He already knew the answer to that question, for Zergh had told him that the age-old injunction to tell the truth within the clan, which had come up from the distant, preliterate past, still held true on the Kolbard. Even through the mindset of the translation implant, he could sense, as well, that certain words could still be traced back to their root, and the references to truth saying and lying were remarkably the same. There was a significant smattering of words whose roots when unknown to him —the translator implant handled them, and he could only imagine that they were of alien origin.

The fifty warriors that surrounded him were silent, all dressed in the same lacquered armor, the only color to them a single red ribbon used to tie their queues. He knew that one of them had to be the kin leader but the gambit was to find out which one. Motionless, he started to hold each in turn with his gaze. Most quickly turned away, some tried to fight his will, and some avoided his glance altogether. From the corner of his eye he noticed the warriors looking to one in particular.

This one did not look like the kin leader, at least not from physical appearance. He must rule by his intelligence and wit rather than strength, Kubar thought, and he will have the strong arm of a sworn champion to defend him.

"I turn to leader who has seen," Kubar said softly, staring over the leader's head to avoid a challenge, "and in your wisdom you must decide if yet another is to die to prove my claim."

The leader snorted and spurred his mount to draw closer. "I have seen, and will not call you an untruth-speaker, but such a claim..." His words drifted off to silence.

Kubar was motionless with Paga at his side holding the silver staff of office. "I can understand your questioning and blame you not, for you must be possessed of wisdom and judgment to lead."

He could sense the inner sigh of relief from the leader. Kubar had avoided a confrontation of proof and a direct blood challenge, at least for the moment.

"Let us eat and talk as the dimming moves, and then perhaps we will see the path to light."

With the third round of the *musa* the mood between the two had started to relax as the soothing effects of the mild narcotic drink coursed through them.

The leader sat on a intricately woven rug, the group surrounded by a windscreen of pale-green cloth that bore the repeated pattern of a single blue flower.

Not a word had been passed between them, for the first to speak would lose face, and each continued to stare at the ground in front of him to avoid direct eye contact, which could be taken as a challenge.

Kubar found this to be of some interest since the ritual was almost the same as from his time—right down to the simple fact that both he and the kin leader had subtly let the hair on their body extend outward, just enough to show calmed assurance—not so much as to be interpreted as a sign of hostility, nor so little, to be taken as a sign of subservience in the presence of a superior.

Finally it was a standard-bearer standing to the side of the leader who spoke first, breaking the silence.

"And you who are Kubar, you have no lesser blood kin to speak first?"

"As you should already know, if my name has survived, my first blood kin died at Mutacha, my second at Vollen, my third—" he hesitated for a moment—"you should know of Cliarn, as well. Therefore your question to me is obviously a trap, but this time I shall not take offense. Is your leader present here the last blood kin?"

He looked up at the one across from him, who gave a slight nod of acknowledgment.

"I speak for Hina co Kalin," the standard-bearer replied, "second to his eldest brother Kalin called taug, who are brothers to Swanika, killed by a fall from his mount, and Uta, killed but a dimming ago by a hairless one."

Kubar detected shame in the speaker's voice, and the statement was greeted by a low murmur. Kubar realized that to die at the hands of a Human was considered dishonorable.

Kubar nodded in the direction of Hina, who was the second of four brothers and thus standard-bearer to the taug. With formal introductions completed by both sides, there could no longer be a killing out of hand, for names had been given and the death stories of brothers exchanged. Zergh had told him that this ritual had survived, as well, so he knew he had achieved the first step.

Hina now unbuckled his sword and placed it on the ground to his left side, and Kubar followed his example, not confident of the symbolism, but feeling that it must be a sign of trust.

"I shall not call you untruthspeaker," Hina began, "but by the souls of my brothers and father, you must see that what you are asking me to believe is almost beyond belief."

Kubar could only smile. Until a score of days past, if someone had walked into his council room and announced that he was the legendary Gretha, slayer of the beast Vis who had once entwined the world in its coils, he would have been hardpressed not to take insult for being lied to.

Kubar chuckled and look up at the dim star overhead.

"Hear me, Hina co Kalin, brother of the taug. If someone had told me that I would be sitting on this world called a Kolbard, five hundred lifetimes into my future, and discussing such impossibilities as casually as this, why, I would not have hesitated to treat him as he deserved. Have you ever heard of Zergh?"

"No."

"Too bad, he is a most remarkable Gavarnian—part thief, part spirit god."

Hina was silent.

"I know that fifteen hundred estas ago your ancestors were travelers from other worlds."

Hina nodded.

"That your ancestors came to this world, and then a great war, a cataclysm, cut them off from their brethren who have never returned."

"That is known by all," Hina replied.

"But did you know that there are Gavarnians who live almost like the gods of our ancient legends, that still journey among the stars?"

Hina was silent for a moment; a look of confusion crossed his face and then understanding.

"Yes, that word is in our Coda. It is a light in the sky that can not be seen. Stars hovered in the sky when the world of our ancestors turned as dark as a cave. Stars . . ." He fell silent for a moment as if looking off in to some great distance.

"All of us remember the stories of our childhood, when our brothers still walked by our side and we knew not which of us would be the first one called by fate. To all of us there are the legends of our sires and our heroes long gone. And first among them—first warrior, first strategist, first conqueror, and then uniter—was Kubar do Ladg, first-named taug. He is our idol, he who united together the various clans of the Gavarn, he who first rose up and set all Gavarnians free, so that together we could leap outward to the stars. He was my dream, and thus your words are either the cruelest of jests or a dream that has come to walk among us."

Hina was silent again, daring to lock gazes with Kubar.

"And somehow, I always thought Kubar Taug to be bigger than life, his voice bolder, and gaze purer, his strength stronger, a radiance emanating from his soul. And instead I meet someone dust covered, someone with an infinite weariness in his eyes, his pelt already thinning, and who stands barely to the shoulder of most of my guards. And that someone claims the name of Kubar Taug."

"And yet Kubar Taug does sit across from you, or I would not be a truthsayer, and then would my strength diminish and I would die."

Hina's gaze would not break from that of Kubar.

"This is Das," Hina said, drawing his blade and placing it before Kubar.

The admiration of the blades, Kubar realized—yet another ritual that had been revived—and he suddenly knew just how important this act would be. It was a ritual, but it could now be a proof, as well.

"And this is Tagak, of purest steel, unknown to your own world."

There was a gasp of amazement as the sword slipped from its sheath, reflecting the light of the dimming sun. Extending the hilt, he leaned over and presented the blade to Hina. Etiquette was forgotten as the warriors gathered around to gaze admiringly at the shimmering blade. Taking the hilt in one hand and the tip of the blade in the other, Hina looked over at Kubar, who nodded his approval.

Hina's muscles coiled as he pulled the blade back until it bent nearly double. The audience was silent. Their own metal would have snapped from the tension. When he released the tip of the sword, the blade snapped back to its original position.

"It is truly a blade of the ancestors," Hina said softly, as he admired the watery lines and luster locked into cold steel, perfect except for a single notch near the hilt.

"Tagak," Paga replied. "And I now carry its sister sword, the blade of Cliarn—Tusta." And he withdrew the sword from its scabbard and laid it before the assembly. The two blades were identical down to the single notch cut into each near the hilt. Hina reached out and touched the single imperfection on the one blade and then the other.

Hina looked up at Kubar, and closing his eyes, he started to recite.

> Coming together, equal to equal,
> Steel flashing fire,
> Coming together, blood to blood,
> Life spilled by brother,
> Thus the joining complete, and the sacrifice made,
> Sacrifice made,
> Death of a brother, a race joined as one.

Kubar fought for composure. The night Cliarn died, he had heard Shesta, the laymaker, first sing those words. And they had survived, along with the dark memory.

Hina reverently picked up the sister swords, one after the other, and presented them back to their owners. By such an act he acknowledged acceptance into the circle of the clan. However, Hina had only displayed his blade to Kubar and had not offered it. Therefore he was not pledged to protect in return.

Kubar made a subtle gesture to Paga not to react to the implied snub. He realized that full and immediate acceptance was of course something impossible to expect so soon. That could only come with time. Even if Hina fully believed what he had said, Hina was not taug. His first brother held that position and thus Hina could not make an acknowledgment that his brother might not accept. He was wise, this one, and cautious, as any of a ruling family should be. Already Kubar liked him, even though he was of this ancient noble system that had returned to life on the Kolbard.

Kubar noticed that it was still getting darker. The light was as dark as if a monsoon-laden cloud had passed before the sun, yet still the sky was clear. He could not help but turn his gaze away from Hina and look to the dark-blue heavens.

"Will the light return again to its former strength?"

Hina laughed. "But of course you would not know that, would you?"

Kubar could detect no testing in that question and knew that the first step toward ultimate acceptance had been passed. He would simply have to prove to them that their greatest legend had indeed come. He looked from the sky back to his arms and legs.

Yes, the legend had come. Even if his fur was thinning out, he thought, and he scratched the bald spot at the back of his neck.

CHAPTER 7

"You there. Yes, you with the sloping forehead. You'll never have the makings of a pikeman of the first rank." Parmenion's voice was cracking with rage. "Yes, stupid, I mean you, step forward!

"And you think you'll be a soldier?" Parmenion stepped closer and leaned forward standing on his tip-toes in a vain attempt to come to the soldier's eye level. "Well, come on, man, speak. Or are you struck dumb, as well?"

The object of his wrath could only look at him goggle-eyed with fright. His mouth was open as if he were trying to speak, but only inarticulate sounds came out.

Parmenion threw up his hands in exasperation, and the pikeman in training jumped back.

"That's it, jump back. I'll see you jump back when you stand your first charge. By all the gods, I'll see you with my sword sticking up your butt if you waver one god-cursed inch. I swear that." His voice was near to breaking. "I swear it by the shadows of my father. I swear it by Alexander himself."

"Try not to drag my name into this."

Parmenion turned on his heels and with a quick flourish presented his pike as Alexander drew closer.

"General Parmenion, if you would be so good as to inspect the latest workings of the smithy, I'd like a word with these men."

"Smithy? There isn't enough metal in this entire stinkhole to make fifty pike heads. And even less intelligence to fashion them."

Parmenion passed through the gate back into the town, the roar of his cursing causing the villagers to bar their doors yet again and to hide their children from view.

"You may rest," Alexander said evenly, and a grateful sigh went up from the three hundred men and handful of women who stood in the ranks.

He tried to imagine them as something different, to see again the serried ranks of his Companions, the five thousand men of the finest phalanx in the world, marching across the plain of Guagamela to dispute the kingship of empires. But there was only the harsh reality.

His "army" was a ragtag, scurvied, thoroughly unmilitary rabble of cowards and thieves. Their city was a hideout for petty robbers who would snatch up an occasional unarmed traveler. They were good for the bludgeon blow to the back, or the even more despicable hunting of their neighbors to collect the Gavarnian reward for heads, but as he had seen not a score of dimmings ago, they routed when a handful of Gafs on horseback decided to chase them for some sport.

This was his army. Starting with this band of scum, he would have to unite all the tribes in a region larger than Anatolia and then turn that force against the Gafs who, to make matters worse, were ruled under a common king of kings, known as the Taugech, or some such thing. Alexander knew as well that if this Taugech sensed but for a moment that a uniter had come to bind the men together, he would not cease until that man had been hunted down. It was of course what he would do if the roles were reversed. Therefore a task that should take years would have to be accomplished in months, otherwise the common enemy would destroy him.

He looked back to the unit.

"General Parmenion is right." He almost stumbled over the words. There had been another Parmenion, most trusted general of his father and right hand to his own early conquests, until he had been accused of treason and then executed. Alexander had never quite forgotten what he had believed at the time was a betrayal, and still his dreams were haunted by that old weather-creased face. So now there was a new Parmenion, a bulging, one-eyed, illiterate guard who was his only link to a different past. A new general Parmenion for a new world.

The men were silent, sullen, and most of all resentful that this stranger, with claims to a legendary grandeur, had so thoroughly mucked up their lives. Alexander knew they'd most likely stab him in the back at the first chance if not for the fact that Neva—who had the strength, both physical and mental, to cower the thieving lot—would kill the first man who tried. He half suspected that when the Gafs had snatched her, the men had run away not in panic, but in relief. Even her uncle, Ivarn Black Teeth, who was the nominal ruler of this filth patch, seemed overawed by her at times. There was something about her that did not fit this place. But now was not the time to ponder that point.

"So far you've fought only as individuals," Alexander said in a voice that he used when he was speaking in a comradely fashion. "For what is to be done you must learn to fight as one. You must move as one, level spears as one, and if need be, die as one. Damn you all, you must realize that if but one of you fails, if but one runs, then the rest of us could die.

"Have no pity for the weak in your ranks, for he could cause your death. Now, I have told you that a hundred times already, but now I tell you something different. Tomorrow we advance against the Kievants. Tomorrow with your newfound skill and courage you will vanquish your foes. All of you have told me how you hate the Kievants, how they piss in your drinking stream and steal your women and young boys for their perverted lusts. With my leadership you will punish them and show them that the men of Ris are to be feared!"

He finished that statement with a rhetorical flourish, expecting a resounding cheer. But they were silent, dumb. After an embarrassed moment, he turned away.

"Now lower those spears, damn you, and advance at the walk pace."

Ivarn, as usual, was already into the latter stages of drunkenness, roaring how tomorrow he would personally cut off the ears of the fallen bandits of Kievant. Alexander sat on the stool across from him, with Parmenion at his back. The room was illuminated by a smokey dung fire that filled the chamber with a choking stench, until finally some of the cloud, after having watered the eyes and fouled the air, curled out of a hole in the roof.

The dimming was nearly half over, but Ivarn was in rare form and already raving.

"And that damned Borst, him will I personally castrate and then hang out on the walls of his miserable dung heap."

Alexander nodded absently and spared another glance toward Neva.

As usual, she was trying her best to give a seductive look toward "her savior," as she called him. He quickly turned his gaze away. The problem with sex was here, as well. Even in his youth he had somehow felt removed from the lusty talk of his comrades. He simply did not feel the same desire, either for the love of another man, so praised by the Thebans, or for the desire of a woman. It seemed to him that he played halfheartedly in a game, more to humor his friends than to take pleasure in the game itself.

And then there was the simple fact that she was the only female relative of the chieftain of this miserable village. The fact that he had rescued her from the "Gafs," as these villagers called them, had raised his prestige, and then his promise to Ivarn to help him destroy the Kievants had, for the moment at least, secured his position. He didn't want to take any risks.

"So tell me again, O legendary one," Ivarn roared, and his half-dozen bodyguards snickered at the witty sarcasm, "how do we do it?"

Alexander looked over at Parmenion in order to stifle any protest or sarcastic comments.

"It's quite simple, O king of kings." Alexander almost choked on the words, but he had to play the part. "I am simply showing you a secret way of defeating your enemies and expanding your glory. By fighting together as one team, you can overcome ten times your number."

"And then I can drive my enemies before me?" Ivarn asked, almost childlike in his tone.

"That is correct."

"And if you fail us tomorrow?" one of the guards grumbled.

Alexander gave him an even smile. "There will be no failure."

"You should hope so," Ivarn said evenly. Alexander knew that he was on a fine balance here. The bow he carried was worth more than all the possessions of this entire village, and it was only the promise of victory against the rivals in the next valley that kept his head on his shoulders.

"Here, another drink," Ivarn suddenly called as he staggered to his feet, offering a sack of fermented goat milk to Alexander.

"Don't you think some rest should be taken?" Alexander asked. "The dimming is more than half passed. It's best to be the first ones moving, for we can expect that the Kievants already know that something is afoot."

Ivarn waved the advice aside and collapsed back onto the stool that he called a throne.

"I think I shall see to the guards," Alexander replied coldly, and rising up, he gave a curt nod to the chieftain and strode out of the hut. His instincts were still expecting that nighttime would be dark, whereas during a dimming the intensity of light dropped only to that of a cloudy day, or the light of a full moon on the snow-covered steppes beyond Bactria. He looked in the direction that in his mind had come to mean northwest, and in the far distance, clinging to the side of Olympus, there floated a flickering smudge of light and a thin plume of smoke. In a few short hours he would march up to them and take the first step toward his new empire.

Again he was flooded by a sense of wonder. He looked to the west, and curving farther up and away he could see rivers of blue, what appeared to be a distant ocean, dark mountain valleys, green forests, and high pillars of white. until the colors merged into a dark blue-green arching up overhead—to be lost in the glare of the dimming sun.

"You know he plans to kill you once you've defeated the Kievants for him."

He turned and Neva was standing by his side. He had smelled her approach, since like all the rest of these robbers she viewed bathing as an insult and complete waste of time.

Alexander realized this girl could be quite attractive if cleaned up and dressed in the way that he was more accustomed to. She drew closer to him and lightly touched his shoulder, pressing her body to his side.

"I could be available to you for the rest of this darkness, if you wished."

"I thank you for the honor," Alexander whispered in reply, hoping that Parmenion at least had the sense to keep an eye on the girl's other hand, which he knew was resting on the pommel of her dagger, "but it is nearly time to rouse the men. And before I go to battle I must have my strength, or the gods will not help me."

"A man such as you surely has the strength to know three women in a night before going out to cut the throats of his foes."

"Ah, yes, of course. But I wish to serve your uncle to the fullest of my strength."

"That old goat, didn't you hear me say he is in there right now planning to kill you?"

"Why are you telling me this?"

"Isn't it obvious?" She started to move her body against his in what anyone but a blind man could see was a reasonable imitation of what she had hopes would occur in very short order.

Alexander suddenly grabbed hold of her and, choking down a gag, he kissed her on the neck. She gave a shudder and groaned with delight. Parmenion, keeping an eye on her dagger hand, could only grin with lewd delight.

"My dear, I want to as much as you," he whispered, "but if I don't win this fight, your uncle will have my head no matter what. I need all my strength and more to win, and then you'll see my reward." He kissed her once more then quickly released her and stepped back.

She looked at him hungrily, her eyes glazed with lust.

"Just look out for Lothar. He's the big dumb-looking one. He'll do anything Ivarn says; the others are too cowardly to try for you in the open."

"Thank you. And know that your desire will soon be fulfilled." He gave a curt glance to Parmenion and muttered, "Let's get the hell out of here." Backing away, he left Neva still panting with desire.

Parmenion started to whisper a ribald comment, but before the first word was out Alexander's gaze let it be known that he would be crossing into very deep waters if he continued.

She watched him disappear around the corner. She was still trembling with desire and now he was gone. Her thoughts centered in on Lothar, who had already staggered back to his hut to sleep off the party. Well, arrangements could be made, she thought, and though Lothar was dumb, he certainly did have a couple of advantages. She smiled with anticipation.

"Remember, at a walk," Parmenion roared. "And be sure your shield covers the man to your left!"

In the distance the horns of the enemy sounded louder. The town looked like an anthill that someone had stirred with a stick, setting the nest into a boiling swirl of activity. The Kievant warriors were pouring out of the gate, shouting and cursing. Alexander could only shake his head in absolute amazement. These people had to be even cruder than the men following him.

It was exactly as Neva had predicted. Combat between the various towns was half blood-vengeance and half blood-sport. When rival sides went to the field, they would meet before one gate or another and spent most of the day shouting insults at each other. To them, that was the civilized way of having a good fight.

Occasionally, she said, someone would work up the nerve and sally toward the other side with much shouting and gesturing. A rival from the opposing tribe, shouting curses in return, would venture out from his camp and then amid elaborate shouts, gestures, and an occasional toss of spears, they would close in. The fight would be joined until either a lucky blow killed someone or one of the combatants was wounded. The wounded man would flee back to the support of his comrades who had been shouting encouragements and, of course, placing an occasional bet on the side. The injured warrior's fellow tribesmen would ward off the spears and random arrow shots of the victor's companions, and the match would be over.

On rare occasions it would boil up into a more general action with a couple of dozen men and an occasional woman trading blows, but that was the extent of organization to their brawls.

After several days of this, one side or another would acknowledge defeat and either pull back inside its walls or march back to its own village leaving their dead, as custom demanded, to be taken as trophies. Of course, the heads would be cashed in to the Gafs for a bounty. If enough fresh heads were presented, the Gafs would take that as a tribute and leave the village alone.

It seemed remarkable to Alexander that men could sink so low that they didn't even understand how to wage a good war, but his own experience with trying to train these men was evidence enough. He thought for a moment of Homer and the heroes of legend who fought one-on-one beneath the walls of Troy—but those men were heroes, these characters were nothing more than brawling thieves.

Alexander surveyed his rag-tag army, marching in a column, four abreast, from his elevated position on Bucephalas. He could well understand how the Gafs had triumphed over them centuries ago and driven them from the fertile valley into the high hills where they were hunted for sport, the way he would hunt for a wild boar.

"Sire, we're drawing closer. I think it's nearly time."

Alexander nodded to Parmenion and gestured for him to order the men from the closed, marching rank into attack formation. He had to keep his own men moving and not let them have any time to consider what was about to happen. Neva's estimates were off when she said the numbers were even. There were at least five or six hundred men pouring out of the fortified village. But the odds could be ten times as great and still it would not have worried him. Discipline against numbers would even the score, as it had on nearly every battlefield he had ever fought upon.

Parmenion struggled, kicked, and shouted to get the unwilling warriors out of their column and into an attack phalanx sixty wide and five deep. Alexander had agreed with his recommendation that with so few men the phalanx would have to be shallower than was customary in order to make it wide enough to wedge the flanks on either side of the ravine through which they were advancing.

Alexander nocked an arrow to his bow and guided Bucephalas to the rear of the advancing column. It galled him to have to lead his troops, from behind, but he realized that his presence in the rear, mounted on a Gaf horse with a nocked arrow ready for the first deserter, would go far toward winning the battle. It was far better to guide from the back of the phalanx than to lead from the front and discover that his "army" had decided to go home.

The chanted insults of the Kievants could now be plainly heard.

"We piss on your heads, you scum."

"You are downhill from us, we are above you."

That one he couldn't figure out. Why the relative location of one to other had any relevance was beyond him. It was an absurdity that even Parmenion could grasp as craziness. But the Ris believed it significant and now cried out in rage.

Parmenion, holding the standard, which was nothing more than a ragged piece of cloth upon which was a crudely drawn representation of Mount Olympus, turned to look back at his men and held the flag aloft.

Alexander looked over his shoulder to where Ivarn, surrounded by his half-dozen guards, sat beneath the shadow of a low-hanging cliff, watching the fight from a safe distance. He knew the dirty old coward would hang there in the back until things were decided, one way or the other.

"All right, Parmenion, let's get this over with," Alexander said, half disgusted at just how ridiculous this motley host looked. A boy standing next to Alexander started to beat out a rhythm on a drum, while Parmenion, holding the standard high, advanced toward the

Kievants who were shouting gleefully at the strange display.

More than one man looked over his shoulder toward Alexander. And a simple gesture with the point of the arrow was enough to convince him to stay with the task at hand.

They advanced up the ravine toward the milling crowd of warriors who stood several hundred paces beyond the wall of their village. The range closed, and individuals could now be easily discerned.

Aldin had the telecams up to full magnification, and was even able to artfully fade between different views as he shifted the scenes back and forth. There wasn't any real serious betting going on over this match; it was more of a professional interest than anything else, but he needed to observe this thing, as well. This was the first time anyone of this age had a chance to witness Alexander in an organized battle. Perhaps there would be some clues that could be applied to later bets.

He knew Corbin would be watching with special interest, and some of the other Kohs would want copies of the action. But with no major fight between the Gavarnians and Humans anticipated for some time, all except a couple of the Kohs had departed the yacht to return home for business or other sport. Once the action started to heat up, they would be back—and a tape of the early fights would be of interest to them.

Somehow it almost seemed a little pathetic to see this once-mighty king reduced to leading such a despicable band. The presence of the man still haunted him. He had, if anything, expected a certain haughtiness, like the attitudes of the Kohs whom he served. There was a certain regal bearing, to be sure, but in spite of that, Aldin could not help but like and finally admire the man. This was not because of the place he held in history, which was cause enough for admiration. It was on a more personal level. Alexander had remarkable gifts, and rather than arouse a sense of envy or distrust, they created instead a desire to like him. At times he seemed like an eager boy confronted with a whole new universe to explore, and yet just below the surface was an infinite sadness. Aldin tried to shake the thought away but he felt as if he, too, supposedly a hard-bitten professional, was somehow under his sway. He could only hope that events of which Alexander was not even aware would not destroy him completely, without a shred of self-respect to soothe his passing.

"To the half left, turn!"

The advancing phalanx, as was typical of such a formation, had started to drift to the right, since each man instinctively moved toward the protection of the shield held by his neighbor.

They were now within a hundred paces of the Kievants, whose shouted taunts had died down to an uneasy silence. Almost all the men turned as commanded, except for a handful who weren't sure of their lefts and rights. The ranks tangled up for a moment, but the men were pushed along with the crowd and quickly faced in the right direction.

"Half right, turn!"

They were now bearing down more or less toward the middle of the Kievants, who jumped about halfheartedly, not at all sure of what was going on. After all, normal men would, at this point, start calling out their individual taunts, start strutting, and generally parade up and down for a couple of hours before working up the nerve to go in. But these men were strangely quiet and came on like a wave.

"Spears down!"

The sight of the spears dropping, more or less, as if guided by a single hand, sent a chill down Alexander's back. It was almost like the old times.

"Don't bunch up, don't bunch up!" Parmenion's voice

was cracking with excitement. It was his first command and he was obviously enjoying it.

The Kievants were absolutely dumbfounded. Some of them cast their spears—most dropping short—but a couple hit into the ranks and a man went down screaming in pain. The advancing formation started to waver.

The timing was all important, that is what won a battle. He knew the time was now, or the men would break apart and revert to their cherished but completely absurd methods of combat.

"Now, my Macedons," Alexander shouted, caught up in a strange fantasy, "charge them at the double."

He spurred Bucephalas into a canter, angling his mount to the right flank, and with his shouted cry the men surged forward—the tension breaking in the release of the charge.

As Alexander knew was all too common in these affairs, the battle was decided before the first weapon was crossed. As the three hundred men shouted out their curses, the Kievants, seeing what was coming, cast aside their shields and departed for a safer neighborhood. Within seconds the battle, if it could be called that, had disintegrated into a footrace as the Kievants, looking over their shoulders and crying in fear, surged toward the protection of their gate, the phalanx hot on their heels.

Alexander surged through the crowd, Bucephalas now up to full speed, which was just about as fast as a man could run. Slinging his bow, he unsheathed his sword and applied it liberally to anyone who came near, using the flat of the blade since he already had plans for these men. As he charged forward, the Kievants parted before him, not daring to face such a man riding atop a Gaf beast.

He arrived at the gate ahead of his own men. The Kievant chieftain who stood by the portal made threatening gestures, as if challenging Alexander to a fight. But when Alexander lowered his sword and acknowledged that he would be more than happy to comply, the chieftain cast aside his shield and fled into the town, disappearing into the screaming mob of women and children who had lined the mud brick walls of the town only moments before.

Alexander turned in the gateway, suddenly aware of the fact that he had surged so far ahead in his cavalry charge of one that the entire Kievant army was now between him and his own men. And since he held the portal of escape, he would have to hold it alone until his men came up.

He turned expecting to face a cornered mob that would fight with desperation to get past him, but what greeted him was something totally unexpected.

The Kievants were falling prostrate, crying out in anguish, raising their hands in supplication, looking back over their shoulders toward the still-advancing phalanx and then back to him. The battle was won before it had even started.

Amazed, he sheathed his unbloodied sword and signaled Parmenion to stop the advance.

It took a couple of minutes to calm the men down, and Parmenion had to knock a couple of Ris flat to keep the excited men from falling on an old rival and slaying him. There was a strange uneasiness as captors and captives looked at each other, neither side having much experience in these affairs and now totally lost as to how to conduct themselves.

Alexander shouted that the chieftain of the Kievants should come out before he could count to one hundred or that he would start to execute all the prisoners, and with that command there was a loud wailing from within the town. He could only hope that they knew how much a hundred was, but before Alexander got past forty the women of the town dragged the chieftain forward, bruised and bleeding, and threw him at Alexander's feet.

Suddenly from the back of the press Ivarn pushed forward, brandishing a massive two-handed club. And with loud shouts and curses he advanced toward the kneeling chief.

"Old scum, thief, one who sleeps with his own sisters, now I've got you!"

The chieftain looked at Alexander and then back to Ivarn, then threw his hands up to Alexander. "Spare me, one who must be a god. And I, Borst, will serve you faithfully."

Alexander looked over at Ivarn. And after weeks of play acting it was a pleasure to let his real feelings out.

"Enough, Ivarn, this man is mine now. In fact, all these men are mine, and not one of them is to be harmed. The Kievants are now the second company of phalanx."

"What? After I won this fight!" Ivarn screamed, and he gave a sly look over to Lothar, who had walked up with his commander and stood by the side of Alexander's horse.

"After I finish this scum, I'll deal with you, you damned foreign upstart."

Ivarn advanced on Borst, club held high, and Borst fell to the ground wailing in terror. Alexander started to turn Bucephalas and bring his sword up, preparing first to take out Lothar and then Ivarn. His only hope was that this wouldn't trigger the phalanx into a revolt when they saw their chieftain killed. But he knew now for certain that Ivarn would have him dead, now that he had learned all he felt that he needed to know.

Lothar moved far faster than he could have ever imagined.

With a leaping stride, the wrestler came up alongside of Ivarn, and with a quick sure movement he snatched the chieftain off the ground and twisted his body into an impossible contortion. There was a loud, audible snap— and Ivarn hit the ground, his head lolling obscenely to one side.

The men were silent, stunned by what they had seen.

Lothar looked to the gathering and then turned back to face Alexander.

"Hail Alexander!" Lothar screamed, raising a clenched fist into the air.

"Hail Alexander!" And the two tribes joined their voices into one shouting his praise.

Already Borst was at his side shouting out that he knew a perfect enemy that lived above them and he pointed "up," toward a ridgeline that shimmered above them in the blue, cloudless sky.

He could see Neva standing off to one side and noticed that Lothar was already standing next to her, whispering something into her ear. So that was the arrangement, he thought, and he gave her a nod of acknowledgment. She was a dangerous one, to be sure, arranging the murder of her own uncle, even though he was a beast. He realized that he'd have to keep a little promise of reward once dimming came, and he shuddered at the thought.

"Tell me, Borst," Alexander asked, trying to be heard above the roaring shouts of the men. "I come from a distant place, and it is my custom to wash with hot water once a fight has been finished."

Borst shuddered and tried to hide a grimace of disgust. "But of course, O Alexander. I can arrange it."

He looked back again at Neva and tried to smile. "And see that there's one available whenever I want it. Even if it's in the middle of a dimming."

Borst shrugged his shoulders at such a strange request, but he was so happy to still have his head attached to his shoulders that he didn't argue.

CHAPTER 8

"YOU REALIZE, THAT SOUNDS REALLY DISGUSTING," Neva said, as if he had just suggested that they engage in some of the practices usually associated with Egyptian royalty.

"But it really is quite pleasant," Alexander replied. "I can assure you that you'll feel like a new person."

"What! And lose the accumulation of dirt and smell that I've built up through several hundred dimmings! Are you trying to say that I'm not attractive to you?"

There was a dangerous look in her eyes and he could only smile at her, hoping that what he was really thinking wasn't too obvious.

"Now that you've had your third bath you should be ready again," she said, reaching out from under the covers, ready to grab hold of him, preferably in one area more than another.

"Ah, yes, indeed if I had the time I would love to, but there are other duties calling. The dimming is almost past, and I should be up and about."

Before she could voice a stronger protest, he quickly

called for Parmenion and exited from what was called "the palace."

Sleepily Parmenion came out of a side room and kicked at the sentries posted to guard the doorway, and who at the first opportunity had slumped down and gone to sleep.

"Damn fools. I'm sorry, sire."

Alexander ignored his apologies and simply looked at the sheepish guards with barely concealed anger that made the men look nervously at their feet.

He strode down toward the gate, his guards stumbling after him.

"Where are we going?" Parmenion inquired.

"To get a better look at that." And he pointed at Olympus, which dominated half the sky above the village. Parmenion fell silent and Alexander knew that he had listened perhaps a little too much to the superstitious sayings about the mountain that Aldin had called a heat exchanger.

Clearing the gate, they walked through the encampment of the Ris army. Some of the men were already rising, and at the sight of their commander they gave a ragged cheer, chanting his name with their curious lisping accent. Alexander motioned for them to be quiet, but their shouts were still echoing as he disappeared up the trail leading to Mount Olympus. The guards accompanying him started to mumble to themselves that this place was known to be the realm of gods, and with a wave of the hand Alexander bade them to go back down the mountain and wait. They didn't need to be told twice, and with a clatter of spears, they took off down the mountain trail.

"You know, one of the Ris told me that there are places up there"—Parmenion pointed up to the brooding heights—"that they say can't be scratched, and shine like the sun."

"You're telling me this to try to persuade me that maybe we should leave well enough alone."

Parmenion was silent, and Alexander looked at his one-eyed companion and smiled. "I've been told that several hundred dimmings past, an oracle came to live up here. These villagers hold the man in awe, saying he serves the gods. If we bring him into my service, it will increase our prestige among all the people of this region. Anyhow, Parmenion, I have to go and see this place and this man; otherwise I wouldn't be Alexander."

Parmenion could only shrug and mumble something about the difficulties of living with legends. Wheezing like an asthmatic in a dustbin, he struggled to keep pace as they followed the narrow path up the immense, white-capped mountain.

As they climbed ever higher, the rushing wind swirled louder and louder around them. It was Parmenion who first realized that there was a faint vibration to the ground, as if an earthquake was starting.

Alexander struggled with his fear, for having witnessed the destructive power of the gods when they shook the earth, he viewed such an event with trepidation. The two of them stood for some minutes, bracing for the shock, but none came, just the steady vibration and the gentle howling of the wind.

He looked up again at the towering height that appeared to go straight up, ten times or more beyond the highest soaring reaches of Asia.

He could not help but wonder why the Ris had not placed their fortress up there where they would be forever "higher" than anyone else, and would thus not have to view their neighbors as having insulted them. But then again they seemed so fearful of the mountain that he could well understand their reluctance to tread its slopes. He understood, as well, that many peasant fears often times had some foundation in fact, and he could only wonder what the mystery was.

A loud roar soon filled the air with deafening thunder, and, after turning at a branch of the trail, they beheld a mighty river shooting out of an underground passage so wide that a hundred men could march abreast into the cavern. Alexander realized that this tremendous flow of water originated from within the mountain, and the phenomenon filled him with awe. Where did the water come from? he wondered. He had seen underground springs before, but never a cataract of such immense proportions, with a flow almost as great as the mighty Tigris.

The light of the sun was already at its peak, flooding the far horizon with its crystalline light. Turning away from the river, they pushed on up the trail, until, pausing at last on a windswept ledge, the two men stopped to rest. The village of the Kievants was far below them, an insignificant speck on the landscape. In the distance they could see the village of the Avars perched on its miserable hillside. Gazing out in every direction, they saw dozens of signs of habitation throughout the hill country. The gentle curve of the Kolbard swept up and away to either side, and now that they were above the low clutter of hills they had a clear, unobstructed view as the twin horns of either horizon cut upward, narrowing into blue-green ribbons of light arching up to the never-moving sun. The two other towers now seemed so close that he felt as if he could almost reach out and touch them, while farther away rose three more towers whose foundations rested in the realm of the Gafs, a hundred leagues away.

With the unobstructed view he now had, Alexander could see the clear checkered pattern of well-tended fields cut by the undulating swirls of half a dozen rivers. The land looked gentle, rich, and full of life. Whoever had created this land must have lived in those distant gardens, Alexander thought wistfully. There was land enough there for all who lived in this region, but as was always the way, he realized, richness was held by a few, while the rest starved.

He remembered yet again the sharp hills and the narrow valleys of his own homeland, and the awe in his heart when first he beheld the great rich plains of Persia, with their well-ordered fields and vast endless spaces—

the realm he had taken from Darius. Darius, he thought, shaking his head at the memory. How he dreamed of meeting him one on one, before the eyes of half a million, to struggle for control of the world; the emperor of the Persians who was his enemy yet somehow the only one in the world whom he could test himself against. But it had ended instead with a squalid murder by the roadside, a dying emperor abandoned by his own men, to lie in the dust, cursed and despised.

"Darius," he whispered, as if the sounding of the name could again conjure his foe out of the dust.

Parmenion looked over at his companion and then leaned back and looked up toward the squared-off peak above them. "Maybe we've already gone too far, and the oracle lives somewhere down there." Parmenion gestured vaguely back down to the lower level.

"If that were the case," Alexander replied, his thoughts returning to the present, "then why does this trail continue on upward? I think you're just looking for an excuse to stop."

"Who, me?"

Alexander didn't bother with a response and, rising, continued on with the climb. The wind swirled around them, plucking at their cloaks, an occasional gust threatening to knock them off balance, so that the two travelers were soon forced to lean on each other for support.

Turning a bend in the upward spiraling trail, they dipped down into a small valley a quarter of a league across, and both of them cried aloud with wonder when they first beheld the sight before them.

It gleamed with brilliant intensity, reflecting the white light of the sun as if it was made of burnished bronze. The wind pushed at their back, trying to push them toward what appeared to be a huge, gaping cavern at the lower end of the valley.

"Well, shall we go take a look?" Alexander ventured. Parmenion was silent, but his expression was more than sufficient to give an answer.

"If I were you," came a voice from behind, "I'd think twice before going on."

Parmenion whipped around, drawing his sword, but Alexander remained motionless, his back turned to the speaker. "If he meant us harm, Parmenion, he wouldn't have given us a warning."

"I just don't like people sneaking up on me," Parmenion replied gruffly.

"Perhaps I could argue that you were sneaking up on me," the speaker replied, stepping out of the shadows to reveal himself.

He stood tall and proud, though obviously an ancient. His hair was gone, his features wrinkled like old parchment, and he leaned on a wooden staff for support, as if the removal of it would cause him to tumble down. He drew closer to Alexander and squinted at him, betraying the dimming of his vision, as well.

"Are you the oracle that we seek?" Parmenion asked.

"What? Oh, no, not another damn youngster coming to seek truth from the oracle." The old man cackled softly. "You searchers are always such a pain in the butt end, coming up here, expecting to hit me with some smart-ass questions and then go back claiming that you found enlightenment. Well, if that's what you came for, then just get the hell out of here and leave me alone."

"Do you know who you're talking to?" Parmenion demanded.

"No. Now let me guess, could it be the new chieftain of the Kievants? Well, if it is, just remember, young man, that I'm higher up than all of you and piss always rolls downhill."

Parmenion started to raise his sword, but Alexander, laughing, beckoned for him to hold his anger in check. "By the heavens, Parmenion, it's good to hear a man speak frankly and without fear. Not since Pindar of Thebes have I been spoken to like this."

"Pindar of Thebes?" The old man looked at Alexander, then turned to his companion. "Parmenion?" he said questioningly as he gazed at the one-eyed guard.

"Sound familiar?" Alexander asked tentatively.

"Why, yes, of course it's familiar. I've read my Arrian and my Renault, which is more than can be said for the rest of the muckers down there." He waved toward the lowlands with a vague gesture of disgust. "And might I ask why you're running around on this climate control and docking tower, speaking in the first person, as if you were an ancient Macedonian king from Earth."

Alexander looked at him with openmouthed astonishment, not sure at all where to start on this one.

"Well, go on. Stop goggling at me like a fish out of water, tell me what all this is about."

"I am Alexander, son of Philip, known to you as the Great."

The old man looked at him appraisingly for some seconds. Alexander could sense that Parmenion would most likely pounce if this man gave what should be a typical reaction.

"Go on now," the oracle replied, and Parmenion held back, not sure if the man's tone was mocking or incredulous.

"It is the truth, old man," Alexander replied in Greek, forcing himself to remember that once-familiar tongue.

"Now you've added a new angle to your argument," the oracle responded, with just a trace of a broad highlander accent.

And now it was Parmenion's turn to be amazed. "How in the name of the gods do you know our tongue? Why, I was getting sick of talking the gibberish spoken by these barbarians. It's good to speak again with a civilized man."

The oracle shrugged, obviously feeling flattered. "Let's just say I've studied the old works. But come, let's get out of this howling gale and talk where we need not shout our words into the wind."

He beckoned for the two to follow him on a narrow side path that led into a cleft in the hills.

"Where does that lead?" Alexander asked, pointing toward the gaping entrance to the mountainside that they had originally been heading toward.

"Watch."

The oracle wandered off the trail and poked at the ground with his staff. After a brief search he scraped up a loose stone and walked to the edge of the valley. With a gentle underhanded toss he lobbed the stone onto the sloping metallike surface. The stone started to slip away, like a river-smoothed rock skipped out onto a frozen lake. It accelerated as it fell toward the cavern opening, driven by the howling wind in its downward slide. Falling through the mouth of the cave, it disappeared from view.

"Care to follow it?"

Parmenion gulped and shook his head.

"If we had stepped onto that surface, that would have been our fate," Alexander said more as a statement than a question.

"Don't go fooling around intake vents, especially where the substructures have been revealed through wind erosion. You wind up in a cooling fin and it's all over. Oh, yes, you finally get pumped back out as liquid fertilizer, but that's a small consolation. No glory, no funeral pyres . . . just fertilizer.

"Quite the system, this," the oracle said, pointing to the mountain around them. "Remote sensors monitor the climate below, feed in the data, and then these mountains act as the regulators. The mountain is honeycombed with heat exchangers that cool the air when needed, and return the moisture either as rain or as a river. If it wasn't for that, this place would have fried out eons ago. Creating a variable star only solved part of the climate control problem. Smart fellows, those First Travelers. I've spent a lifetime figuring out how they did it. Now, you definitely don't want to go near the moisture dump system farther up, that place is a real killer."

The two Macedons looked at the oracle as if he were speaking some sort of alien tongue that their translator implants simply could not pick up on. The oracle, realizing that he had lost his two visitors, stopped short with a shrug of his shoulders.

"Oh, anyhow, hold your thanks for my saving your lives. You'll pay me back later, I'm sure. Now let's get out of this damn gale. Come on, you want enlightenment, I'll give enlightenment. If you don't want enlightenment, then get the hell out of here and go mumble your Greek someplace else. It's all the same to me."

"You still don't believe that I'm Alexander?"

"Well, let me put it to you this way. If I came wandering into your court, and said that I, Yaroslav, the most brilliant oracle and wise man of my realm, had traveled across space and time from a ring-planet, made by a race known as the First Travelers, and they built this place for the hell of it, what would you think?

"And then to top it off, I told you that I'd been transported by some man named Aldin who gave me this mission to unite all mankind." He stopped for a moment, leaned back in his chair, and took another swig from a wineskin. "Now, where was I? Ah, yes, if I showed up with a story like that, what in the name of Zeus would you do?"

Alexander could only shake his head.

"Now, those simpleminded fools down there might buy it, but me?" He shook his head and chuckled.

"Let's leave this old dodderer," Parmenion said gruffly. "We don't have to prove anything to him."

"Nor do I intend to," Alexander replied evenly. "So sit back down, Parmenion, I've still got some questions."

"Listen to him, Parmenion," Yaroslav said, again

speaking in Greek. "After all, he is the great Alexander, so show the proper respect."

"You know, your Greek is really quite good," Alexander replied good-naturedly.

Yaroslav waved away the compliment as if he did not need such things. "Here and there some small centers of learning still survive. I spent a lot of time studying what you claim was your time."

"Where?" Alexander inquired.

"Never mind that, but anyhow, do you have any idea just how big this structure is?"

"I think I have a grasp of it."

"Even I, who've spent a long time studying this place, still have a hard time getting a grasp of it."

Yaroslav stood up and walked to the far corner of the room that he called his private study.

The room was richly appointed, and did not give any feeling whatsoever that it was in fact a cave. The walls were paneled with what appeared to be oak, the leather chairs that they sat upon were heavily padded and, to Alexander, seemed out of place somehow for a hermit living atop a mountain. If Yaroslav was an oracle, he certainly was a comfortable one. Alexander could only wonder as to how this old man had managed to haul so much material up the mountain to this distant cave.

Yaroslav pulled open a cabinet door and, mumbling a series of curses, he rummaged around inside the walk-in closet for some minutes before reappearing, dragging a massive scroll as thick around as a man's waist. Grabbing hold of one end, he gave it a toss and the scroll unraveled across the floor—only a small fraction of it was revealed before coming to a rest on the far side of the room.

"Now, where are we?" he mumbled meditatively. "Damn thing's always so big, it's such a pain working with this damn parchment. Damn primitives."

"Is that a map?" Parmenion asked, standing up and peering over Yaroslav's shoulder.

"Of course it's a map, you idiot. Can't you see that?"

Parmenion made a significant and age-old gesture at Yaroslav's back, then got down on the floor beside him to look at the details.

"No, no, not here." Yaroslav pulled the parchment across the floor so that it continued to unravel from the far corner.

"Could it be there, where it's marked in red?" Alexander ventured, pointing to a section that had just unraveled from the scroll.

"Ah, yes, that's how I marked our particular region in question."

"Now, to give you an idea of what we are dealing with," Yaroslav said in a pedantic tone. "Remember first of all that this world was built by a race we refer to as the First Travelers."

"Who were they?" Alexander asked. "Were they gods?"

"You could call them that, at least in your classic Olympian sense, as beings who still had the foibles and desires of men. You see, I believe they built this ring simply as an exercise, an amusement. The way a child might build a huge sand castle simply to prove to himself that he can do it."

"Do they still live here, then?"

Yaroslav hesitated for a moment, as if judging his response.

"I don't think so," he replied slowly, "though there are legends among the current inhabitants that the 'Ancient Ones' still live beneath, in the subterranean passageways."

"The what?" Alexander asked.

"Remember this Kolbard is of artificial construction, like a massive building. There are literally millions of tunnels, access ways, cooling fins exposed to open vacuum, and repair ports honeycombing this entire structure."

"Are we near an entryway now?"

"If you ever get curious, just go through that opposite door. Though after a couple of leagues I can't remember which way to go," Yaroslav said quickly, his voice full of warning. "So you might not get back."

Alexander eyed him with curiosity.

"Is it locked?" Parmenion asked suspiciously, as if the opposite doorway was an entry to the dark underworld —which in a sense, it was.

Yaroslav only smiled in response.

"Where are we on this map?" Alexander asked, pointing to the section outlined in red.

"Ah, yes, now let's see." Yaroslav leaned forward and after a brief search he pointed out the high range of hills that ran along what he called the "northern" section of the continent.

"You notice a scale line down there." He pointed to a series of graph lines. "Distance is measured in versts, and comes out to about three versts to one of your leagues. Now, there are several hundred continent areas on the Kolbard; some are smaller than Europe, while others are ten times that of Asia."

"How are they divided apart?"

"There are oceans, to be sure. From up here you have no problem seeing the Iras Sea to our west. That is nearly a million square versts in area, with a number of islands on it. So, like Earth, the various continents can be divided by oceans, but they are also divided by barrier walls that soar up beyond the upper levels of atmosphere."

"Why the walls?" Parmenion asked.

"To break up wind-flow patterns. Otherwise, due to the coriolis effect, there would be hurricane-force winds building up, if the terrain didn't interrupt it. In some places the wind has gradually stripped away the topsoil. The locals around here refer to it as the Anvil."

Alexander couldn't understand some of the terms, but grasped what the old man was saying.

"And what is this 'Anvil'?"

"You noticed the open shimmering area down toward the Iras Sea? It's the bare metal of the support structure. Strong stuff, that metal, damn near impossible to scratch, and definitely impossible to pull up and use. That Anvil down there is a small one, only a hundred versts long by a hundred wide. Now picture an area like that a hundred times larger. In some regions it acts as a barrier from one area to another. Nothing grows, it's damn difficult even to move on it. Nothing gets across except for an occasional nomadic merchant. It's as good as an ocean to divide things off."

"Nomadic merchant?" Alexander asked. "Does that mean that all the wheel is occupied?"

Yaroslav smiled.

"I think so, but it is so massive it is hard to tell. Nearly three thousand years ago, more than halfway back, in fact, to your time, mankind first made landfall here. Colonists settled it at a number of locations. Those muckers down below came from north of your original empire. They've pretty well reverted back to precivilized standards, thanks to the Great War, which cut off thousands of worlds and left them isolated. What made it even worse was the fact that the First Travelers had stripped most of the planets of their resources a million years ago, and thus there was next to nothing as far as basic materials to rebuild through the various technological levels.

"Here, as on innumerable other places in the Magellanic Cloud, we found ourselves competing with the Gafs, along with another race, for control of all the inhabitable worlds. I can only speak for this area, but there are rumors that there are dozens of different races living on the various continents, for the First Travelers seemed to take delight in dropping off interesting specimens to populate this little project of theirs, long before we ever arrived on the scene.

"Damn it, I've heard of plantlike creatures in the next continent over, and insectlike beings that breed humans for food and as slaves. Why, there're almost limitless probabilities to this place."

"What I'm interested in now," Alexander interrupted, "are the Gavarnians."

"Ah, yes, we call them the Gafs. So why the interest?"

Alexander stood up and smiled at Yaroslav. "I'm Alexander, should not that be answer enough?"

Yaroslav chuckled, more to himself than to his guests. "So another war of conquest. And those scum down below are to be your army, is that it?"

Alexander nodded in reply.

"It's a far cry from your Macedons. And your foes will have no Darius to hamper them."

"Yes, Darius," Alexander said softly. "Do you know then of their leader, this Kubar Taug?"

"Ah, no, can't say that I do." And he fell silent.

Alexander noticed that Parmenion was watching their host intently, but he voiced no opinion.

"So you plan to unite the tribes into a host and to train them to your task?"

"That's the general idea."

"Ah, well, I best be packing then."

Without another word Yaroslav walked into the next chamber and the two wanderers heard the sound of drawers opening and slamming shut, with occasional mumbled curses and groans. After some minutes Yaroslav reappeared with a pack slung over his shoulder and a fairly good imitation of an archaic Greek helmet on his head and a rounded shield at his side.

"Best be off, then. I shan't miss the fun of this, so I guess I'll tag along."

"Old man," Parmenion mumbled, "in your condition, one day's hard march will leave you dead. Stay here and live off the offerings of the fools that come to hear you."

"Old man, is it?" And Yaroslav advanced on his taunter. "Look at that belly," he roared, poking the overweight guard in the stomach. "It's a wonder it hasn't sagged to your feet so that you trip over it when running from your foes! I'll outmarch you, outwench you, outfight you, and outdrink you. All this clean living of a hermit has worn a little thin. I've been waiting for an adventure like this, now let's be off."

Alexander was silent, looking closely at this newest recruit.

"Look, Alexander son of Philip—and yes, I do believe your tale, no matter how improbable it sounds—like Augustine once said about his religion, 'It's so damn improbable, I have to believe it.' I can read, I know this world, and I'm passably good as a healer, as well. Besides, you need a chronicler for this tale, and that I shall be, because you're not going to find anyone down there that can hold a quill correctly, let alone have the intelligence to know how to use it. And believe me, I'll write a far better history than some of the damn fools who've scribbled out a pack of lies about you. So let's take the map, you'll need that, and be off."

"We can't carry the whole thing," Alexander said, looking at the impossibly long parchment roll. With a quick flash of his sword he cut out the area marked in red.

"Just like with Gordius," Yaroslav replied philosophically as he gazed on his mutilated trophy. "I'll come back with some bearers later to bring the rest, along with my library and easy chair." And then he turned away and strode out the door without a backward look.

"So, this is the army of the great Alexander." Yaroslav groaned sarcastically.

"My father's grandsire had not much better than these when he started," Alexander replied, and Parmenion could sense the touch of despair in his master's voice.

The Kievants, after a dozen dimmings of intense training, had been judged ready to serve as the second phalanx and were now drawn up in battle formation beside their former enemy. The cavalry force had been doubled, as well. A Ris hero—that at least is how Alexander had named him—had come in with a report of a lone Gaf scout who was mounted and searching the area where Alexander had made his first encounter. The sighting of the Gaf could only mean that his opponents were out looking for him. Parmenion had taken a contingent out and returned three dimmings later, mounted uneasily atop a towering horse. His stature now was second only to Alexander's, for all soon were told how he bested the feared warrior alone, one pikeman bringing down a mounted swordsman.

Several of the Ris were bloodied from the foray. Not by the Gaf, but by the sound thrashing Parmenion had given them for breaking and running when the warrior charged. And as was sometimes the case with such men, they now held him in high esteem as a man to be reckoned with and one that had near-mystical powers. And they were quick to pummel any man who spoke out against the fat chieftain of the "golden one," as they now called Alexander.

Alexander nodded to Parmenion, and his second in command nudged his mount to a canter. Parmenion trotted down to stop in front of the regiment of Ris and a spontaneous shout went up from that command.

Good, Alexander thought, already we are accepted, and some of them must sense, as well, the start of what comes here today. He looked out at eight hundred men assembled before the gates of the city. They were still filthy and ragged; there was no semblance of uniforms except for brown headbands on the Ris and dirty white for the Kievants. Their armor, if they were fortunate to have any, was a boiled leather tunic backed with felt or wool. Only one in three carried a metal-tipped spear.

But he could remember the stories the old soldiers had told him in his youth, and somehow he could see here the resurrection of those legends from his past when the Macedons were nothing more than barbaric shepherds and thieves. Yes, these men could be a start after all.

He stood up in his stirrups. "Soldiers! I call you soldiers, for now, for the first time, you are soldiers and worthy of that honored title."

Yaroslav gave a sarcastic sniff, but Alexander ignored the oracle.

"Once you called yourselves Ris and Kievants. Once you fell upon each other and squabbled like ignorant children in the dirt. But no more. Look now to each other. When divided against yourselves you were nothing. But now, united, you are powerful. Can you not sense the strength here? Can you not sense the power that can be yours as long as you are united?"

He stopped for a moment, and there was a gentle murmur in the ranks as the men turned and looked at each other.

"Behold!" Turning to Yaroslav, he took the single stick that the oracle offered to him.

Alexander grabbed hold of the stick at both ends. His muscles knotted, and the stick snapped in half. Again he held out his hand, and this time Yaroslav gave him two sticks. Holding them together, he tried to snap them also, his muscles knotting in a great show of force—which was indeed show, for he did not want his lesson to suddenly break. The two sticks held.

"Thus in the two sticks is your lesson. Alone you are like a twig to be snapped, united under me you cannot be broken. And stronger yet you shall be before we are done, as stick after stick is added to the bundle."

A mighty shout went up from the assembly.

"You, the Kievants, have told me that the people of Novgor piss downhill on you. Today we march on Novgor."

A wild cry greeted his words, for both villages had managed to maintain a longstanding feud with their other neighbor, as well.

"We go not to destroy them, but to take them, so that

in another dozen dimmings there will be a third regiment in our command, adding to our strength."

There was some quiet muttering at this, but Parmenion merely had to urge his horse forward a couple of paces and the complaints died away.

"Listen to me, soldiers. For I, Alexander, shall tell you all. Once the Novgor are at our sides, we shall split our army, half marching to Avar, the other half to Boroda. Then in a dozen more dimmings there will be yet two more regiments, and they in turn shall conquer and recruit yet two more, so that soon there shall be a hundred regiments. And when we gather together at one place, our shouts shall drown out even the roaring of the cascade coming from the mountain I call Olympus."

The men were silent, enrapt at the realization of what he was proposing. Some of the wiser men started to cry out about whom they should attack next, once the conquest of the Humans was complete.

"Already some of you can see where I shall lead," Alexander shouted in response. "For when we are strong enough, we shall march down to the sea. The oracle Yaroslav has told me that where the Anvil meets the sea there is a great hill of iron that fell from the sky eons ago. This is where the Gafs get their metal, and there we shall meet the Gafs. We shall face the Gafs and take from them the mountain of iron and the flowing sea, and the rich lands, to call our own. I, Alexander, son of Philip, called the Great, promise this."

They stamped their spears upon the ground, roaring their approval.

"Listen to me now, Ris and Kievants. From today onward you are no longer two people. When you joined me in this cause, your old names of the past were left behind. From my realm there was one people above all others, and henceforth all that join me shall be known by that name.

"From now on you are Macedons!"

The men looked one to another, saying this new word

tentatively at first but soon chanting it proudly, as if it were some spell or talisman.

Drawing his sword, Alexander pointed to the goat path that led off toward the village of the Novgor, and the ranks fell in behind him. As he rode past the wall, which was barely higher than his head, Neva leaned over, revealing her ample charms to him. He had convinced her to stay behind as his regent. That way she would be out of sight, and smelling, for several dimmings, at least. With a well-acted look of pained parting, he gazed at her for a moment and then cantered past.

Yaroslav was trotting by his side, and reaching down, Alexander hoisted the old philosopher up behind him. For several seconds the old man gazed closely at Neva with an intent curiosity, as if he had suddenly seen a woman for the first time.

"Really, that rabble back there, Macedons indeed," Yaroslav said, turning away from the woman. "Scratch that thin layer of bravado off them and they're still a pack of thieves. Macedons indeed."

"They will be," Alexander replied, his voice distant, "they will be."

And no one noticed at that moment the look that so many had seen on another world, when his followers would say that he was gazing toward a glory that only he could somehow see.

"And what do you make of this report, Kubar Taug?"

Long he had waited for this question. For the passage of four-score dimmings he had waited, as if in Binda, for a question regarding the current situation. Here at last they had finally recognized him at a clan gathering. The game of waiting that he had been forced to play was now entering its next phase.

Upon his arrival at the court of Kalin, Hina's brother the Taug, Kubar had withdrawn into solitude and waited. He knew that if he was to lead these people it would not be as someone who came bearing warnings and calling to lead. Rather it must be that they should come to him in the end and ask. And now they were asking for the first time. It was only a simple question, delivered in a slightly mocking tone, but it was the start nevertheless.

"First, Kalin," he said slowly, as if stirred from deep sleep, "first tell me what you yourself think, and then I shall speak in turn."

Kubar stopped speaking and looked around at the assembled Gavarnians. Nearly sixty warriors were present, each of them representing one of the noble families that inhabited this region of the Kolbard they called Kia Valinstan, "the realm of blossoming flowers."

They were all dressed almost identically wearing the traditional lacquered-armor tunic that flared into a long hanging skirt of shining leather that reached nearly to the ground. Upon the right breast of each was painted the family standard—for some, flowers; for others, geometric designs; and for yet others, symbolic representations of honored ancestors who had been the legendary first settlers in the murky, distant past.

Having come from all points of the realm, they now were gathered at last in the central courtyard of Kalin's castle, the main bastion of Sirt, the single large city of their realm. Cities were anathema to those who ruled the land from their own private fiefdoms; Sirt's status had grown merely because it was the personal domain of the taugs, the acknowledged elder family of their world.

To some from the distant marches, this was the first visit to Sirt in their lifetimes. The pagodalike central keep that rose high into the air and the sloping battlements of stone that covered nearly a square verst in area filled them with as much awe as the fact that they were in the presence of Kalin Taug. Some, as well, though they kept the fact hidden, were in awe of this stranger who claimed to be legend come to life.

Kubar returned their curious stares with a polite nod and then faced back toward Kalin.

Kalin turned and looked back at his personal court,

who were members of his immediate family and the family retainers. He knew what they already thought of this meeting, for few of them believed, himself included, that the one who sat before them was the Taug of the legends of the past come to them. But word of this stranger's presence had spread through the city, and at last, bowing to pressure, Kalin had allowed him to attend the clan meeting.

Kubar noticed the two females who were allowed to sit in the council. One was Kaveta, the wife of Kalin. Kalin, as the eldest, was the only one of his four brothers allowed to marry. But he already noticed that her eyes rested more often upon Hina than her spouse. Judging, so far, between the two, he could well understand why. But he knew that as a Gavarnian of noble rank it would stop merely at looks, for to do otherwise would be the worst possible disgrace for her, and one of the ultimate betrayals possible for a brother.

He noticed, as well, the looks the other one gave. Her name was Liala, the one sister of Hina and Kalin. She was attractive beyond measure, her almond-shaped eyes unusually large and full of vibrant life. He had found himself looking forward to their brief conversations as they passed each other in the corridors of the castle. He could not help but see the look in her eyes when she gazed upon him. But he could only think that he was already old and graying, and that her looks were one of simple admiration, and he thought no more of it.

Kalin rose up, his red-lacquered armor creaking, his gaze straight at Kubar, as if waiting for a challenge.

"It is simple enough," he said gruffly. "The hairless ones, the scum beneath our contempt, have found some leader. He has united together a score of their filth-covered clans, and even now moves to bring the entire hill region under his control. If we moved against them today, we would face an organized foe of perhaps ten thousand. It is reported that he is doubling the size of his force every thirty dimmings. They call this one Iskander, the name you first mentioned upon your arrival here. It is obvious you knew of him before us, and that mystery in and of itself is troubling."

Kalin fell silent, as if he had spoken too much already by acknowledging Kubar's foreknowledge of the threat. Kubar realized this was not the time to press his case so he quietly changed the direction.

"How many can he draw upon in the end?" Kubar asked evenly, not staring straight at Kalin, to avoid an unnecessary challenge.

"We keep no count of the scum. They are there for our sport when we wish it, or when we need to punish their thieving. After all, they are only hairless ones, not even worthy of this formal attention they now receive."

"Be that as it may," Hina interjected, "they are in need of our attention now. My border watchers report that maybe forty, perhaps as many as sixty thousand, can be brought together. That is more than all the nobles and landless servants in our entire realm."

"To bring together that many in one place up in the hills would be impossible," came a voice from the back of the room.

Kubar smiled and looked to the shadows behind Kalin, where the speaker stood. It was Wirgth, the court advisor to the taug clan. Such a position was an old and honored one in Gavarnian tradition. The advisor, or Kaadu, was traditionally the closest friend of the sire who ruled before the current taug. Upon the death of his friend the Kaadu became the most cherished advisor to the son who ruled. Thus a ruler chose his closest friend carefully, looking for one who was loyal, intelligent, and with the moral strength to speak forcefully and with truth at all times.

Kubar recognized those qualities at once when he met Wirgth. The graying, ascetic-looking Gaf had spent many a long dimming with him, questioning carefully, endlessly probing Kubar and his story. Kubar knew that his presence at the meeting was Wirgth's doing. The Kaadu had accepted him as the true Taug.

"Explain, honored Kaadu," Kalin said coldly.

"It is simple enough," Wirgth said, advancing to the center of the room. "The hairless ones need at least a wreth weight of food per day in order to keep their strength. Thus if their army came together in one place, they would require sixty thousand wreths of food a day. In one day they would devour everything in even their largest village. We've denied them horses, taking the breed for ourselves with that consideration in mind. Without horses and wagons it's physically impossible for them to supply a large number of people in one place.

"Thus they must do one of two things. They must either disperse, or they must move down out of the hills and into our richer lands, where they can gather enough forage to stay alive."

"They'd be fools to dare us," Kalin roared. "I don't give a good damn if they organize in their hills, they can stay there and rot, for all I care. But they would never dare to face the shock of one of our mounted regiments."

"But I think they just might," Wirgth interjected. "For this unifier, whoever he is, must be unifying for a reason. If he allows his men to spread out once again, he shall lose control in short order. Therefore I believe that his only logical move is to come forward with the intent of driving us."

"Hairless ones driving us," another underlord shouted, coming to his feet. "That is beyond all reason. Your reading has addled you, Wirgth. Whoever heard of a hairless one driving one such as us? They are there for our sport, not as a challenge."

"Arn, they might have been sport for you in the past," Wirgth replied, "but the days of sport with the hairless ones are over."

Wirgth fell silent, and before Arn, the lord of the northern marches, could reply, thus starting an argument he was obviously looking for, Hina interrupted.

"Kubar, I am curious as to your response regarding Wirgth's comments."

"Iskander, as you call him," Kubar interjected cautiously, "has come to this world for but one purpose—to organize the hairless ones and then to turn them against us in a war of conquest. That is why I am here at this time. There is no coincidence in this. It is a simple logical fact. Iskander will invade. He must invade and do so shortly, and when he comes there will be sixty thousand men behind him. Do not underestimate this man, for he is the best in the entire history of the Humans—conjured from their past to destroy us."

There was a low rumbling of growls from most of the underlords. Kubar gave a quick hand gesture to Paga, who was sitting behind him, as he sensed his standard-bearer's anger.

"Let them come then," Kalin roared. "We shall carpet the ground with their dead!"

The vassals in the courtyard came to their feet, shouting their approval.

"It shall be a hunt like no other," Kalin screamed. "We shall drive our enemies before us until the hills run with blood. Let them dare to come down, and then they shall see the wrath of the Gavarnians. I have said all along that this is a race beneath our contempt. Let us exterminate them and have an end to their filth!"

Knowing better than to try, Kubar still felt compelled to give warning. Standing, he turned to face the family heads behind him. Their wild demonstration lasted for some minutes, but one by one they saw his visage, and as if sensing his power they fell quiet in his presence.

"They'll send out a decoy on the extreme right flank," he began softly. "The flank farthest removed from our center of concentration. Thus as we advance out to meet them our own flank will be exposed to their position in the hills. Then their main force will cut in from behind, forcing us to give battle.

"I must warn you now, do not underestimate them."

His voice now rose up and those around him could sense the cold calculation and determination in it. He was speaking as if he had already read a history of what was to come.

"They know nothing of your honor, the way you fight, or the way you expect your opponents to fight. They will laugh at your conventions, the calling out of family names, the seeking of a worthy foe. Do not underestimate them."

"Are you the taug of my people?" Kalin replied harshly.

Kubar turned and looked back at Kalin.

"No," he said evenly, trying not to betray the despair in his heart, for it was obvious to him where the arrogance of Kalin might lead. It was the same arrogance the nobles of his own time had shown when first he had stood up to face them.

"Then are you the general that shall command our army?"

"No, I am not the taug of your people, or their general. For I have not been asked."

His phrasing was well calculated and revealed to all present what he would finally expect. They would have to come and ask him to be the taug.

"You are nothing but an impostor," Arn shouted, coming up to Kalin's side. "An impostor, a charlatan, and I would rot before serving you instead of the true taug."

"Paga, hold," Kubar shouted. Arn had offered a direct challenge, which in moments could descend into a bloodbath. The moment was dangerous. And it was Wirgth who finally retrieved it.

"For your service to our taug, in offering him advice, I thank you, Kubar," Wirgth said evenly, stepping forward to place himself between Kubar and Arn.

"You have the courage of a Kaadu to speak as you now did, offering fair and honest advice. It is the same advice I now give Kalin Taug. Do not underestimate this one called Iskander."

The words of a Kaadu were considered sacred, and the tension in the courtyard started to ease off. Hina, who was standing by his brother's side, looked to Kubar as if offering a warning not to speak further. Kubar could see the anxiety in the younger brother's eyes and nodded in response.

"I know you believe him," Kalin snarled, watching the interplay between his brother and Kubar.

"I can believe him and his words yet still be loyal to he who is the same blood and flesh as I," Hina replied. "I will ride by your side and serve, as I am sure Kubar and Paga shall do as well."

"But of course," Kubar responded diplomatically. "And of course I wish the honored Kalin luck and the blessing of my brothers departed when he goes to meet them. Know that I shall be there when Kalin goes to meet Iskander."

"Goes to drive them," Kalin snarled.

"But of course," Kubar replied evenly, without a trace of emotion.

CHAPTER 9

From: Aldin Larice
To: All participating Kohs
Subject: First stage completion report for the Alex-
             andrian/Taug Encounter

The primary campaign of Alexander has been completed as of game day 127, standard. His accomplish-
ments are as follows:

As of the date of this report the last active resistance
to his consolidation has been eliminated. For all practical purposes resistance to his unification drive collapsed
by the start of his fifth campaign when he was capable of
fielding ten regiments. From thenceforth, except for one
or two minor cases, the Human inhabitants flocked to
his banner, throwing open their gates. Most all of them
already accept the fact that he is indeed the Alexander
sent from their historic past to redeem them.

The northern hill region measuring nearly a million
square kilometers in area is under his sway (see enclosed
maps).

At this date he can marshal nearly fifty regiments of heavy pike, twenty of skirmishers, one of ballista artillery, but less than half a regiment of cavalry. Full tote records evaluating performance of each regiment is enclosed, along with evaluation of command structure and control.

Several skirmishes have developed, but the Human forces have yet to venture into the lower plains where the Gavarnian cavalry is most effective.

Intelligence reports indicate however that the Gavarnian advance into the northeastern hill region is in fact a full-scale penetration. As you can observe from evaluation printouts, Alexander's forces are reacting in an appropriate manner, which indicates that they are fully aware and deploying for a counterstrike. Therefore this memo should be considered a full-scale battle alert. Primary odds have been computed along all lines. As is standard operation, all considerations have been fed into the game standard evaluation program. Any and all bets can be processed through access code 23-alpha—alpha—873. Portfolios of all corporate assets wagered will be evaluated by a blind system-three program for total worth. Security clearance to data is through coded access only by party or parties responding to bet offer.

Duplicate reports of Kubar Taug's progress, as submitted by Zergh, are enclosed with cross-comparison evaluation of results.

As of this date, standard, daily tote odds will be printed. Today's odds are as follows:
Survival of Alexander—day, standard 87:1
Survival of Kubar Taug—same 1,221:1
Battle to occur within seven days, standard 3.7:1
First victory to Alexander 2:7
Submitted—Larice

"A little short on the odds, there, my dear Aldin, aren't we?"

Aldin looked up from the navigation board and,

standing, offered his chair to Corbin Gablona, who could barely manage to squeeze his massive bulk through the doorway.

The pleasure yacht had cost him an even fifty million, a value greater than some planets, but for some foolish reason the master designer had never considered the bulk of its owner when it came to the command and control area of the vessel.

The designer was currently dealing with a most unpleasant job retrofitting organic fertilizer ships.

"Do remember, my lord, that conflict analysis through statistical measurement is a complex process. Take for instance the question of Alexander's death."

Aldin looked closely at Corbin as he spoke, but there was no response.

"Yes, Alexander's death."

The two men turned as Bukha Taug came into the room with Zergh at his side. Zergh nodded politely toward Corbin and then came up to Aldin's side, extending his huge paw to his fellow game master.

"I was just discussing such an event with my Koh Bukha," Zergh said evenly. "My analysis of course matches yours as to the odds of his death, which shows the ability of our programs, along with our own skills at data gathering and profiling, but one does not always agree with analysis, even when it is your own. Do you not concur, my friend?"

"There is the possibility," Aldin replied smoothly, "that our mathematical models of Alexander are not precise. Remember that I merely provide data input with some judgments of possibilities, but the computer is the one that analyzes this data and produces the final outputs. A Game Master of the First Degree, of which there are only two"—Aldin nodded to the Gavarnian who was his only equal—"can only provide probabilities. We cannot calculate a particular arrow or its flight and how that will intersect at a given moment with the line of Alexander's life."

Corbin was silent.

"In my analysis," Zergh interjected, "which was interplayed with that of Aldin's, I gave a slightly higher probability of death or serious injury to Alexander. But the computer rated Aldin's projections higher due to his specialization with this particular warrior. But I daresay, either way, it could make an interesting side bet."

Corbin nodded toward Bukha. "Rather than the private bets through the computer, shall we say a little public wager?"

"I do hate betting on the death of a Human I could almost admire, but the loyalties of race are thick."

Bukha looked straight at Corbin as he spoke, but there was no response.

"Shall we say control of your Cersta System?" Corbin said. "If I'm not mistaken, the automatic mines on the three worlds there are showing a significant return on your initial investment. For my part, I shall wager my pleasure world of Marrakesh; the Human females there might even meet with your approval."

Bukha, as was befitting a properly repressed Gavarnian, hid his revulsion at the mention of interracial sex, which was in fact practiced but viewed by the moral of both races as bestiality.

Bukha nodded to Zergh, who pulled out a pocket unit and ran a quick financial check.

"Relative worth comes out more like one point eight to seven," Zergh reported.

"Throw in the Dias Consortium, as well, then."

"But you are merely co-owner along with Zola."

"If I lose, I daresay that effeminate lout will be more than happy to sign me out and you in."

Zergh ran another quick check and nodded his approval.

"Two point three to seven."

"I'll draw the documents," Aldin said matter-of-factly.

"Come, come," Corbin replied smoothly, "we are all gentlemen here, are we not?"

Bukha smiled evenly, even though to his own race a smile was an act of hostility.

"My lord Alexander, they are responding as you said they would."

Alexander looked up at the sweat-covered courier who sat astride a small Gavarnian mount.

"Where did you get the horse, boy?"

"I took it in the ambush." The boy beamed with obvious pride.

"Parmenion and his troops?"

"They're not a verst behind me. Staying just ahead of the pursuing force."

"Good, very good. Go to supply, draw yourself some wine, you've earned it."

"I should return my lord Alexander."

"Follow my orders, rest yourself. They'll be here soon enough."

The boy saluted and kicked his mount to a canter. Alexander looked up from his map table and smiled at Yaroslav. "Did you hear that, he took it from a Gavarnian."

"Only someone as young as he would be crazy enough to mount such a beast."

"I've got fifty horses now. Already the men are learning that taking a horse means an end to walking—they've lost their fear."

"They'll soon get it back," Yaroslav said pensively, looking at the rolling cloud of dust approaching from the east. "Best you start the final briefing." And Yaroslav stepped out of the tent to beckon for the regiment commanders to come in.

"Do you all know your positions?" Alexander asked, looking to the regiment commanders once they had gathered around the raised sandbox that was used to illustrate their position since most of them still were not used to the idea of symbols on parchment representing hills, rivers, and men.

The men were silent. He could sense their fear. It was one thing when they had come to his banner, one after another to march against other Humans, but this was their first go against the Gafs. They were petrified, and at this moment it was only their greater fear of him that kept them to their task.

"Remember, it will be simple enough, we just let them come to us. They'll deploy in the way that Yaroslav here said they would, for war to them is as much ritual as it is a matter of death or victory. Just let them come. They have only eight thousand mounted and five thousand retainers on foot compared to our forty thousand deployed here. But if one of you breaks, the rest of you will break, and we'll all be slaughtered, for you can't outrun them. And besides, you have no place to run."

There was a faint rumble from the back of the crowd, but his look of challenge silenced them.

They were indeed in a trap. Nearly a fortnight ago the Gaf army had marched from their capital and advanced northeast, into the hill country. Alexander had led his force out into the plains after the Gaf army had passed, severing their lines of communication, thus forcing them to turn back and attack his prepared position. A lesson he had learned from Darius at Issus. But he had positioned himself in the fork between the Volsta and Benazi rivers, thus eliminating any hope for retreat. If they broke and ran, the rivers would block any chance of escape, and everyone in his army now knew this.

There was no way out, and some now looked at their leader with hatred and suspicion.

"Go to your posts, and those on the left, remember. If you show yourself before I come to lead, I'll personally take your heads. If any of us are left alive. Now go."

The men turned and left.

"If the battle goes against us," Yaroslav mumbled, "they'll seek you out first and cut you to ribbons before they themselves die."

"I'm not worried," Alexander replied almost cheerily. "You see, my friend, if I don't plan to lose, I won't."

"Oh, just grand, next thing I know you'll be telling me that your father Zeus assured you of this victory."

Alexander merely looked at him and smiled.

"My lord Kalin, they've stopped their retreat. See, just before the crest of the next hill."

Kalin, commander of the first host, reined in his horse and looked to where his aide was pointing.

"Still only fifty or so, and they've backed into the fork of the river rather than make for the last ford. The stupid fools are trapped."

"We've yet to sight the rest of their forces," Wirgth cautioned.

"Oh, they're in there, behind those hills and waiting. He's not sure of his men, this Alexander. He knows he has cowards, so he has trapped them into a position where they must fight or die. This makes it far easier to finish them even before the dimming."

"So why attack?" Hina replied. "If they're trapped, let's bottle them up. Within several passings we can starve them out."

"What! Even against the hairless ones I would not do such a thing. Have you no honor at all? Let's slaughter this rabble and go home."

Kalin turned in his saddle and looked at Kubar, who sat silently behind him. "Or does the most ancient and honored Kubar have another opinion?"

" 'Tis your host, not mine, therefore I merely observe and speak not."

"With such a lofty claim as yours, do you wish to announce first?" Kalin sneered.

"It is your army, your fight, and pray, your victory. Therefore I shall not partake from your honor but shall merely observe."

"Wise enough," Kalin said coldly, as his staff snickered at the apparent cowardice of an obvious liar. "Hina and Wirgth may stay with you, by the way."

The two turned and started to voice their protest.

"It is only as tradition demands," Kubar replied softly. "Hina as the last surviving youngest brother should not ride into the same conflict as the eldest lest the family line itself be threatened, and the Kaadu must not risk his life, either, less his advice be put to peril."

"For once we agree," Kalin said coldly, but there was a strange look in his eyes as he spoke, as if he had himself been pushed into a trap that he was only now becoming aware of. Kubar held Kalin's gaze for a moment and then bowed in a show of respect. The warrior turned his horse and galloped away, leaving the three to the rear as the army of nobles jostled for position in the advancing line.

"Classic formation," Yaroslav said, as if observing an academic problem on a sheet of parchment, rather than the maneuvering of thirteen thousand warriors.

"No logic to it, though."

"Ah, my Alexander, by your standard, not theirs. Remember, the nobility rides, as is their birthright, the non-noble marches. Titles and rank must be given and exchanged, that is the proper way. Thus the mounted unit deploys in forward line ahead of the infantry, highest rank closest to the west, lowest to the opposite side, and then the swordsmen behind."

"Foolishness. The same waste of cavalry that Darius used against me at Issus."

"Perhaps. But they can still fight. Look, that must be Kalin." He pointed to the far left of the enemy line where a single horseman had detached himself from the line and advanced across the open field that separated his serried ranks from Alexander and his troop of fifty horsemen that lined the low crested hill that stretched like a barrier in front of the river fork.

Like a rippling wave the line started to advance from

the Gavarnian left, each horseman waiting until the one to his own left had started forward, thus not riding ahead of someone decreed to be higher in rank.

When he was less than half a bow shot away, Kalin reined in his mount and then stood in the stirrups.

"Human, I give you honor by addressing you. I am Kalin, eldest of Kalin's son, called taug. I am the eldest of the eldest for eight generations, and the sword arm of my people. Thirty-eight of your kind have I hung inverted from my saddle. You are not worthy of my blade, but today I shall give you the taste of it. You without honor or love of brother, you whom they call Iskander, come forward and give unto me your history before you die."

Even before he had finished speaking, the next Gaf in line drew up by Kalin's side and started the same litany and then the next one and the next one so that soon the wild growling of hundreds of voices echoed against the hill as the noble Gafs advanced, shouting their family names with pride.

The sound gradually thundered away down the line while Alexander remained silent and motionless in the saddle.

An expectant hush settled across the field, for the Gafs now believed that histories would be given in turn, even if they were only hairless ones, and once given the Humans would advance in single line to meet them.

Alexander rode forward for a dozen paces and, reining in, he stood in his stirrups. He looked back to Yaroslav, wondering for a second if this were not some elaborate ruse to humiliate him, but the aged scholar simply beckoned for Alexander to go ahead, even as he started to back up in anticipation of the Gaf response.

Reaching down, he prepared himself, and when his gesture started to be obvious, an angry growling came up from the Gafs.

"I now piss," Alexander shouted, his voice echoing

even above the angry roar. "Kalin, hear me, for I piss on the honor of your brothers, and may their bones be rubbed in it!"

He never had a chance to complete what he had started and Bucephalas snickered with surprise at the sudden soaking as Alexander hurriedly tried to finish, for an earsplitting roar came up from the Gafs. As if guided by a single hand, they drew scimitars and charged.

Reining his horse about, Alexander urged it into a semblance of a gallop and headed back for the crest of the hill. Already his cavalry troop streamed before him; panic-stricken, they looked over their shoulders. Parmenion hung to the back and came up by his side.

"Lucky we are in a trap," Alexander roared, "otherwise those bastards would keep on running."

Parmenion looked over his shoulder at the advancing host, for now their infantry, enraged at the ultimate insult, was surging forward, as well. From the look of blood lust in the advancing host of wolflike giants, Parmenion found himself half wishing there was an escape route after all.

The troop of cavalry crested the hill and surged between two fluttering pennants, with Alexander and Parmenion bringing up the rear. Pulling up the pennants, Alexander followed his horseman carefully in order to stay between the chalked lines that marked the safe path.

Coming over the top of the slope, he could see the raw slash of entrenchments that ran more than half a league to the north and ended in the far riverbank. Nearly every foot of the entrenched line was faced by sharpened sticks that would hit a Gaf at chest height. At regular intervals the barricade had small openings, like the one he was now making for, which were flanked by three-meter-high ramparts of earth. The roar behind him grew louder and suddenly burst over them as a wave of horsemen crested the hill.

A thundering shout came up from his own line, but he could sense that it was a cry of fear more than of rage.

Clearing the gate, Alexander turned and watched as a dozen men dragged an entanglement of sharpened logs out and quickly threw them across the open barrier.

He stood in the saddle then leaped up to the platform where Yaroslav and several regiment commanders stood, awestruck by the rampaging advance.

"Told you it would make them angry," Yaroslav shouted, his voice barely heard above the outraged roar that was sweeping down upon them.

Alexander was silent, intent on watching the opening stage of the battle. Parmenion was already galloping down to take command of the center, prepared to rally the line if it should start to give.

Alexander looked to the broad, open trench behind the stockade and moat where his men stood three ranks deep and then back over his shoulder where the reserve attack phalanxes were drawn up, each in a column of eight. At least they were still holding, even though most all of them were white with fright.

"Here it comes," one of the commanders shouted.

The wave of horsemen, having crested the hill, were now picking up speed as they advanced down the slope, with Kalin at the head.

"There goes one!" And a shout of triumph went up. It was as if the earth had opened up to swallow both Gaf and horse. Suddenly another, and then another went down, falling into the concealed traps. Yet still they came on, chanting their family names. Kalin continued to push forward as if guided by fate, heading straight for the battlement where Alexander now stood.

He was oblivious to the disaster around him, as singly, and then by the tens and the hundreds, the advancing wave of cavalry fell to the checkerboard pattern of traps, pitfalls, and hidden entanglements of rope.

Alexander watched as the enemy captain somehow found his way onto the safe path through the line.

"I must meet him," Alexander shouted, pulling out his sword as he prepared to leap off the battlement wall.

"Wait," Yaroslav shouted, even as he pointed at the enemy captain whose horse had veered from the safe path.

Caught by a trip line, the horse spun over, hurling its burden forward. Kalin hit the ground hard, right at the base of the tower. From the way his head lolled to one side Alexander knew there was no need to face him now.

"So brave, yet so foolish," he whispered sadly.

"Shall we go forward to see?" Hina asked quietly.

"There is no need," Kubar said sadly. "For we can sit here and yet still know all, even when we see it not. It is far too obvious. And the words of that Human were but a confirmation of their plan. How I wish I could have warned your brother and have him believe me, for there is nothing worse, Hina, than to see disaster coming yet be powerless to stop it."

Hina tried to suppress his desire to go forward in order to blot out the insult that had been given. It was obvious by now that a disaster of undreamed-of proportions was taking place on the other side of the hill.

It had been some time since the last of the infantry had swarmed up over the slope into the thundering roar of battle. Now there seemed to be a continual stream of riderless horses and wounded warriors staggering back down the slope. Something was obviously going wrong. There had yet to be a paean, the unified shout of victory at the striking down of a rival chieftain. Instead, there was just a wild and constant roaring that somehow held in its turmoil a note of growing fear.

"Clear the barrier," Alexander roared as he finished his gallop down the line to the position on the far left.

Turning in the saddle, he looked back at the serried ranks of the Ris, who held the position as the farthest most regiment on the left.

"Remember not to break ranks!" he shouted to them, his strong full voice carrying above the thundering roar of battle. "And follow me."

The last of the logs having been drawn back, he pushed his way forward, keeping pace with the skirmishers who poured out in front. They were on the extreme right of the enemy line, faced only by an open deployment of infantry.

For what must have been an hour or more, the Gafs had thundered against the entrenched position. Those who survived the deadfalls and entanglements had pushed against the fortified lines, all semblance of control forgotten. It had been a maddening assault that was terrifying in its intensity, but useless for any practical purpose.

As the casualties piled up, the enemy formations had contracted to the center. Alexander had been up and down the line, helping to plug the few breakthroughs that were made, and had finally worked down to the extreme left where his final punch was concealed.

As he cleared the gate he looked farther up the line and signaled for Parmenion to start his regiment out, as well. The plan was simple enough: punch through the crippled right, pivot, and roll up the enemy line. Clearing the last of the entanglements, his men shook out their line to form a phalanx a hundred men wide by ten deep. In a minute they were ready, and pivoting forty-five degrees to the right, they set out at a double pace.

The few weary Gafs that were before them broke at the sight of the inexorable wall bearing down from the north, and the sight of their enemies' backs heightened the spirit of the men. In staggered formation Parmenion's regiments fell in on the right flank of the expanding line, and half a dozen more regiments swung in as reserves.

Looking down the enemy line, Alexander could see that they were well extended beyond the Gafs' position. Holding his sword up high, he pointed for them to pivot another forty-five degrees. They were now a wave, rolling down the length of the enemy line, curling it up like rotten wood collapsing beneath a razor-sharp blade.

The roaring anger of the Gafs now gave way to fear.

Here and there a lone warrior, beyond caring, held his ground and was washed over, taking a Human or two with him, but the once-proud host was pushed beyond all their ability to comprehend. Gafs were supposed to fight as by the law. Humans had always run like animals of prey, for that was what they were. But now the beast had insulted them, then fought in ways beyond all comprehension.

The men behind him knew, as well, that somehow this strange warrior who claimed to come out of the past from the legendary Earth had created a new thing. It was a moment beyond their wildest imaginings. And in it they took courage, and found themselves, after all, to be men.

The chant started from the back. A single voice calling out the name to the beat of their advance, their accent changing the word, but still recognizable.

"Iskander, Iskander."

It swept like thunder down the line, so that thousands of voices cried as one.

"Iskander, Iskander."

And counterpointed to it came the dismal shouts of the Gafs as they broke and ran in a stampeding herd toward the river, which was their only hope of escape, now that their flank was completely turned.

As they ran their weapons fell, wounded were abandoned, horses left to capture, and the Human wave bore down upon them.

"Iskander, Iskander."

Reining in his horse, Alexander let the ranks pass by. His practiced eye noticed that already the formations were breaking up, but that was beyond control. He had to remind himself that these were men under arms for less than a score of weeks, and not the thirty-year veterans he had led out of Bactria and the Indus.

"Iskander!"

The cry came from his left, and turning, he saw a Gaf driving a spear through the body of a man who stood by his side. Alexander instantly knew that the man had leaped in front of a spear that had been meant for him.

Spurring his horse around, he came up on the Gaf and with a single blow finished off the enemy who had let the Humans march over him in order to get at their commander.

After leaping from the horse, he came up to the dying man and knelt by his side.

"Iskander," the man whispered, "it is a good day to die, for I have seen them run." And then he was gone.

"A glorious day," Parmenion shouted, coming to his captain's side. "By Zeus, it's as glorious as Guagamela!"

Alexander came to his feet, that curious, distant look in his eyes.

"Yes," he whispered, "even I will say it was glorious." And unfastening his cloak, he laid it across the body of a beardless youth.

CHAPTER 10

"BROTHER KALIN, GO NOW TO OUR BROTHER SWANIKA. Brother Kalin, go now to our brother Uta. Oh, my three glorious brothers, wait for me in the hall of Binda beyond the shadows. Oh, my three brothers, wait for me, until at last I cross over the shadow, as well, where again we shall be joined as one. Together we shall be joined and face then the mystery of the Unseen Light, for together from the light we came, and at last, together, we shall return unto it."

Choked with grief, Hina turned away from the crackling, blazing pyre. The four keepers of the flame, dressed in red robes, bowed to the heir and took from his hand the flaming torch that had ignited the blaze.

Kalin's body alone had been given the honors that were proper. It had come the dimming before, under Human guard with a message from Alexander saying that he wished to return the body of an honorable warrior to his people. The courier had then inquired as to the proper custom of disposing with the other ten thousand corpses of the host.

Hina's guardsmen wanted to tear the Humans apart on the spot but he had prevented it, for to do so would be a loss of face. And he had allowed the envoys to depart.

He looked at the few survivors of the once-proud nobility. Nine out of ten had fallen on the field. As custom demanded, a place was still kept in the line for the slain during the mourning period, but where sixty family heads had once stood, only five were left. Half a dozen younger heirs stood in the place of older brothers or sires, but for the other families every male heir of the direct line had been lost, for the convention that applied to the heir of a taug was not practiced for lesser titles. Besides, they had only been hunting Humans, and as such, none had wished to miss the sport. If there was no heir to stand for a fallen nobleman, the vacant place was occupied instead by a sheathed sword set upon the ground.

Hina composed himself. First he nodded to Kubar, who stood silent by the flaming pyre, then he bowed to the assembly.

"Honored nobility, the mourning time for all of us shall continue as is our ancient custom, but still we must prepare."

"Prepare for what?" came a shouted taunt from the back. Hina recognized the graying speaker as Arn, the Wu-taug, or family leader of the Paka clan, whose family estates encompassed the region now occupied by the Humans.

Arn stepped from his assigned place in the assembly and walked to the foot of the dais that Hina occupied. That action alone, which implied a challenge, drew a murmured response from the nobles.

"There was no honor for those who fell at the forks," Arn roared. "There was no name giving with the Humans, and no blood debt paid by the victors so that families would be satisfied. What honor was there, answer me that?"

Hina was silent while a murmur of assent greeted Arn's words.

"They were slaughtered by Humans, by cattle that we hunted for sport and for meat at the time of holy days. The Humans did not fight, they denied all honor. And then to add insult, you suffered this envoy, the voice of this Iskander, to live even when he was in our camp, sword about his waist."

"Is it not said," Hina quickly replied, "that the head of an envoy, the voice of a family, is sacred when he comes to your fire? Even if he is a man, I will follow our law."

Arn ignored the quote from sacred tradition. "They have done something new, something strange beyond our understanding. They have taken the honor of war and torn it asunder like the peeling of the bark from a tree. There is no honor left. It is time for us to chant our names, and return back to that cursed hill of death—and there to end it, once and for all."

The survivors of Arn's clan gathered around him, shouting their approval at his suicide plan.

Hina extended his right arm, and even though the sun was dim, still the object in his hand glinted in the shadowy light.

"This is the circlet of the taug," Hina cried, and the warriors fell silent at the sight of the sacred object. Kalin had worn it into battle and it had been returned with his body.

"This crown," Hina shouted, "is the symbol of the taug. On your naming day you swore an oath of loyalty to it. Remember the oath is to the symbol of the taug, not simply to he who wears it. Two score lifetimes ago we came to this ring in the great migration, and then our brothers who crossed the stars disappeared in the Great War with the hairless ones. For two score lifetimes we of the hundred first families grew in numbers about the Iras Sea, and always did we honor the rule of the taug.

"It was the rule of the taug that set the rules of war, thus preventing us from destroying ourselves, and taught us that war is an honor of nobles who serve the one taug. The symbol of the taug is sacred and must be obeyed, else we shall disappear into the night of legend, where there is no light and none may see."

Arn knew that age-old tradition would win out over the discontent of his followers. He bowed his head in acknowledgment.

"Of the hundred first families there were but sixty left before the Humans changed. Now there are but eleven. If we follow the desire of Arn and march back to fight yet again as we did, there shall be none.

"War was once for honor and the reputation that a Gavarnian took to his pyre. Now it shall be different, it shall be for the survival of us all."

"War and honor are one," Arn replied coldly.

"That must change." As Hina spoke he held the crown up so that all were silent. "And I am not capable of the task," he said evenly.

Arn looked into his rival's eyes, looking for the weakness, but there was none.

"How can that be?" another cried. "The clan Brug has been above all rivalries since the migration. Your clan alone is bred to be the final judge."

"I know nothing of the new warfare that has to be fought," Hina replied. "And we must learn this and acknowledge who shall teach us, if we are to survive."

There was an expectant feeling in the air. Hina stared at Arn and could see a sudden look of hope in the old warrior's eyes.

He turned away from Arn and walked over to Kubar's side. "At this moment I hold the power that you are all sworn to obey. I am the last heir of the Brugs, thus whatever I do shall be the law. Watch now what I do, and obey this decision."

Before anyone could voice a protest, he turned and placed the circlet of steel on Kubar's head.

"I acknowledge the truth of this one's words. Once before in legends past there came the first Taug, whose very name became the title for all since who have ruled. He was the first Taug, and from out of legend he has been sent again to save us as he did our ancestors. Kubar Taug is the one Taug of the Kolbard."

A scattering of cheers arose from the assembly, but most were silent. As oath-bound, they were sworn to serve, but they were not sworn to love what most of them believed was an impostor. And believe him as taug, or not, all knew how the first great Taug had ended the rule of the landholders and thus united his people ages ago. Such things were fine when they were legends—but legends were difficult to live with when come to life.

Kubar looked over to where Liala was standing in the corner of the courtyard. Their eyes locked for but a moment, and he could see that her look was simply not one of admiration. His wife, who had been a wife in name only, was dead now for four thousand years, but she was still a memory alive but a brief time ago. Liala's interest created a momentary confusion on his part and he turned away to look back at Hina. He could imagine that his friend was suffering from the same confusion, since by tradition, if the older brother was married, the wife of the brother remarried the younger one. But Hina had other things to concern him at the moment; they would talk of it later.

Hina was looking to Arn, awaiting a response. The clenched fist was finally raised, but the eyes glowed a defiance that was evident to all. Kubar noticed, as well. It was a look he had faced a thousand times, and it was a look that more than once had nearly led to his death.

"Close one for Kubar," Zergh said quietly, staring into the brandy that Aldin had poured for him.

"You had it plotted out well in your initial prognosis. And it followed remarkably close to what you had said," Aldin replied to his old friend.

"You are a Human; the inner weavings I can expect you to know here"—Zergh pointed to his head—"but in the heart, that is something only a Gavarnian can truly understand. They want to believe that he is Kubar, sent to redeem them. But have you ever admired someone who was too perfect? You want to be by their side, yet at the same time they are a living proof of your own limited abilities, and thus create pain."

Aldin, as usual, looked like he had taken one drink too many, and Zergh wrinkled his snout when Aldin pulled out a less-than-pleasant-smelling cigar and lit it up.

"You sure the room aboard this ship has been debugged?"

Aldin nodded in response and pointed to his own countersnoop, which rested on the sideboard alongside the half-empty bottle of brandy. The stasis field, which blocked out all sound and was impervious, as well, to laser sensing, was already locked on, but it was possible nevertheless to have a microplant floating in the air and inserted into the room before the stasis had been turned on. Corbin was noted for such little forms of trust and hospitality.

"There's been an interesting ripple in the betting flow," Zergh began cautiously. "Why, just on that last fight alone, nearly eight percent of all the real estate in the Cloud changed hands. If that much went up on the first battle, I can imagine how it will run when we get down to the last encounter."

"Now's when the real action starts," Aldin replied, pulling on the cigar and watching the pattern of smoke as it hit the edge of the stasis and flattened out.

"After that last battle the free-float odds chart shifted three point seven three to one in favor of Alexander."

"I know that, Zergh. It's my business to compute it."

"But there's been no sign of Corbin's money coming into the game. Sure, he's placed the usual handful of bets, a world here, a multisystem business there, but no reports of anything major."

"What about Bukha?" Aldin replied.

"He's a Gavarnian of the old school. He'll bet some on Kubar out of loyalty but so far he's been slow to enter, as well. But come now, Aldin, what about Corbin? You know what kind of man he is. What's happening with him?"

Aldin turned his gaze to Zergh and fixed him with an even gaze.

"I'm in the employ of Corbin as his master vasba. I trust he'll abide by most of the rules. But beyond that . . ." He shrugged his shoulders.

"Aldin, I've watched you grow in your profession for thirty years, or have you forgotten you apprenticed under me? You're a damn good historian and gaming analyzer, but a piss-poor judge of Human qualities. Corbin must be up to something. This game's turning into the biggest gambling operation in history, and I've suspected from the day Corbin first mentioned this project that he had something up his sleeve."

"A Gavarnian trying to tell me about Human qualities?"

"I've tried to tell you more than once about Corbin, but oh, no, you wouldn't listen. So the son of a bitch robs you blind, and that cousin of his soaks every last ounce of alimony payments out of you. Then yesterday you told me that his royalty payment to you will be partnership in the Zswer Mining Consortium. Come on, Aldin, that's a sucker's deal if I ever heard one. He'll skin you clean out of that in six months' time and then where will you be—broke and on the beach with nothing to show for three years' worth of work."

Aldin was silent, ignoring his friend's words as if to listen would cause him to betray the trust of yet another friend.

As Aldin finished up his cigar, Zergh finally arose complaining that he needed a breath of fresh air. Aldin did not even acknowledge his departure as he prepared for yet another shot of brandy.

"The nobility is dead," Kubar said quietly, and looked across the table to his friend on the other side. "I'm not saying that because I relish the idea. Always remember, Hina, that I was of noble birth, as well—the same as you."

Hina leaned back in his chair and grimaced.

"You can say that around me," Hina replied, "because I know that. Remember, I saw them go down to their defeat. The nobility died in the field facing this Iskander. But don't ever say that around Arn, no matter what his oath of allegiance to the circle of steel." He pointed to the thin crown of metal on Kubar's brow.

Kubar barked softly and grimaced. "Remember, I had an entire world of nobility to deal with and to unite. And, oh, how they wanted me to end the slaughter—and to still keep their titles once the slaughter had ended. I think I know how to tread softly around Arn."

"Realize, though, that if Arn ever comes to truly believe that you are the Taug, then he'll have the lesson of our distant history, as well, to show what remained of the old orders once you had finished. Your contemporaries did not have such an advantage. Don't count on your legendary status too much with Arn. Remember, close exposure to a legend tends to lower him a notch or two into the realm of mere mortals."

Kubar chuckled at the thought. So he was a legend, placed even higher than Narg of the Shining Blade and this other Gavarnian of over three thousand years past who, according to Zergh, had discovered the means to jump from star to star.

"So why do you accept me?"

"Because I guess you could say I'm a romantic. It was assumed even when my brothers were still alive that Kalin would be always the one to rule. He was first from the womb of my mother, and thus it was his right to start with. It was I of the four who was the one allowed to read and to dream of distant glories."

Kubar thought it a curious throwback, that reading should one day be viewed with disdain, a compromise with the strength of a warrior's word.

"I dreamed that we were not the only Gavarnians to survive the Great Wars with the Humans and the other races. And your presence here, and your story of this Zergh who flies through space and time like a servant of the Unseen Light, have proven that, at least. I dreamed of greater things and knew in my heart when I met you that your coming was the sign I had hoped for."

Kubar could only smile at the romance in his friend's mind. Hina reminded him of those first comrades who had rallied to his banner when his revolution was young. They had all been so young, so full of dreams for tomorrow. And all of them, except for old Paga, who sat sleepily in the corner of the room, were now dead. He muttered a silent prayer for his friend that the dreamer of fate would not dream of darkness for this companion.

"Tomorrow we shall start," Kubar said evenly, drawing the conversation back to the practical concerns that faced them.

"If this Iskander is any type of commander, he will not let the initiative for this campaign pass into our hands. The stone walls of this city and the fact that we face the sea and can thus gain supplies from ships most likely will prevent him from launching a direct attack and siege."

"Then where do you think it shall come?" Wirgth finally interjected, entering the conversation that until now he had been observing silently.

"An army that big devours supplies like the bottomless stomach of the giant *Gress*. His men must spread out and forage the countryside."

"Why not come straight on to the city and finish it?"

"Ah, I must assume that this Iskander is good. Never underestimate your foe, even if he is a hairless one.

Always believe that he knows everything you think and is smarter than you in all things."

"Unlike my brother," Hina said darkly.

"Your brother fought in the way he thought all wars should be fought," Wirgth replied diplomatically.

"As I was saying," Kubar continued, "Iskander must assume that we shall not make the same mistake again. If we pull back to the city, the walls of stone will require a long siege. With the harbor behind us supplies are no problem, for as yet the hairless ones have no ships. No, I think he is too shrewd to attack us in that way. Besides, a siege requires engines and supplies of metal for equipment and weapons. Most of those men we faced were still carrying wooden-tipped spears. You can't take a stone-walled city with that. Even with the supplies they looted from our army, they still do not have enough to mount a proper siege. And, besides, it will take several score of dimmings to rework the weapons they've taken to fit Human hands."

"Then he must gain three things," Hina ventured, "before he can make his killing blow. While we need but one to win."

"Go on."

"Supplies for his men, ships to close off our harbor, and metal to equip both men and ships."

Kubar barked a muffled tone of satisfaction. With the tip of his finger he pointed to a black oval on the map before them, two hundred versts north of the city.

"The wrecked ore carrier that rests thirty versts to the northeast of Mount Lequa, that is where he shall drive for. That destroyed vessel of ancient spacefaring Humans has enough iron ore to supply an army a hundred times the size of Iskander's. Your own people have been mining it since you first settled here. Where it rests on a bay of the Iras Sea, it is just south of the hill country that the Humans can withdraw back into if they are attacked and defeated. Yes, that is where I think he will come. But do not neglect the southward approaches, either, for there are some of our richest farmland. Now that they have horses, they are sure to raid in that direction to take supplies, as well."

"You mentioned the three things for the Humans," Wirgth interrupted, "but what is it that we need?"

"We need to relearn the art of war," Hina replied coldly.

"Never call it an art," Kubar responded as if he were suddenly too tired to continue. "Rather it is learning how to butcher on a massive scale.

"Your ancestors on this ring were wiser than all but a few realized. They knew that if ever massed warfare was allowed to take hold with their descendants who were marooned here, the slaughter would be catastrophic. So they changed the equation, made combat a highly ritualized thing that would kill but a handful before it got out of control. Now you all will have to relearn the older, far more efficient way, and that is why I am here."

Kubar sat back for a moment, the thought suddenly taking form, a thought that he had been far too busy to consider in a serious way. It was this Iskander who had united the Humans and taught them the new way, which in fact was as old as their history. And he had been brought across time to do yet the same service, if service it could be called, to his people, as well. Why? For what reason was this bloodshed escalated? Granted, in the end it would settle the difference between Human and Gavarnian on the Kolbard once and for all, and across ten thousand dimmings, more lives might be saved than lost. But still there was the nagging question of why. Such endless rounds of slaughter, and for a moment his memory drifted back to Cliarn and the fields of his last battle—that last battle that finally united Lhaza. Cliarn.

"So how shall we do it, then?" Hina asked, interrupting Kubar's line of thought.

"We shall raise up the landless laborers and those of the city."

"They'll not fight as a noble would," Hina replied

evenly. "They serve as border warrens, but you saw how useless they were in that fight. Most of them broke once Iskander's Humans came out of their fortress and charged."

"Because, in the end, they had no real reason to fight. They are landless peasants, without title or respect. Really, Hina, there is an entire continent we can give them out there as reward for fighting."

Hina was silent, understanding the implication, knowing it was needed, but still frightened by the revolutionary impact of what Kubar was leading to.

"As of tomorrow there shall be no more landless class. Each shall be given his estate to work by the sweat of his own labor. They will fight for such tangible reward."

"But what about the nobles?" Hina replied coldly, and in his words even Kubar could sense a tone of identification with his own class.

"If they do not agree, then they doom themselves anyhow, for without an army to face the hairless ones, Iskander shall win and there will be no estates, period. Besides, there will be rewards for the nobility, new titles to have, decorations for valor to wear, and pageantry to lull them. The first draft of levies will come from those family estates that were wiped out in the battle of the forks, or from lands already overrun by the Humans. We'll leave the others working, for now, to bring in what harvest they can before the Humans arrive.

"With the passing of this dimming, we shall start. The training will be essential, for the troops must learn to fight as a unit—their bodies subject to the will of but one mind."

Again there was the old paradox. Here he wished to create a society where each was equal to another, yet in order to achieve that he would first free the landless and then immediately set out to bring them under his unshakable will, so that they would finally be willing to die at his command.

"Arn will try to block you," Wirgth said. "He's too shrewd to fall for a mere bauble or decoration to ease him while you dismantle an entire social order."

"I assume he will. But you shall be surprised how quickly some of the other nobility will be willing to rush to their death in order to earn a hunk of metal hung on a useless ribbon. As for Arn, I shall let him assume that once the war is won he'll be able to eliminate me and reestablish the status quo. I need him and his nobility too much right now, to train and lead the new levies of troops."

With a yawn Kubar stood up from the table and stretched. "This world without a night is too confusing to me. How I miss the twilight that filled the sky with a lavender glow."

To Hina, who had never seen such a thing as night or the stars, Kubar's words sounded as if they came from the world of myth. And then he reminded himself yet again that he had just given his crown to a myth. A myth who while saving them would most likely destroy them, as well.

With a polite nod to Hina and Wirgth, Kubar started to the door, and Paga, roused from his nap, came in behind his master.

Tomorrow they would start in earnest. There were a few other things that he planned to start, as well, but best not to overwhelm Hina with those little experiments that he had in mind. He had already placed a request for the lightest sheets of fabric to be found, along with enough copper to nearly strip the kingdom of every pot and pan. But that would be his little secret, for now.

It would be an interesting diversion from his other tasks. Long before, he had found that working with such things cleared his mind so that he could better deal with the far more important problems. And problems there would be. Iskander, of course, came above all else. He would have to fathom how this Human made war and then find a way to counter it. There would be the training of the levies, the preparations to defend the ore carrier, and of course Arn. But for the moment his thoughts were centered on Zergh. He knew that to waste time contemplating the one who brought him here was foolish. But the question of "why" would not leave him, even as he tried to settle into a restless sleep.

"Not a bad arrangement, so far," Corbin said lazily, as he examined the contents in his goblet. Leaning back, he drained off the rest of the brandy and smiled at his companion.

"Sure you wouldn't care for a drink?" Corbin asked.

"No, I'd rather keep my head clear."

"Ah, Tia, my shrewd little mistress, you never did care for drinking."

"Just because, from no choice of mine, Aldin is my uncle does not mean that I inherited his cruder vices. Besides, he's my uncle from my mother's side of the family, which makes you my third cousin. If I've inherited any vices, my dear, it comes from our mutual blood, not his."

Corbin threw back his head and laughed. "You inherited your mother's sharp tongue, at least. But let's not quarrel about such trivial things. How goes your work with Aldin?"

"He's fat, he never washes, he's of the lower classes and acts it. Why you respect him as a vasba is beyond me."

"I never said I respected him. I use him because he is useful, that is all."

"So why have you forced me to serve this man you use?"

"Because you had no choice. With your mother gone, you are family obligated to obey my wishes. It's that simple. Anyhow, I did have a significant investment with the Alexander game and I wanted someone close to me to observe him, with my interests in mind. Your report was quite concise and informative."

Tia was silent, waiting for the real reason for this required visit to come out.

Corbin smiled in what was a caricature of loving indulgence. "Knowing the arts of the vasba can't hurt you. In fact, it can help make you wealthy as you get older."

"Since I'll never inherit the family control, I'll need that knowledge, won't I, my dear, or have you finally decided to declare which of the mistresses you'll make your legitimate wife?" As she spoke she drew closer, running her hands up and down his bloated body.

"Now, I never said that you were not the one in my will," he said laughingly, while returning her caresses in a more direct manner.

"Don't patronize me," Tia responded, suddenly pulling back.

"Ah, Tia, my darling, you'll be well taken care of, just trust me. Anyhow, I think there is a little something you might be interested in. You have shown a decent knowledge of how the games work, as well as a certain desire to give me any pleasure I desire."

She leaned forward again, ready to hear what he was going to offer. From the beginning she had suspected there was something more going on behind the scenes with Corbin, otherwise his placement of her with the recovery team for Alexander would have made little sense.

"Ah, now my greedy young child is all ears for what Uncle Corby has to say."

"Just get to the point, and don't call yourself Uncle Corby. It makes my being your mistress sound a little too perverted."

Corbin extended his hands in an innocent gesture, as if he had been wrongly accused. "Well, let's get down to business then, shall we? First off, I needed somebody in the family to learn a little more about this vasba business. I see a big future in it now that we've discovered a way to harvest old Earth for interesting arrangements.

Yes indeed, there are endless possibilities for gaming in our future."

"But you have Aldin to run that angle."

"Your uncle or not, he is getting old."

"What you really mean to say is you want to cut him out of his ten-percent commission and keep it in the family."

"Did I say that?"

Tia could only smile knowingly. It could be a lucrative agreement. She knew Corbin had been cheating Aldin on his royalty statements for some time. With the commissions from the Alexandrian game, Aldin could find himself to be a very rich man. So that was Corbin's offer, for a start, at least.

"So I've learned something about being a vasba. It's a dirty lower-class job; what else do you have in mind?" Tia said, smiling. "Come on, I know you well enough to realize there's something else."

"All right then, girl. I need you to make a special arrangement."

"Go on."

"First off, I want you to report on anything suspicious about Aldin."

"I assumed I was to do that from the start. And I daresay that he assumes that I am to do that, as well."

"Things are going to get a little tense very shortly," Corbin said, leaning over to fix Tia with his gaze. "I need your help, and the reward will match the help."

"Such as naming me your legitimate spouse?"

"Don't push your luck," Corbin replied coldly. Then leaning back, he smiled again. "But anything is possible, once this is over with.

"You see, betting is running strongly on xenophobic lines. Now, the Gafs have some interesting worlds, to be sure, but it's the possessions of old Sigma Azermatti that really interest me. His systems sit astride the jump point back to the home galaxy. I think this little time device can have some interesting implications for going back to trade markets not yet exploited—and Sigma would get the duties. Also, the worlds he now owns are rich in and of themselves."

"And besides," Tia interrupted, "he vexes you simply because of the respect all the other Kohs have for him. Along with the fact that he's the wealthiest Human Koh in the Cloud."

Corbin grunted angrily. She was right, he had always hated Sigma for the air of disdain that he had shown for the "Gablona upstarts," as he termed them when Corbin was not within hearing distance.

"I plan to wipe him out in this game."

"His estates are four times the size of yours," Tia responded, "you can't match him on bets. Secondly, he's betting on Alexander, the same way you should be. After all, the trends indicate a continued win on his part."

"Oh, really," Corbin said knowingly.

"All right, what's the scam, dearest?"

"Your overall analysis report was perhaps far better than you thought, and, if anything, confirmed what I believed would happen all along."

"And that is?"

"We're betting on two societies in conflict, but we are also betting on two personalities, as well. But there is a significant ingredient to victory for either side that's being overlooked."

Corbin leaned back, beckoned for Tia to fill his brandy snifter, and then continued.

"You see, for Alexander to succeed it will be through the strength of his own character that will mold a shapeless society together, giving it order. For Kubar, however, victory comes from merely transforming a complex social system already in place. Up until the first battle, I had my suspicions as to the overall outcome, since Kubar had to deal with an entrenched system of nobility. Oh, they might admire him as a legend, but they damn sure weren't enthused about having that legend bearing witness against them. But conveniently for me, that social system died in the first battle. Kubar has an open ticket now to transform the Gafs into the only type of army that could beat Alexander—an army modified to defeat phalanx tactics. Once he's trained them, it doesn't matter if he lives or dies."

"But if Kubar should die," Tia replied, "Alexander's superior generalship would win the day."

"Oh, of course, if Kubar should die first."

She looked at him suspiciously. "What are you driving at, Corbin?"

"Come now, Tia, do I need to spell it out?"

"I suspect that there's a deal in this for me. There damn well better be. But before I get dragged in, I want to hear it straight from you."

Corbin leaned forward and suddenly his voice was full of menace. "There'll only be two other people besides myself who know about this. Let me tell you the negative first, if you should decide not to cooperate."

"I'm dead, just like the plastacement contractor."

"His little accident, at least, was quick and relatively painless. There could be far worse things."

Tia reached over and picked up Corbin's hand and rested it lightly upon her breast. "You were the first to touch this, Corbin. When I met you that's all I had to offer. That's more than can be said for that cheap slut Regina, whom you seem to be favoring more than me."

"She's got bigger teats than yours, Tia, but not the brains. That's why I'm talking to you and not her."

She certainly did, Tia realized, and the dirty old lecher in front of her, like most men, considered an extra ten pounds of swollen glands to be far more significant than a woman's brain. Damn, she knew he'd wind up cutting her out in the end for that swollen, shrill-voiced, vacuum-headed cow. But maybe this scam was the way out she had been looking for ever since she allowed herself to be dragged into Corbin's net. Corbin was a path to prominence in her family. In fact, he was the only path since he did have a propensity to squash any of his relatives who had pretensions of grandeur, especially if the relative was a woman.

"I know what you'd do to me if I failed you," Tia replied, putting on her best seductive smile. "So go ahead and tell me, dearest."

"Cut the 'dearest' crap. This is business, plain and simple, and you fit the bill. You're Aldin's niece, even if it is only through marriage. The old dodderer has a liking for you and always has. At the same time, you're part of my family, so there's a self-interest there. And finally, I sleep with you."

Corbin leaned back and smiled his cold, sinister grin. "I plan to murder Alexander and thus throw the game."

Her expression did not change or flicker, and she returned the smile that he gave her.

Good, he thought quietly. No moral outcry, no whining, because if she had, her next drink might have been her last.

"How long have you been planning this?" Tia replied evenly.

"For over two years, right after my research people started to show some promising results with the time travel studies and I realized the game might be feasible.

"I came across an obscure paper, printed by some fool academician back at one of the universities that I endowed for public relations purposes. It was a study of the Kolbard and an examination of some of the cultures. The old fool who wrote it made some good points, and he created a scenario outlining how the Humans we finally chose for the fight could win or lose. The model fit Alexander and Kubar, since he pointed out that both societies needed some sort of charismatic leader to transform them.

"It was the classic great man theory all over again. But once transformed, the Gafs would most likely win, since they would still have a better organizational structure. In fact, the historian actually cited Alexander, comparing his empire built around one man to that of the

Romans, which was more of a societal team effort. I must say, that paper helped to center my attention on Alexander. That paper was the inspiration, Alexander and Kubar are merely interesting window dressing to draw the suckers into the biggest scam ever played. The author was quite the intellectual; I could have used him, but the stupid alky disappeared right after the paper was published."

"So in spite of the current Gaf setbacks," Tia said hurriedly, "you still plan to kill Alexander?"

"The setbacks make it all the better, and again, it's just part of the scam. As I said, I plan to kill Alexander after secretly wagering a fair portion of my fortune in favor of the Gafs. I've held off till now since the odds were fairly even, as I anticipated they'd be. But I also anticipated that Alexander would have little difficulty organizing, while Kubar would take some time. Thus Alexander would win the opening rounds. Those opening victories would drive the odds up maybe as high as five or six to one in his favor. Now that that is happening, I plan to start to funnel my money secretly into the Gaf side. Once the market has been driven as high as it can go in Alexander's favor, I'll trigger his death. The Human side collapses, since as was pointed out in that paper, the Human society will be built around just one man."

"The same as in the Wars of the Succession," Tia replied. "Once Alexander died, his empire disintegrated into civil war. The dream of unification was lost."

"Ah, Tia, you have been studying then, as well."

She smiled quickly and shrugged her shoulders.

"With Alexander dead, the Humans lose and I clean up."

"Against whom," Tia replied, "and how are you planning to filter this money in without anyone knowing? After all, if word got out that you were betting against Alexander, it would blow everything wide open. All the Kohs would be hot on your trail to find out why. When

Alexander gets it, even if they couldn't prove it, the bloody finger would still be pointed in your direction."

"Ah, Tia, Tia, so now we come to the point, and that's why I'm bringing you in. For the last two years I've been quietly creating a large number of corporate fronts, creating holding companies that hold other companies in turn. Hell, that plastacement contractor still holds controlling interest in nearly a hundred worlds through a dozen companies held by one of my dead bodyguards. It's all been cleverly arranged, my dear, all of it. But I cannot act in this little drama directly. The risk is too great. My every move is being monitored by the other Kohs. As of yesterday, nearly ten and a half percent of the total wealth of the Clouds was tied into the game. With that much money floating around you can be sure that large amounts are being spent just trying to figure out who is doing what, looking for the inside angle on the game.

"Therefore I have to remain above all suspicion, and assume that everything I do is monitored. I want you to handle the portfolio and to filter the money in. It will merely mean that you'll act as the middleman, so to speak, dumping the corporations into the betting when I give you the signal. No one will ever meet you, it will all be handled through your contact to the controllers of a particular firm. Code systems have been set up, and it will appear as if a consortium of minor Kohs have learned of the game and are stacking their life savings on the action.

"The bets will be placed anonymously through you, and they all must be specifically targeted against the holdings of Sigma Azermatti."

"When you win, though, it will finally come out that the Gablona Family is holding the Sigma fortune," Tia replied.

"Oh, eventually, but by then any attempt at tracing the death of Alexander will be impossible. In fact, I want

Sigma to know, two or three years down the road, that I, Corbin Gablona, finally cleaned him out."

"Of course, my dear," Tia said smoothly, "I'll do it. I'd do anything for you. But this will take a lot of effort on my part, and there is some small risk involved."

"Ah, yes, the payoff," Corbin replied smoothly. "How does one percent of all winnings sound to you? One percent can make you a minor Koh in your own right."

One percent! The cheap bastard. That simple offer in and of itself showed what he felt for her. So, Regina or that twosome of Mpnoa and Bithila, who would work on Corbin together at the same time, would be the ones that wound up with the bigger bucks. She fought to control her anger. She could see, as well, that making her his mistress had nothing to do with desire or love. She had often wondered about that, since she had always felt so insecure about her own appearance. The other women around Corbin were simply voluptuous while she was all skinny angles with a bobbed, upturned nose and hair that could never get past shoulder length without looking like a home for various vermin. So that was it all along—he had picked her for her superior intellect, the knowledge taught to her by Aldin, and her innate ability to help pull off such a scam.

He was certainly a cheap bastard, but then she had known it from the very start.

"It's agreed then," she replied smoothly.

"Ah, I knew you would see the potential in this for you," Corbin replied, smiling.

"But one question. How do you plan to kill Alexander? That playing field down there is crammed with surveillance equipment. The Xsarn's done a masterful job at insuring that everything is legal and that all contact is impossible. Even our own trip to Earth and every contact with Alexander were scanned to make sure no slow-acting agents might be introduced by either side. So how do you plan to do it?"

"As I said earlier," Corbin replied, "only two people

will know about the plan. But neither of them will know more than they need to. Don't ever ask about Alexander again."

She backed off, sensing the threat in his words.

Smiling again, Corbin turned and pulled a bottle of champagne from the sideboard, leaving the alternate bottle, the one he would have used had Tia balked, in its place.

After the bottle was uncorked, the two smiled at each other as the drinks were poured. So now she knew and apparently had taken the bait. This woman was a good choice, as he had sensed years before when she was still but a young girl first flowering into adolescence.

She'll do well, and he almost regretted what he'd have to arrange once this was over. Give women too much power, he thought, and they start to run amok. That's why in the end he preferred the dumb ones who knew their place. It'd be a shame to use the other bottle of liquor on her the way he already planned for the other participant. He smiled again at Tia, wondering what she was thinking.

Looking over her glass, Tia returned his loving gaze.

CHAPTER 11

"BY ALL THE GODS," PARMENION ROARED, "STAND ON that flank or I'll kill you myself!"

The wavering men looked in his direction and then nervously back to the approaching line of Gaf infantry.

"You've got to hold!"

They were really outnumbered this time, and the enemy was pouring around the flanks, ready to threaten the small fortified camp that guarded their toehold on the edge of the Anvil.

At Alexander's orders, Parmenion had led two thousand men ahead of the advancing column with orders to capture the strange mountain of iron by surprise before the Gafs could reinforce it. Half of them were all of Alexander's mounted strength, the other thousand being the elite Ris and Kievant phalanx that had ridden across the Anvil double-mounted with the horsemen. But even as he reached the edge of the Anvil, he knew the hope of surprise was lost. Gafs by the thousands poured out of the fortress to meet them. Somehow the enemy must have second-guessed their intentions and reinforced the position that had been reported near empty only half a dozen dimmings before.

Looking back behind him, the Anvil glimmered even in the dimming. He could see the dozen columns that marked Alexander's approach. Distances were hard to measure though, and he guessed that at best they were more than a half day off, but one column on the left did appear to be closer. He could always break off and withdraw back across the Anvil, but to do so would mean the loss of the one prize he had managed to take.

The Anvil—to the men in his command it was nothing out of the ordinary. Merely a desert of bare windswept metal that stretched for thirty leagues. But in his mind it was still a fear-shrouded dream. He had heard often enough that this was a world created by the godlike First Travelers. But gods made worlds from dirt and stone, not metal that could barely be scratched and was flat as a griddle for as far as the eye could see.

They had crossed it in two dimmings, riding hard, their march guided by the lump of darkness that as they approached took shape into a collapsed structure that was larger than many a town he had seen back on Earth.

Parmenion was still amazed over the fact that he was looking at a ship that once flew through the air like a winged chariot, bearing more iron ore than all the mines of Anatolia could have produced if worked for a hundred years. Yaroslav said that it was an ore ship, sent to bring desperately needed raw material for the first crew of Humans who had landed on the Kolbard. Yaroslav said that such vessels had been ships that sailed without men aboard. The vessel would land on a world, carve out the side of an ore-bearing mountain, then fly away to bring the ore to a world that needed it. But the ship had somehow crashed, perhaps destroyed by one of the sky-chariots of the Gaf demigods. Such knowledge made Parmenion feel as if he were living in a drunken nightmare where all truth had been turned upside down. Alexander could smile his curious smile when confronted with the new and strange, but not he. It damn near was driving him mad.

The iron city was less than a league away from the position they now occupied with their backs to the Anvil. Parmenion had been amazed to see that a town was built into the ruins of the ship, complete with watchtowers shaped from ore rock, and ringed with walls of that same metal. Why, there was enough metal there—"

"They're charging!"

The Gafs had learned quickly! The heavy line of infantry was advancing on the run. His infantrymen, who had ridden across the Anvil clutching the backs of their mounted comrades, lowered their spears.

"Right flank horse hold. And don't let them get around you!" Parmenion roared to a messenger who wore the headband of the Avar horsemen.

The rider saluted and galloped to his young commander Sashi, a youth barely able to shave, but who had demonstrated such skill with the Gavarnian horses that he quickly earned the respect of all who aspired to Alexander's mounted arm.

Knowing that the only way to win in this form of combat was to attack, Parmenion drew his sword and cantered up to the left side of the Ris and Kievant phalanxes.

"Front spears down, and watch your spacing," he roared.

As if guided by a single hand the weapons dropped, the spears in the second, third, and fourth ranks coming forward past the first line, so that the approaching enemy would have to face a wall of sharpened death.

Gaps were opened at regular intervals so that the slingers could pull out from the front and reach the protection of the rear, where they would continue to hurl their missiles of death over the heads of the line.

The Gafs were surging forward, and in imitation of Parmenion's own formation, the Gavarnian cavalry was posted to either flank, rather than follow their older concept of lining up in front of the infantry.

"Macedons! Forward!"

The two phalanxes, a hundred and twenty men wide by eight deep, stepped forward while the cavalry extended its screen to either side.

Parmenion let the men advance while dropping to the rear, where he could better survey the action as it unfolded.

This endless probing and skirmishing had been going on since yesterday's dimming without any chance for rest. A dozen times the Gafs had swarmed out from the fortress to threaten them. The first eight times they had broken and retreated before contact could be established.

The last three times, however, they had ventured closer, and along a number of points had actually come into contact. The vast majority of them were still nothing more than a formationless mob of five or six thousand warriors. But Parmenion feared that they were about to introduce something new.

An hour ago, a new unit of Gafs had come up from the southward road, which led back to their capital. And this formation marched and had deployed in near-perfect imitation of a phalanx. The only thing different was they were armed with swords.

The marching cadence of the Gaf formation started to falter as the Ris and Kievants raised their battle chant.

"Iskander, Iskander."

Damn them, Parmenion cursed, they were supposed to stay silent so that the signal horn could be clearly heard.

"Parmenion!"

He turned to see a squadron of mounted men galloping in from the edge of the Anvil. Several of them were pointing off to the south, and rising up in his stirrups, he saw a shimmering dark column coming out of the heat. It had to be Alexander, leading a flanking march, but they were still a fair distance away. The couriers drew closer.

"Alexander commands that you fall back, if need be."

"And abandon that?" Parmenion roared, and he pointed down toward the edge of a small lagoon at his back.

"What in the name of the world-makers is that?" the courier cried, goggle-eyed at the strange device.

"It's a Gaf ship," Parmenion shouted, "beached here for repairs. We took it before they could burn it."

"A ship? What is that?"

Parmenion ignored the boy and turned his attention back to the fight.

The discipline of his regiment was holding, they were continuing down the slope toward the Gafs, who had almost come to a stop. Good, maybe they'd pull back again without a fight and then he could detach his cavalry to cut up the flanking forces.

"Damn them, here they come!"

With a wild roar the Gaf line suddenly surged forward, losing all cohesion and semblance of formation.

Urging his horse forward, Parmenion came up to the rear of his line, which was starting to waver. "Hold them, hold them, my men!"

With a deafening shout the Gafs rushed forward, waving their scimitars, and the impact came as several thousand Humans and Gavarnians smashed together in a wild cacophony of roars, curses, and dying screams.

The weight of the impact shuddered the Human line, pushing it back half a dozen meters as the alien warriors pushed against the men, who seemed almost childlike when fighting against their roaring opponents.

"Rear rank spears," Parmenion cried to his signaler.

The horn sounded high and clear, three piercing notes, and the last four ranks of spearmen lowered their weapons, leaning into them as if advancing into a storm. More than one Ris or Kievant was speared in the back by his own men, but most of the men were able to guide their ungainly weapons through gaps in the line where their sharpened steel points, fashioned from trophies from the Battle of the Forks, pierced through the leather armor of their opponents.

The line of impact shifted and pushed as some Gafs gave ground against the impenetrable wall, while others, caught up in the old way of battle, leaped into the fray regardless of orders.

To either flank of the main fight the Gafs held back, kept at bay by the cavalry forces that stood like anchors to either side of the fight. But this anchor was weakening, as well, as squadron after squadron was detailed off to screen the enemy flanking forces that spread out wide to either side.

Parmenion could only hope that Alexander was pushing his forces forward as rapidly as possible. The Gafs were learning far too fast the art of engaging a phalanx.

"Call them off."

"But my lord Taug," Hina ventured, "their line is starting to buckle! We just might destroy them."

"That's not what we're fighting for today," Kubar said quietly. "Remember, never let the scent of victory blind you to the possible stench of defeat."

"Look over there." He pointed toward the advancing block of men coming in off the Anvil.

"The Humans are still several versts away. By the time they come up..."

Kubar looked at Hina and the half-dozen staff members by his side. "This battle is a lesson to us, we watch and learn. Twelves times we've attacked them, each time to watch how they deploy, to see how they use their weapons and combine their men on foot with those on horse. It is a lesson to understand the mind of their commander."

He stopped for a moment and looked again at the distant man on horseback who commanded from the back of the Human wall formation. Was that the one called Iskander?

"That is why we have fought today. And be sure you remember what you've seen."

"But the ship on the beach?" Wirgth said. "I'm not at all comfortable with their possession of that."

"It is an unfortunate loss," Kubar replied. "In battle one must weigh the gain against the price. We could retake it, but in doing so, that column,—he pointed toward the advancing Humans—"could close our retreat back to the city. We have but one group of warriors trained to fight as a unit, that group down there, which is earning its first blood. Those warriors are to return to our capital to train the others.

"The recapture of the ship is not worth the loss of their experience. Now pull them out before it is too late."

Seconds later, half a dozen kettle drums started a rolling beat, to be picked up by the signal drums of the unit commander.

Still not disciplined, Kubar thought, watching as a significant portion of his warriors still surged forward, even as the rest of their unit started to pull away.

"Senseless," he mumbled, "what senseless waste." The Humans gradually swarmed over those who continued to fight, while the rest of the formation backed away and then, turning, started to run back up the hill.

"This is the hard part," Kubar said, as if lecturing a group of students in the classroom. "Going into a fight is always easy. It is the backing away that requires real discipline, elsewise your warriors might break and just keep on running."

"A true Gavarnian never runs from a Human," Arn said coldly from the rear of the assembled staff officers.

Kubar was tempted to retort with an inquiry as to how he had survived the debacle at the Forks, but let it pass.

"A true warrior," Paga said softly, looking straight at

Arn, "learns to defeat his opponent in the end. All that happens before is without meaning."

Arn was silent, knowing that those around him were completely under the influence of this newfound leader who fought without honor.

The flanking units started to pull back, as well. As planned, the cavalry that Kubar had held in reserve swung out from their concealed positions behind the hill to screen the retreat of the infantry. That had been a hard lesson for Kubar to explain—the need to keep cavalry in reserve, in order to exploit a victory or cover a retreat. To the Gavarnian warriors, there was no logic in not throwing all your strength in at once. But he could see those around him nodding and speaking to themselves as the cavalry did its job of stopping the Human advance. Good, this little affair was having precisely the effect he wanted. Without committing to a major battle, his future officers were learning in the field the truth of his lessons. Now it was time to follow up.

"Good, we've learned much today," Kubar said quietly. "Now what have we seen?"

"They never fight as individuals but always as a group," Wirgth replied. "It makes good sense. One to one we could kill them out of hand, but a wall of spears, that is hard to argue with."

"Very good," Kubar replied. Realizing that there was little time left before the relief column arrived, he decided to convey what he had seen himself, rather than let his pupils say it for him, and thus feel that they had discovered it on their own.

"Note the following and remember it. The cavalry stays on the wings, covering the flanks of their formation. They wait until their opponent wavers and then send it in for the killing blow. Your cavalry *reserve* behind the center can be shifted to either wing, attack up the middle, or can cover your retreat as you've just seen. They would have done that now to us, if their commander had not been so anxious to protect the prize they've captured.

"I can see now that swords against lowered spears are useless. The weight of our attack almost took them, but the length of their spears prevented that."

"Therefore we should use the same weapons?" Hina ventured.

"I don't think so. It takes time and training to get a large group of warriors to fight in formations like that. One or two warriors losing their head in the heat of battle could cause a line to crack wide open. They only barely hold themselves, we could see that. The blood of our warriors is not cool enough yet to fight so coldly. We must figure out how to break those formations before we hit them."

"Archers?" Hina asked.

"That was a sport of nobles; it takes a long time to train one archer and even longer to make the right bows. We have not the time nor the skilled warriors in numbers. But those we do have shall be used accordingly. At least that will be a sport our noble warriors will enjoy."

Arn was silent.

"Hina, it's best that you rejoin those men now. I need to think on how to break the Humans' formations; I'll send my ideas to you by the messenger birds that I brought with me."

The staff looked at Kubar incredulously.

"But you're coming back with us to the city, are you not?" Wirgth cried.

Kubar barked softly, as if they were joking. "This mountain of ore behind us must be held. If the Humans take it, then they have another ingredient toward their victory. It will take time yet to train our army back at the capital. If this citadel falls, then they can form a living chain to haul all the ore they need back up into the hills where it can be forged into stronger weapons. No, I shall stay here."

"No, Kubar," Hina replied anxiously, "I'll stay here and you go back."

"Listen to me. This is where the battle will be fought for at least the next thirty dimmings. Here I can observe how they fight and plan for the time when our forces march out to meet them. Besides, you here might accept me as taug, but it is you, Hina, who in the eyes of many are still the true taug, no matter who wears the crown. You alone have the force to counteract those who would oppose our plans. Now go."

As he spoke the last words, Kubar looked significantly at Arn, who returned his gaze with defiance.

The others hesitated for a moment, then bowing, they turned to leave.

"Oh, by the way," Kubar said as an afterthought, "I could use one or two of noble birth to aid me. Would you be interested, Arn?"

The warrior turned and grimaced at him. He knew he was trapped, for to refuse would be a mark of cowardice. Silently he turned away and, mounting his horse, he started back alone to the citadel.

"And, Wirgth, I could use your help, as well, if you would wish to be of assistance."

The Kaadu, for once allowing his emotions to show, nodded with delight. Bowing low to Hina, who signaled his approval, Wirgth stepped over to Kubar Taug's side.

"Now move before those men cut off our retreat."

"Kubar, I still don't like this," Hina said. "If they should block the harbor, you'll be cut off."

"Then train your army quickly. I'll look for you in thirty dimmings."

Mounting their horses, Hina and his retinue cantered back down the slope where the battle-tested regiment was drawing up.

Thirty dimmings, Kubar thought, as he looked at the iron fortress. If Hina failed, or the nobles revolted, or Iskander tried some new trick, then all would be for naught, and he would die at last. Would he then return to the time he had been snatched from, to rejoin his brothers at last?

Feeling the bittersweet ache for his departed kin that only a Gavarnian could understand, Kubar Taug mounted his horse and rode back to the iron fortress that he knew would soon be drenched in blood.

"They're learning how to fight," Alexander mused, between gulps of warm beer that one of Parmenion's aides offered him.

Guiding his horse around the clumps of dead, he worked his way across the open field that had been a scene of nightmarish chaos less than an hour before. "How did our men stand?"

"Not bad for raw recruits. Ah, but if only I had but one regiment of our old troops," Parmenion replied gruffly, "I could have had that fortress for you as a present."

"You're turning into quite the general. Almost as good as my old Parmenion back on Earth."

Parmenion was silent. He was already forgetting his old station as a lowly drunken guard back home.

Across the valley, almost within hailing distance, Alexander could see several mounted Gafs looking in their direction. Was one of them the Taug?

"From what you've said of their fighting, I daresay they were observing us, seeing how we react and then forming their plans in response. So far they're responding to us. I wonder when they'll finally be forcing *us* to respond?"

"The fact that they brought that regiment up, fought it but for an hour, then sent it back to their capital almost confirms that suspicion. It leads me to believe, as well, that they knew we would strike here first."

Again he looked across the open field at the Gavarnian horsemen.

One of them moved his horse forward by several paces and then raised an arm into the air. It almost looked like a salute.

"Well, that must be him, damn it," Alexander said,

smiling, and raising up in his own stirrups, he returned the salute.

The Gavarnian turned and galloped back toward the city.

"Is the encirclement complete?" Alexander asked, looking up from the rough charts that he had drawn himself.

"We've completely surrounded the fortress," Yaroslav replied. "The men are starting to dig the defensive positions facing the enemy capital."

"Position that blocking force on the southern road correctly. Make sure they have a clear field of vision, so they have several hours' warning of an approach."

"I've already seen to it," Sashi replied. "As you advised, I'm moving patrols up to within sight of the city. We should have at least one dimming to warn of any approach from that direction."

"But there is still the sea," Alexander said quietly. "As long as that line is open to them, they'll have supplies. We must cut off the sea."

"We can post artillery at the narrows," Parmenion interjected. "I already have men working to construct ballistae. When posted on both sides, it can sweep the main channel."

"Still not enough, damn it. We need more metal for the ballista fittings. Oh, we'll smash some of them, but even two or three ships a day getting past our blockade will make a difference. I'm racing time here," Alexander replied wearily. "Every day we wait gives them another day to train for our method of war. I would not want to see what would happen if they fielded an equal number of phalanxes trained like ours. We must take that mountain, and quickly. Then we must convert its metal into weapons and siege equipment for our entire army if we wish to take their capital. Damn it, if we give them six months, they'll drive us back into the hills, and then the war could drag on for years. I want to end this thing now!"

"Sire, the unit we faced yesterday was hardly trained," Parmenion replied, "if that's what you're worrying about. They came on in formation, but once we closed, all cohesion broke down and they fought like Gafs."

"Even then," Yaroslav interjected, "our casualties were almost equal, and our line damn near cracked. Even you've admitted that."

Parmenion was silent.

"Even so, there is still the question of cutting off their capital from the sea. If only I had some Cretan shipwrights with me."

"What are Cretan shipwrights?" Sashi asked.

"Oh, nothing we have here, boy," Alexander said sadly. "When I heard they had a regiment at least partially trained and then pulled it out, I knew then that we were in trouble. Those Gafs are starting to learn how to fight like Macedons. That regiment will be used to train the others. Therefore we haven't got much time. We need to seal up this ore city tight, take it, and then use it. What might very well tip the scales is that the Gaf have metal and we don't."

"So why not march straight on the Gaf city?" Sashi replied.

"I've thought of that, boy. But the fortifications there are immense. We would need heavy siege equipment to breech it; they could hole up there by the thousands while we're spread out in a circle twenty versts in length. Besides, if we leave this place in our rear, it could cut us off from the hills. Finally, we need to cut them off from the sea if we're to take that city.

"I need ships, Parmenion, otherwise this will be another Tyre, a year-long siege we can't afford. I had hoped, my friend, that your lightning strike could take the mountain in one quick march, but the gods did not will it so."

"Ah, yes, Tyre," Yaroslav interjected. "Bit of a rough time taking them before you got a navy together."

Alexander had to remind himself again that this man had read the history. And that thought alone chilled him. He was *history*—five thousand years old.

"Do you have any suggestions, Yaroslav?" Sashi asked hopefully.

"Too bad we don't have any sulfur," he said quietly, as if musing to himself, "but then again . . ."

The others were silently looking at the aged philosopher, who merely smiled and then changed the subject.

"Now, the Romans in the first Punic War faced the same problem."

"Romans. Too bad things didn't work out the way I planned," Alexander replied. "A pesky little people, them. Arrogant as anything. I had hoped to pay them a visit."

"Now, that would have been interesting, too bad it couldn't have been arranged." Yaroslav fell silent again for a moment.

"But as I was saying, the Romans faced a similar problem and introduced a little something called the assembly line, since they, like you, didn't have a skilled shipwright in the lot."

"What's this assembly line?" Alexander asked.

"Simple enough. The Romans were fighting with—" He hesitated for a moment. "Well, never mind that, just say that they discovered a wrecked ship of their enemies. They took it apart plank by plank, right down to the last peg, then trained several hundred men to make one part and one part only.

"Now, each man could turn out a number of parts a day, which then were numbered. The numbered parts were put together by other unskilled laborers, and behold, within days they had a replica of the first ship. Within a month they had half a hundred ships, within six months they had a fleet of half a thousand. Granted the vessels were made of unseasoned wood, but they did sail. Meanwhile, the Roman general set up rows of benches and trained the men how to row and keep the pace."

Alexander's eyes were gleaming. "We only need half the men here to develop the siege lines and launch probing attacks. We could turn our least trained regiments to the task."

"But, sire," Parmenion interjected, "the Gafs don't seem to have any warships. That vessel we captured is simply a miserable sailing craft."

"So we'll just remove the mast, punch in holes for oars, and mount a ram up front. Yaroslav, you'll be responsible to start on it at once. I'll sketch out the changes we'll need."

"Maybe I should have kept my mouth shut," Yaroslav muttered.

"Come now, I hereby appoint you admiral of my new fleet."

"Oh, thank you, sire," Yaroslav replied evenly. "It's just the title I've always wanted."

There was a solution as he always knew there would have to be. With a nod to his staff, Alexander left them to their planning for supplies and stepped out of the tent. For a brief moment he felt disoriented. The fact that he was exhausted made him think that it should be night, but the sun as always was motionless, forever hovering in the same spot.

It was the middle of a dimming, and the heavy overcast that had set in caused the light to have an early-twilight cast to it. In fact, it was the darkest he had seen the countryside since his arrival.

The clouds stretched out from Olympus and its companions, which still dominated the entire northeastern horizon even though they were now well over a hundred leagues away.

For weeks there had been little if any rain, only an occasional thundershower, and the temperature had slowly climbed to near summer heat. Now, with the cloud cover spreading out, he could already notice a slight cooling. He wondered for a moment if the mountains to the northeast and their twins to the south had something to do with the change.

Walking to the crest of the hill, he saw that his army was resting, except for the occasional patrol that rode far afield in a giant protective arc. The center of all his attention was the ugly cylinder of what had once been a ship that sailed between the stars. It seemed a honeycomb of caves and scaffoldings, while around it rose a wall that stood three times the height of a man.

He was tempted to storm it once enough engines and towers had been built to sweep the battlements. Was that Kubar he had seen earlier? Two hands suddenly wrapped around him from behind, nearly locking his arms to his side.

With a cry he whirled around, breaking free from his assailant's grasp.

She greeted him with a laugh, and then he recognized his attacker.

"Neva, I thought you were back running the villages!"

"I grew lonely, and besides, those stupid oafs can run themselves now that you've managed to drag away all the quarreling men. In fact, it was so peaceful it started to get boring. You remember Divina, the girl who had an interest in Parmenion. Well, we kept talking about the two of you and finally decided there was only one way to solve our problem and get the treatment we've been needing for some time."

"I'm sure Parmenion will be happy to hear this," Alexander replied, imagining how useless his second in command would be once Divina had finished a night with him.

"Just do me one favor, tell Divina not to wear him down too much. I need him."

"Maybe you should worry about my wearing you down," she said softly, moving her arms up around his shoulders.

At least she's bathed for the occasion. Alexander, smiling, looked into her eyes.

For a moment he thought of Roxana and the devotion she had for him, then his thoughts turned even to Bagoas, the Persian eunuch boy who had been his lover, as well. Again he wondered why the pleasures of the flesh had not held him slave the way they did the other men he had known. Perhaps because he had truly loved but one thing—the pursuit of glory, the conquest of a world.

Neva gradually let her hands slip off Alexander's shoulders and drift the length of his body. For the moment, at least, the obsession with glory disappeared, and he led his eager companion to his tent.

CHAPTER 12

"My lord Taug, what in the name of the Unseen Light is that?" There was a note of awe—edged with fear—in Wirgth's voice as he pointed to the drawings spread out on Kubar's desk.

"Perhaps we should not discuss that just now." Kubar returned to his desk and hastily rolled up the sheaf of drawings.

"It looked like some giant bubble. Is it a new weapon?"

"One could call it that. Now, why don't you tell me what it is that has brought you here unannounced?"

"Oh, yes. Arn reports that a dozen ships approach, running close-hauled to the wind. It must be the supplies and reinforcements."

"Fine, fine."

"He also says that there is some unusual activity going on across the bay."

Kubar looked up from the drawings that he was concealing. "What sort of activity?"

"We can hear horns and such—that, and a column of

men was seen running off the hill and disappearing back into the bay that the hairless ones have been protecting so carefully."

That didn't sound good. Something had been going on over there. He had attempted to run some scout ships up, but the Humans had mounted half a dozen huge rafts at the bend of the bay, each carrying one of their giant bows, thus making approach almost impossible.

"I'm coming," Kubar replied, tossing the drawings into a cabinet.

Leaving his study in the center of the ore carrier, he stepped out into a small open area surrounded on all sides by shear walls nearly fifteen meters high. It had at one time been the central core of the ship, and the Gafs, when they had started to mine the wreck, discovered that the central section of ore was a remarkably high grade of iron nickel. Thus they had left the other sections nearly intact while clearing out the best of the metal.

Down in the lower courtyard nearly a hundred women, the only ones in the fortress and most of them wives and daughters of smiths who lived there, were still busy at their work, stitching the layers of silk that Kubar had taken with him from the capital before the siege had started.

A light rain fell upon them as they sat beneath make-shift shelters, the object of their work spread out, filling nearly the entire floor area of the chamber.

"This damnable rain," Kubar cursed softly. It had been falling nearly constantly since the siege had started thirty dimmings ago.

"My lord Taug," Wirgth said softly, "Arn is up there." And he pointed to the high watchtower built into what had once been the stern of the ship.

Following Wirgth's lead, Kubar ascended what appeared to be an endless series of ladders. Coming out onto a high platform, he stopped for a moment to examine the new heavy crossbow that had been installed within the last dimming. Its proud crew bowed toward him as he nodded in their direction.

The workmanship was not bad at all. "Any luck?" Kubar asked.

"Nothing today, my lord Taug. We've tried a couple of shots on that group over there." The warrior pointed toward the ten-meter-high siege towers positioned four hundred paces back, near the lowest part of the wall. "They're moving men up, it might mean something."

Kubar looked to where the soldier had pointed. Half a dozen wooden towers covered with leather were positioned just out of bolt range. There did seem to be an unusual level of activity. Turning his gaze across the bay, he saw a flurry of activity in the Human's secretive position over there, as well.

Damn it all, if only his secret was ready. But he knew wishes were useless in the face of war. Yet he did not need any secret weapon to surmise what might very well be happening. Turning to the west, he could see the convoy of a dozen ships rounding the outer point and then he looked back at his opponent's preparations.

"Sound the alarm," Kubar said softly, looking over at Wirgth. "I think the Humans are preparing some sort of surprise."

"By all the gods, I get the sickness of the sea." Parmenion groaned.

"Shut up and lead them out," Yaroslav shouted, jumping up and down excitedly from the shoreline.

"I never should have tackled that damned Aldin, *never.*"

A horn sounded from atop the watchtower guarding the passage into the narrow channel.

"Remember, steersmen, just keep them at a steady pull," Yaroslav cried.

"Yaroslav, we can still trade places."

"Are you crazy? I'm the philosopher, you're the warrior, now get going."

"All right, you bastards," Parmenion roared, "let's get this over with."

A feeble shout went up from the twenty galleys drawn up in line along the shore.

"Come on, you scum," Parmenion cried, looking to his own crew. "Start the count." And he nodded to the drummer boy who stood by his side.

The boy brought a mallet down against the leather head of the drum. Most of the rowers managed to pull together on the first stroke, but several of the men tangled up as their oars bit the water for the first time.

They had been practicing on land for thirty dimmings, sitting on wooden benches and pulling their shafts against thin air. And while they had practiced, the assembly line had developed around them, turning out the first score of rams based upon the clumsy design of the Gaf sailing cog. The shipyard had been constructed in a narrow channel with no room to practice, and the assigned crews dared not go out into the bay where the Gafs would have observed the birth of Alexander's new navy. The launching of the attack would be the first attempt for all the men who had come down from the mountains to now fight upon the sea.

The drummer kept a slow but steady pace, and even though some of the oars tangled up, Parmenion managed to keep them guided toward the channel opening while Yaroslav ran along the bank shouting encouragement.

"That's it, that's it. Remember to back up once you ram!"

"If I don't get back from this," Parmenion cried, "my ghost will haunt you forever!"

"Nonsense," Yaroslav shouted. "Pure superstition."

But Parmenion had no time for a retort as they approached the sharp bend in the channel that led out into the open bay.

"Left side stop," Parmenion cried, forgetting the nautical terms that Yaroslav had tried to teach the new sailors. Fortunately most of the men knew what he was referring to, and as the other side continued to row, the galley pivoted through the channel.

"All oars and increase speed!"

The bay opened up before them. Half a league away the Gaf fortress rose up from the waterline and he could hear the distant horns blowing. They must have guessed something was up.

Off to his right he could see the convoy running the narrows. One of the ships was on fire, having been hit by the artillery posted on the bluffs, but the other twelve ships were already clear and running for the protection of the enemy harbor.

He spared a quick glance back over his shoulder. Damn it all, one of the rams had simply continued on straight and run clean ashore, but so far most of the others seemed to be keeping pace. Already half a dozen of them were out of the channel, advancing in a more or less ragged line.

He had seen such a sight before during the siege of Tyre when hundreds of ships had maneuvered as if guided by a single hand, and Parmenion knew that this was a ridiculously poor imitation of that. They had all known that any attempt to organize the maneuvering of their raw fleet would be absurd, so each ship's commander had simply been told to head for the nearest enemy ship and to ram it and then back away.

He could only hope that they all wouldn't turn coward and run, or worse yet, completely forget how to maneuver their vessels.

"Bring up the speed," Parmenion commanded, and the drummer increased the beat.

Most of the rowers were keeping together, but there were several who were hopelessly out of rhythm and tangling their comrades ahead and behind them.

"You there, Gris, pull your bleeding oar in and stop rowing," Parmenion cried. The uncoordinated rower did as he was commanded and looked up at Parmenion with a foolish grin on his face.

"All right lads, I'm steering for the lead ship now."

Several of the men slacked their pace to look over their shoulders.

"Don't look, damn you." The ship skewed to starboard due to a sudden tangle of a half dozen rowers.

"Don't look. I promise to give you plenty of warning before we hit 'em."

Within minutes they had closed to the point that he could see individual Gafs running about the deck of their lead ship.

Looking back over his shoulder again, he could see that over half his fleet had made it out of the channel. The remainder, however, were either tangled up with the beached vessel, a knot of them completely blocking the channel, or they were spinning about in circles like a fly with one wing broken off. Two of them had managed to roll over, and their terrified crews were clinging to the wallowing wrecks. Not a single man in his command knew how to swim properly, and he cursed aloud at the graphic reminder. He couldn't swim, either.

There was a loud shout of triumph off to his left and he saw that the ram crewed by the villagers from Kievant had pulled ahead of his own men from Ris. These two villages, being the first of Alexander's army, had expressed their insult when first passed over for the new navy. Realizing that such esprit was essential, Alexander had agreed that they should be represented in the fleet. Parmenion cursed them silently, believing that their loudmouthed insistence had resulted in his own assignment as the attack admiral, allowing Yaroslav to sit back on the shore. "All right, lads, *ramming speed!*"

The range was down to a long bowshot, and the Gaf fleet was in a panic; several of the ships to the rear were attempting to turn about and run back through the narrows, while the others ran as close into shore as they dared. Since they had yet to come abreast of the Gaf fortress, the catapults that Alexander had positioned in anticipation of such a move were already firing, sending their flaming bolts out across the water.

But Parmenion turned his thoughts away from all other concerns as he aimed his vessel on an intersecting path with the first Gaf ship.

It was obvious they had no experience with rams, otherwise the captain of the other vessel would have turned his vessel to meet them, Parmenion thought. They must assume we'll just come in alongside and then try to board.

He gripped the tiller tightly; it was less than half an arrow-flight to go.

Half a dozen bolts arced out from the ship; one of them skimming in low caught a rower square in the back. With a scream the man stood up, the bolt sticking out of his chest, and as he tumbled forward, his oar tangled up with several others.

The ram skewed to port and Parmenion fought to bring it around.

"Ramming speed!" Parmenion cried. "Keep at it, men, ramming speed."

A hundred paces, now fifty. He was looking up at the deck now. A Gaf archer stood up and fired, the bolt slammed into the deck by Parmenion's feet.

Twenty-five paces.

"Ramming speed!"

Seeing at last what was about to happen, the Gaf commander pulled the tiller hard over. It was too late.

With a thundering impact the ram drove into the Gaf vessel close to the stern. Rigging lines snapped, splintered planking rose into the air, and every rower was knocked from his bench into a tumbled, squirming mass of men.

Screams of panic and rage echoed from the Gaf ship.

"Up, damn you, up," Parmenion roared. "Back to the oars."

He jumped from his perch astern and charged down the narrow deck kicking the men back to their positions.

A Gaf archer appeared above him. Parmenion dodged to one side as a bolt skimmed past him. After picking up one of the spears stacked on the deck, he hefted the shaft and hurled it upward. The Gaf warrior disappeared in a shower of blood.

"Now pull, damn you," Parmenion cried, "pull us out or we go down with it."

Less than half the men were back in their positions, and working feverishly, they foamed the water with their oars. Parmenion could feel the stern of their ship rising slowly out of the water, as the Gaf vessel quickly filled from the hole torn in its side.

"Pull!"

With a shuddering groan they snapped free. As they backed away, they exposed a gaping hole in the enemy's side, and the vessel slowly started to roll over.

Gaf warriors and sailors spilled off the deck, screaming with panic.

"*Back!* Get us the hell out of here!"

The ram swung backward, but due to the imbalance of rowers, the vessel swung to port cutting an arc around the ship.

"Now forward," Parmenion cried. "All together, pull!"

The rowers reversed the direction of their oars, and the water foamed around them as they stopped their backward drive and then started to move forward.

"Harder!"

With slowly increasing speed, they pulled away from the sinking ship.

"Parmenion!" The cry came from forward, and looking up, he could see Gris, the clumsiest of the rowers, struggling with his oar.

A Gaf was clinging to it. The creature was fighting desperately to hang on, a look of wild panic in its eyes.

And in that gaze Parmenion saw a mirror of his own panic if he were to be suddenly cast into the ocean.

"Hold the tiller steady, boy," Parmenion commanded. Giving the helm to the drummer and running forward, he came up alongside Gris, who hung on to his oar, looking like a fisherman who had suddenly hooked a whale.

The Gaf had worked its way up the wooden shaft, so that it was nearly alongside the boat. Before reason or logic could show him the possible danger of reaching out, Parmenion extended his hand and the Gaf grabbed hold.

For a second he thought the creature was trying to drag him in, and he pulled back with a fierce desperation, but the Gaf hung on, coming right up over the side.

A look into its eyes, though, showed that it was filled with panic and terrified beyond all reason.

He pulled it up and over, and the Gaf, dressed in a long red flowing robe, collapsed onto the deck.

"Tie it up," Parmenion commanded to the rower next to him, and turning, he rushed back to the stern.

Taking the tiller back from the drummer, he suddenly had enough time to look beyond the range of his own personal struggle.

At least half a dozen other ships had been rammed. The Kievant ship had already disengaged from its target and was rowing desperately after another ship, which was drawing nigh the protection of the enemy harbor. He could see where one ram had buried itself so completely into an enemy ship that both of them were going down together, their crews struggling against both each other and the deathlike embrace of the sea.

The three Gaf ships that had turned about were already running back through the narrows. Another one was aflame from the batteries on the hill, while several enthusiastic ram crews pursued them.

There wasn't much left to do, other than to help pick up survivors and shepherd the fleet back to their base. The second phase of the assault was up to Alexander, and Parmenion looked off toward the position where the half-dozen siege towers had been constructed.

"Parmenion, I tied her up."

It was the rower from up forward.

"What?"

"The Gaf, I tied her up."

"What do you mean?"

"I think, sir...at least it seemed like it, sir. You know, I think she's a woman."

"Most ingenious on their part," Kubar said softly, looking out at the wreckage of the supply convoy.

Even as he spoke he could still hear the distant sounds of the fighting. Two ships had managed to break through, one of them with its port side railing below the water. The pursuing rams were already turning about and heading back to their base on the other side of the bay, while off in the distance the two ships that had managed to break free of the trap had cleared the narrows, leaving two flaming companions in their wake.

"Is that all you can say?" Arn shouted. "We've lost several hundred reinforcements and the precious supplies, and all you can say is 'most ingenious.'"

"What else can I say?" Kubar said, turning to face the raging noble. "One must remember, more than anything else, that a commander must never let rage rule his emotions. Kalin learned that lesson, but too late."

Arn looked for a moment as if he would strike the Taug, and the hair on his neck bristled. A soft growl of challenge came from Paga, who stood by Kubar's side. Arn looked to the others for support, but they averted their eyes—a sign that he had shamed himself by the outburst.

"Come now, Arn. I feel your pain at our loss." Kubar walked to Arn's side as if to put a hand on his shoulder, but Arn shrugged the gesture off and stalked to the other side of the watchtower.

"So they know how to fight now upon the water. I

should have forseen these ram ships, but our history had no warfare upon the open sea..." He turned his eyes landward.

"I must assume that this Iskander has let but one-half of his plan fall." He looked at the siege towers. "They'll hit us there. Now let's see if it's our turn to spring a little surprise."

Even as he spoke the signal horns from the enemy camp sounded and a mighty shout went up from the Human army.

"Forward, my Macedons!"

Dismounted, Alexander marched to the left of the advancing siege towers, each of them pushed by a full regiment of five hundred men.

He knew the attack was still premature, but he hoped that the Gafs would be demoralized by the victory of the fleet which combined with the sudden assault, would result in the Gafs' capitulating. He had but one fear for a capitulation, that the army, still only half disciplined, would turn a surrender into a massacre, thus hardening the future defense of the capital city. He needed a surrender with honor to use as a lever to weaken the resolve of the last redoubt.

All around the perimeter, the Humans raised their battle cries, as the ten regiments of heavy troops advanced at a slow walk toward the metallic ramparts that surrounded the ore carrier. Having the advantage of a slight downhill slope, the six siege towers advanced without incident.

As he stepped in front of the ranks, Alexander turned and looked back at the advancing line. Swinging up his shield, he raised it high as a signal, and all across the front the wooden shields of the heavy infantry were raised up in response.

The towers were slowly gaining momentum as they rolled down the slope, so that the men were now braking the ungainly mountains of wood.

The attack was within arrow-shot range now but still no response, and not a Gaf was to be seen on the battlements. Alexander knew that no Gaf resistance at all was too good to hope for; there must be some preparation. He could sense the nervousness in his men. The silence from the other side was unnerving, and here and there along the line some of the men started to falter. But most kept moving forward as if drawn into the conflict by the six mobile platforms. Suddenly from all along the line, pillars of hot sparks showered upward.

The men hesitated, many of them crying out in fear. But no weapon was seen. There was another outburst of sparks, and then another, in a slow rhythmic pattern. Yet no weapon was seen.

Alexander leaped to the fore of his line. "Forward, my Macedons! Forward! They're setting fire to their own city." He knew it was a lie, but this was the moment to set his men into motion. Drawing his sword he started forward, his blond hair streaming out from under his helmet. For a moment he was alone, a sole warrior rushing toward the enemy, plainly visible to all the thousands on either side. It was a fitting stage for the glory that had always been his dream.

As if caught up in the power of their commander's vision, the host surged forward shouting his name, so that it echoed from the walls and the hills beyond. "Iskander, Iskander!"

The siege towers rolled forward, gaining speed, their crews not wishing to be left behind. More than one man stumbled before the advancing juggernauts of wood and was crushed, yet the engines of war pushed relentlessly forward.

The line swept onward, commander to the fore, and the base of the wall was gained. The race was over and he had grasped the fleeting vision yet again for an all-too-brief moment.

As if dazed, he looked about him as his host crowded beneath the battlements. Ladders were raised up and down the line. The towers were nearly to the wall, and the men struggled back to avoid being crushed, while their crews struggled desperately to stop the vehicles before they crashed into the wall. And then the reaction came.

Up and down the line, hundreds of Gafs suddenly appeared, their deeper growls cutting through the shouts of the Humans. A shower of rocks cascaded down, while a volley of spears arced out, smashing into the upturned shields of the defenders.

"The towers!" Alexander roared. "Drop their drawbridges!" But his words were lost in the wild crescendo of screams, curses, and shouts of pain.

The first tower reached the wall and the Gafs revealed their response.

The showers of sparks became continuous along the wall. Alexander, as if sensing that something was wrong, started to look straight up.

A blinding sheet of fire and smoke arced out over his head, hissing like a red-hot sword thrust into ice. The sheet of fire came down behind him, and turning, he watched as dozens of men fell to the ground, thrashing and screaming. A garish light exploded to his right, and looking over his shoulder, he saw a river of flame cascade down from the nearest tower.

For a moment he thought the untanned hides from slaughtered Gaf cattle, hung on the sides of the towers, would repulse the fire. But so intense was the heat that it ate right through the green leather, and the wood beneath it burst into flames.

The shouts of triumph from the Humans changed in an instant to that of panic, as the army stood beneath the battlements, unable to respond.

The river of fire over his head stopped for a moment, and after sprinting out from the relative protection of the wall, he pushed his way over the burning thrashing men on the ground.

A shadow passed over him and he ducked down,

holding up his shield, but nothing struck him. Looking up, he saw a log swinging out over his head, suspended by a series of cables. At the end of the log dangled a series of grappling hooks.

The log smashed into the tower, the hooks snagging into the structure. To his amazement the log started to move straight up, and stepping back, he saw a heavy cable was tied to the front of the log. The cable stretched back up to a high battlement up on the ore carrier, where half a hundred Gafs were turning a windlass. With a creaking groan the tower lifted up onto one side and tottered, leaning over in his direction.

All at once the Gafs released the windlass, and turning, Alexander started to run. The tower crashed down not two meters behind him, sending a thundering shudder through the earth.

Another river of flame hit the ground in front of him, and looking up, he saw a fire-wreathed nozzle sticking out from the battlement, while a shower of sparks rose up behind it. A jet of flame arced out again, and he dodged backward, realizing that the Gafs aiming the nozzle were trying to hit him. A searing pain whipped across his legs and he stumbled backward, holding his shield up to protect himself from the scalding heat.

Even as he struggled to survive, he knew the assault was lost. All around him the men streamed to the rear, most of them throwing away their shields and spears. Half a dozen pyres of flame leaped into the air—all the towers were lost. Unlike his old Macedons, these men would not rally by a personal display of bravery on his part. None of them would even bother to look back over his shoulder until they had reached the encampment atop the hill.

Turning, he started back up the hill.

The roar of the Gafs thundered behind him and then died away, to be replaced with a deep guttural growl that sounded like a chant that he could almost distinguish.

"Taug, Taug, Taug."

Alexander turned again and looked back at the battlements a hundred meters away. Another river of fire shot from the wall to reignite a smoldering tower. Lowering his shield, he looked at the bossing. It was covered with beads of still-warm metal, and he looked again at the rhythmic showers of sparks, as if they were coming from a forge.

They must have used a massive series of bellows to shoot molten metal out onto the troops, while using some sort of combination of logs and ropes to lift the towers and toss them onto their sides.

He noticed that the Gafs were looking toward one individual who stood upon a battlement, next to one of the crews that had lifted a siege tower from the ground.

Alexander felt that this one was looking straight at him, and on an impulse he raised his sword up in the air.

There was a flash of metal from the other side as a scimitar was raised in response.

So that is the Taug, Alexander thought, and turning, he followed his demoralized men back to the encampment. He knew that it would be a long night of bracing up the morale of his defeated army. But his having had a sea victory first, before the defeat, would help to balance that out.

But there were any number of other problems, as well. And he knew that the Gafs were only just beginning to show that the war was not over yet.

"My brother Kohs," Sigma Azermatti said, looking around the monitor room at the assembled gamblers, "there's a problem with the game."

"How can there be a problem?" Zola shouted. "A sea battle—imagine, an actual sea battle!—too bad it wasn't worth betting on, though. But still it was interesting nevertheless."

There was a general murmur of postgame comments from the other Kohs gathered around the room. Zola, in a ridiculous attempt at merriment, had appeared wearing a flowing robe in the Grecian style with an olive wreath perched jauntily on his brow. The Humans thought it was rather immature and shocking, but several Gavarnian Kohs had quietly asked him who his tailor was. Sigma turned away from the panoramic window that provided a magnificent display of the world below Mount Olympus and stared angrily at the Kohs.

"Come now, Sigma," Corbin began lazily, "we have the Xsarn's oversight of the action, and it has reported nothing amiss." He turned. "Have you, my friend?"

The Xsarn looked up from its feeding trough and wagged its head in what it felt was a good interpretation of the negative, which coincidentally was used by both Humans and Gafs.

"See, Sigma, if there is a problem it would be the first to report it."

Sigma settled back into his chair. "My concern is that the betting is getting, how shall we say, somewhat out of hand. The latest public tote sheets report that nearly eighteen percent of the total capital investments and corporate wealth of the entire Cloud is committed to this game. Eighteen percent! This damned thing is tying up an outrageous part of all our operating capital. Capital investments in general are now on hold, for no one is sinking anything into their projects once the assessments are made for betting purposes. Gentlemen, this is getting way out of hand."

"Come, come, Sigma, it's merely a game," Zola remarked.

"Merely a game, you say!" Sigma replied heatedly. "In some areas the economy is at a standstill, for without capital investments entire heavy industries are on hold, with resulting financial disruptions and unemployment. Gentlemen, the Overseers are bound to notice this, and seeing that it is out of the usual pattern, it can result in their getting curious."

"Let the bastards get curious, we've covered ourselves," Corbin replied. "We've got good security on the Kolbard, they'll never find us out."

"But that's just part of what I'm concerned about," Sigma replied coldly. "With eighteen percent of the total wealth of the Cloud now resting on the lives of one Human and one Gaf down there, the situation is ripe for someone to try to take advantage."

"Oh, come now," Yeshna interjected, "we are honorable gentlemen."

There was a chorus of "well saids" and "here, heres."

Sigma realized he was not being heard, and taking his brandy in hand, he rose and started for the door.

"Go ahead then, gentlemen. I've fallen prey to this game lust, as well, far too much so, I daresay. And I'm not happy about getting sucked into it. If it all comes crashing down, don't say you haven't been warned."

He stopped at the doorway and then looked back coldly at Corbin. "And might I add that if Alexander dies, I shall suspect the worst. And if ever I can prove it, then Overseers be damed, I'll have my revenge." He slammed the door behind him.

"How dare he," cried Zola.

"I *never*! And to think, he is a gentleman, no less," shouted Gragth.

But Corbin was silent, smiling as if to himself as he poured another drink. So Sigma was starting to feel the pressure. Tia had been doing her work, all right. Odds just before the day's action had stood at 4.1 to 1 in Alexander's favor. Granted the battle was a draw, in a tactical sense, but strategically they could all see the implications when Alexander had started to build his fleet. Overall, the odds would continue to climb in favor of the Macedonian. Sigma's little tantrum was, most likely, a clever ploy to scare off some of the pro-Alexander money so he could suck up a bigger share for himself.

Clever son of a bitch, Corbin thought. Tia was doing her job properly—and Corbin's other player was all primed and ready.

* * *

"Did you send a message that you wanted to see me?"

Aldin looked up at the open doorway as Zergh bent low to enter the room.

The old Gaf stopped speaking as he noticed who was sitting across from Aldin. "I didn't know you already had company."

"Come now, Zergh, I can remember a time when you'd sit me on your knee and delight in telling me old Gavarnian legends."

"That's before you grew up, Tia." She could not help but notice the sarcasm in his voice.

"Come, come, Zergh," Aldin said softly, "I don't like it, either, but our little Tia had to reach maturity some time."

"Stop being so protective of me, Uncle. I can take care of myself."

"It's just that I've worked for Corbin for thirty years, that's ten years longer than you've been around. The fact that you've allowed yourself to become his mistress—"

"Look, Uncle, girls have sexual desires, too."

The old Gavarnian, embarrassed as all Gavarnians were by the predilection of Humans to openly discuss sexual activities, rose up again as if making to leave. Among male Gavarnians sexual longings were suppressed, for only the oldest brother, or the last surviving brother, had the right to mate, since the male-to-female ratio at birth was four to one. Some males did engage in homosexual activities, but that was something no Gaf would ever dream of openly discussing with another Gaf, let alone a Human.

"Don't leave, Zergh, there're some things I want to discuss."

Zergh looked back over at Tia, who returned his gaze with an even smile.

"I know," she replied to the look of distrust in his eyes, "now that I sleep with Corbin you'd rather not talk about certain things in my presence. I can take a hint."

Without another word she rose and left the room.

Shaking his head, Aldin pulled out the bug scanner and gave a quick pass of the room, as if Tia might have left a listening device behind. Satisfied that all was secure, he motioned for Zergh to close the door.

"Listen, Aldin," Zergh said, settling down in the chair next to his friend, "I've been running some discreet checks on that mining consortium Corbin promised you as part of your royalty payment. It happens I've a friend in an accounting firm that reports to the Overseers. Now, those guys doctor the books like mad for the do-gooders, but they know the inside news, as well. The damn thing's a dummy. Its assets were stripped six months ago then transferred over to an Eldarnian World bank account, and Eldarnian World accounts are handled strictly by code words, no names involved."

"So you're saying that Corbin is cheating me once again," Aldin replied dejectedly.

"What I've been telling you from the beginning. Once this game is up, you'll get taken and then dumped."

Aldin could only shrug his shoulders and pour another drink for himself.

"Enough of that damn drinking," Zergh replied. "That stuff's killing you, man."

"At least that's one thing Corbin keeps me well supplied with."

"Yeah, 'cause he knows what it does to you. You'll fall into another binge, he'll come along after the game is over, help you to dry out like the last time, and then take you for another ride.

"There's more you should know about, as well," Zergh continued. "My friend in accounting says that he thinks *billions* of Katars are being laundered through the Eldarnian banks. *Billions*, all of it impossible to trace. I can't help but think that Corbin is up to something."

Aldin shrugged his shoulders.

"And you let your niece, the girl you practically raised, hang around with that bum."

Again Aldin's shoulders shrugged.

"By the way, was there any reason for that visit of hers? I haven't seen her since the two of you got back from picking up Alexander."

Aldin looked over at him and smiled. "Just family business."

"You mean she was just checking up on you?"

"You could say that. It was just family business, as usual, that's all."

CHAPTER 13

Alexander looked at the Gavarnian female and smiled. He had learned in recent days that such a gesture in Gaf society did not hold the same meaning, but she had already explained that in her thirty days of captivity she was learning the nuances of Human gestures, as well.

This was so like Darius again, he thought. After Issus he had captured Darius' mother, wives, and concubines, and from them learned the subtleties required of a Persian emperor. The female before him was the only sister of Hina, the Gaf who would have been the taug ruler if not for Kubar.

The language implant had quickly allowed him to converse with her, and she in turn was learning Human speech. She was shrewd, to be sure, revealing nothing of military value. Nevertheless she was showing him the way of the Gafs, and thus providing information that would be needed in the days ahead.

"So, I am honored again by your presence," Liala said, beckoning for Alexander to sit by her side.

"You are comfortable?"

"Captivity is never comfortable for a Gavarnian. But I had assumed all along that I would be tortured and killed if I fell into the hands of the hairless ones. So in comparison I must confess that you have made me comfortable. But tell me, why have you come to me in the middle of the dimming?"

"It's just that I've had a suspicion, and now I wish to confirm it."

"And that is?"

"Ever since your capture you've never told me why you were aboard that ship. I would never have known you were the only sister of Hina if you had not made the mistake of speaking to yourself while I was standing outside your tent."

"Iskander, that was a violation and most rude. When a Gavarnian speaks to the Unseen Light, they do so with open voice. To listen while I called for the protection of my brother was shocking."

He could see that she was gently chiding him, and there was nearly a sense of playfulness in her voice. He could not help but like her. She was intelligent, straightforward, and dignified. In their conversations, she had spent hours reciting the Balda Hista, the great ballad of Kubar Taug, which had been passed down across four thousand years of Human time. He realized that if anything this woman was putting a face on the Gafs, revealing them as cultured, with a history and tradition as rich as his own. They were no longer beasts in his eyes. They were opponents truly worthy of respect.

"But you were saying that you wish to venture another guess as to why I was aboard that ship, so do entertain me with your assumptions."

"It took me some time to learn to read the emotions of a Gavarnian: I had to learn the inflections in the voice, the interplay of words with facial expressions, and the look in your eyes while you spoke. I think now that I'm beginning to see."

It was the same, he realized. Until Issus, Darius was nothing but an image to him—a distant warrior sighted across a field of battle. But then he saw him at last through the eyes of someone who loved him, and through Darius' mother he learned to see Darius as someone's son.

"Go on, Iskander, tell me what it is that you've surmised."

"Without your brother's knowledge you hid yourself aboard that ship. For no brother would allow his sister to go into the peril you chose to face."

She started to grow uneasy.

"I realized it last night when you were reciting the part of the Balda Hista that spoke of the last meeting between Kubar Taug and his wife, just before his final battle and the betrayal. I knew then that you loved him, and that is why you tried to reach the city we now lay siege to."

Liala was silent and turned away.

"Thank you for sharing Kubar Taug with me," Alexander said softly. "You know it is my fate to face him and to cast him down, but know that you shall always have my protection. I have sent a courier to your brother telling him that you are safe but that I cannot release you until this thing is over. For you have seen too much of our armies, and far too much of me, as well. If you wish, I shall inform Kubar Taug of your safety."

Liala turned back and looked into the eyes of the Human who would try to kill the one she loved, and saw far more of him than he would ever reveal to any of his comrades.

"I thank you for your truthspeaking, but I ask that you not send a message to Kubar since he thinks I am still safely back in the city," she said softly. "Now leave me. For now that you know, I wish to pray for the safety of Kubar Taug."

"I tell you, it leaves a trap wide open."

"It sounds like cowardice to me."

Kubar was glad that Paga was not in the room, otherwise a blood challenge would have been offered. He desperately fought to control his own exasperation. Just once, if only for one time in his life, he truly wished that he could give way to his temper and let his true feelings surge to the surface. All his life he had met illogic with calm reasoning, never had he raised his voice in anger to those who followed him. He turned back to face Arn and the other half-dozen nobles.

"Let me try to explain this simply. What is the purpose of our defending this fortress?"

"To deny it to the hairless ones," a section commander growled.

"And you've all done that most admirably. But there were some other reasons, as well. First of which was to act as a bait, to draw Iskander's army out into the open while preventing it from ravaging our croplands to the south, or from threatening our capital. That purpose has been served."

"And we need but hold for another half-dozen dimmings and then we can catch him in the vise between our army and Hina's. We know that Hina's ready to march."

"So we wish," Kubar rejoined. "And if it were that easy, we could end this campaign in a dozen dimmings. But never underestimate what Iskander is."

"He's hairless scum," Arn's sword-bearer snarled.

"And brilliant—otherwise could he have come as far as he has against the best we can offer?" Kubar replied slowly.

There was no response.

"Now listen to me. We did not want him to take this sky-ship, since he could mine it to make more weapons.

We've held it for nearly sixty dimmings, and from our last messenger hawk we know that Hina marches in but three more dimmings."

"To our relief and then to victory."

"Our relief, yes; victory, I doubt. Look at the map, just look at it." He unrolled the soiled parchment across the table.

"The Anvil is an open plain to the east. The Horth estuary a barrier to the north, our capital to the south, and the sea to the west. If Hina advances, Alexander will not meet him, he will in fact withdraw back across the Anvil and there will be no final confrontation."

"Then he is a coward."

Kubar, struggling with his emotions, let the comment pass.

"Why would he run?" Wirgth inquired.

Kubar almost breathed a sigh of relief for the timely question. "Because it is what I would do," he replied, knowing that such a statement would draw a scoffing response. But there was only silence in the conference chamber.

"He will not advance to meet Hina because to do so would leave a fortified position at his back, threatening his line of retreat and supply. On the other hand, he could throw everything he has against us, but the victory might be so costly that again he would be forced to retire in the face of Hina's fresh units. Either way he turns, there'll be an enemy at his back. Therefore, if this fortress holds, there is only one alternative for him—withdraw back across the Anvil and promise his men the booty that can be looted from our farmlands to the south."

"Then we'll meet him there."

"On our own farmlands?" Kubar asked quietly. "You don't know what that means, I do. Far too many times I've seen it. We'll be forced to scorch the land, then they will burn it, in kind. It will be raided and counterraided as each side grapples for position. It will take an endless cycle of dimmings before the issue is brought to grips. And when finally one side has triumphed over the other, there will be little if anything left for the victor.

"Believe me," he said coldly, "I've seen war, real war —without honor or glory in it, and I know what it produces. I've seen the farmlands burning from horizon to horizon. I've seen the numbed looks on the faces of defeated armies retreating at night. And I've seen the families, the thousands of families—waiting, forever waiting for a return, when all hope is already dead. Yes, my friends, I've seen that. I spent a lifetime helping to produce it—and I don't want it again."

He fell silent and looked away from them for a moment, as if wrestling with the memory. So strong was the conviction in his voice that none dared to respond. Even those few who still doubted his authenticity as the true Taug paused for a moment.

"I want this war ended here and now!" Kubar roared, smashing his fist down on the table with such force that the wood beneath his iron hand cracked.

"Honored nobles, it is no coincidence that this Iskander and I arrived on this world at the same time. I, from our legendary past; I must assume that the demigods of the Humans have done the same in the choosing of Iskander. Therefore I also must assume that he is their best. I say this without false pride or that even more dangerous trait, false humility. It is merely a point of logic, nothing more.

"Therefore I want all of you to realize, I want every warrior in a position of command to know, that Iskander in his Human form, no matter how distasteful, is equal to me in all abilities. If Hina marches and this fortress still stands, he will withdraw."

"But why abandon this fortress?" Arn said slowly, as if he had conceded the logic of Kubar's argument.

"As the hook in the bait. There'll be too little time for Iskander to mine this place, but once he's taken it, he will be loath to leave it. With the threat gone from his back, he will feel confident to use this as a base as he turns to meet Hina. From the beginning I assumed that his plan was to take the fortress, mine it, then turn southward to meet Hina before the walls of the capital. One ingredient is missing—the ability to mine it. For when we leave, we shall smash our forges and drag the tools with us. There will be little time to use this resource, and then he will be forced out to meet Hina.

"He will not retreat once this place is his, since he will not be willing to come take it once again. And, besides that, there is the question of morale of his men, for a retreat after a string of victories will be beyond understanding to his troops, and he knows that, as well. No, we cannot let him deny us this battle. We must give him the fortress."

"But couldn't he hole up in here?" Wirgth asked.

"Not likely. Too many men under his command, first of all, to fit in here. He most likely understands that his control of the sea is tentative, at best, and that we will respond. No commander will allow himself to be pinned into a siege deep inside enemy lines. When we do defeat him in the field, he might even fall back here, hoping that he can lure us into another attack on a fortified position. Then we can finish him off."

"If he doesn't march into our capital first," Arn replied.

"Then it will not matter for any of us, including myself."

Kubar looked around the room and sensed that the logic of his argument was taking effect. He must act now before there was chance for any opposition to regroup.

"When the next dimming comes, we move."

"That is one point you haven't clarified," Arn said smoothly. "Or have you forgotten that we are surrounded and our sea route is cut, at least for the moment? Must I assume then that you simply plan to cut your way out of here?"

"Wirgth has told me there is a chamber into the underworld that leads down to the coastal tower."

There was a loud murmur of dissent.

"No one has gone in the catacombs and survived," Arn shouted angrily. "No one!"

"But Wirgth has the maps."

Wirgth nodded, and with a quick snap of his wrist, he unrolled the parchment atop the plans to the fortress and the surrounding countryside.

"The diagrams have been in my family line for generations and clearly plot a course directly beneath this fortress. The entryway is connected into the catacomb we have been using."

The others mumbled quietly, not wishing to show their fear.

"It could be a trap, or some such foul machination, of the gods who made this place," one of the warriors mumbled while making a sign to ward off evil.

"I doubt that," Wirgth said quietly.

"Do you doubt the word of one of our most valiant captains?" Arn replied.

"But of course not, sire, Wirgth replied. Only Kubar noticed that the pronunciation Wirgth used for the word sire was in fact an archaic form not used since his own time, when such a term, for a while at least, was only used derisively.

He looked at Wirgth closely, but the old Gavarnian only smiled at him, his rheumy eyes twinkling as if they were sharing a private joke. But how could he have known such a thing? Kubar wondered.

"Then if we can march out," Arn inquired, "why not move Hina's army in here in force and catch Iskander by surprise?"

"The tunnel path comes out to the north side of the great mountain," Wirgth replied, "a good five leagues from our own line. I've not mentioned it before simply because it would be useless to bring supplies or a large army up through it. But a thousand of us appearing out of it will cause quite a stir. If Hina has already passed, then we'll simply follow up behind him."

"It still sounds like witchery to me," one of the other warriors said.

"I've already been there," Wirgth said offhandedly, "and I certainly wasn't afraid of any godspirits or ghosts. Now, my good sires, surely if they didn't frighten me..."

The others could not respond without sounding as if they were afraid of something that the old Kaadu viewed with disdain.

"There are nearly a thousand of us," Arn interjected. "How do we propose to pull out without their overwhelming us?"

"But that is the final point," Kubar replied. "You see, in fact, I *want* them to overwhelm us."

"What?"

Control your temper, Kubar thought desperately, control it, and he attempted to force a smile.

"Iskander!"

He was already buckling on his armor, even before Parmenion had torn the flap aside and burst into the tent.

"They're sallying?"

"They've already hit the line in front of the main gate."

"There shouldn't be that many," Alexander stated, trying to give an outward appearance of calm, even as all around him the camp was in an uproar.

"It's not the men," Parmenion cried. "They have another of their machines."

So this Kubar had invented yet another device to confound them. His interest aroused, Alexander grasped his sword and strode out into the chaos that surrounded him.

"By all the gods," he whispered softly.

The first siege line was already breached, but there were no Gafs in sight. Instead the Humans were confronted by what appeared to be a tortoise shell the size of a small shed. And already a second one was emerging from the gate.

"It's merely a type of siege tower," Alexander said out loud in an attempt to calm those around him.

"But look!" one of the men cried, and even as he spoke a tongue of molten metal arced out from a nozzle mounted on the side of the tortoise, sweeping the trenchline with fire. Panic-stricken men burst out from the escarpment and ran for the rear, while from the fortress walls a volley of arrows and catapult bolts rained down, catching half a dozen fleeing Humans in midstride and pinning them to the ground.

Alexander looked for the commander of the Ris and Kievant phalanx, whose men served as his elite bodyguard. Catching the man's attention, he gave the signal for the phalanx to be formed.

As he waited, the second tortoise cleared the gate, and a third one appeared behind it. Having the advantage of moving downhill from the elevated gatehouse, the machines moved along at a fair speed while playing out a heavy cable behind them. Alexander's artillery opened fire with a shower of bolts and rocks, making a number of strikes, but without effect. A number of Gaf skirmishers sallied out, as well, and Alexander could see where a heavy unit of horse was forming up just within the fortress wall.

"Do you think they're trying a breakout?" Parmenion cried, trying to be heard above the ever-increasing roar of battle.

But Alexander was silent. They had managed to pierce his first siege line but there were two more beyond that, and then two leagues farther out was another series of protective ditches facing southward toward the enemy capital. If they were trying a breakout, it was certainly a desperate move. But this was a time of desperation, both for him and the Gafs. He assumed that their preparations in the capital would soon be complete.

He was planning to assault the ore carrier before the Gafs marched, but now they seemed to be coming out, thus possibly eliminating for him the need for a desperate assault, since the earthen ramp that he was building toward the east wall was still six meters from completion.

"Sire, we're formed," the Ris commander shouted, and the Kievant nodded his assertion.

"We charge straight at them, open formation," Alexander shouted. "When we've closed be sure to stand clear of the nozzles then drive your spears in through the slits or try to jam them up underneath the wheels. There, do you see it, it's being pushed by Gafs walking inside. Pass that back to the men."

Damn it, if these men were his real Macedons there would be no need to explain, they'd simply do it, the same as when they faced the elephants of Porus. The men had opened ranks and let the beasts pass, and then attacked them from the flanks and rear. He could still remember the cries of the wounded creatures—he blocked out the thought.

"Forward!"

The phalanx swung into a four-rank formation behind him and advanced down the field at a walk. The skirmishers deployed to the right flank in an attempt to deliver harassing fire against the wall and thus keep the enemy archers down.

The third tortoise stopped in the gate, having skewed to one side and then crunched down, as if its forward axle had broken. Suddenly he could see his chance.

He looked back up to where Parmenion was watching the action, but there was no need to point out the enemy's plight.

Parmenion was already shouting to his signalers, and within seconds the horns sounded five steady notes and then a sixth note an octave higher, to be repeated again and again as the camp stirred into action. Up and down the line the men saw what had happened and a wild shout rose to the heavens.

"To the right flank in column," Alexander screamed. "Follow me to the gate!"

Half a hundred Gafs were gathered around the tortoise, trying desperately to push it out of the gate. But the harder they pushed, the more the front edge dug into the ground.

The damned fools, Alexander thought, they should push it back, not forward.

"Faster," he cried, "before they close the gate, faster!"

The other two tortoises stopped and the back ends split open—a score of Gafs poured out of each and dashed up the slope even as the phalanx came down from the flank.

It would be a near thing, and some of them, falling behind, turned in desperation to trade their lives as dearly as possible.

One warrior, singling out Alexander at the head of the column, drew a scimitar and charged. As he bore down, Alexander braced for the impact, driving his shield in low in an attempt to knock the towering creature off balance.

He felt as if he had run into a stone wall. A crashing blow numbed his arm and sent him staggering backward, but the host pushing down behind him charged over the Gaf and bore him under a tide of shouting men. Alexander was pushed to one side, but nothing could stop him at this moment. Casting aside his shield, he pushed to the front of the charging column.

The Gafs, seeing the tide of men bearing down upon them, backed up, forming under the portcullis.

"Forward, my Macedons!"

And the line at the head of the charge smashed into the wall of screaming Gavarnian warriors.

Panting for breath, Kubar looked over his shoulder. The reserve line was gone, the last of the warriors were off the wall and had retreated into the inner citadel.

"Go on, Wirgth. Paga and I will stay here only a moment longer."

"Not until you leave," Wirgth replied, his eyes locked on Kubar.

Kubar quickly turned and looked back at the fighting that was raging in the gateway a score of paces away.

"Those are all first or second brothers," Wirgth said coldly. "They pledged to hold the gate and put on the fight to deceive this Iskander. They want to die here and you cannot stop them, nor should you blame yourself. Now leave."

But Kubar did not move, and his hand rested on the half-drawn sword in his scabbard. It was one thing to order warriors to battle, it was far different to ask men to go to certain death. But a hundred would have to stay and die, and he had been forced to ask. Those who had older brothers still alive had cried for, had almost begged at times, for the honor. Again their damned glory and honor.

"You are the soul of our fight," Wirgth said softly. "If you die then we all die at the swords of the hairless ones."

He looked back at the gate again. A lone man was battering his way through the gate, ducking beneath the blows of the Gaf warriors and coming in low with an up-driven blade. But the man was lost from view as Paga, Wirgth, and half a dozen guards forced their commander away from the fight.

Suddenly they were out of the courtyard and into a rough stone passage that cut downward into the heart of the ore ship.

Every twenty paces they passed a torch stuck into a socket, and the last guard in the detachment knocked the torch down after they had passed.

The downward descent leveled out as they came into a low vaulted chamber. It was quiet, cool, and damp—a startling change after the heat and roar of battle aboveground.

They stopped for a brief moment before a jet-black stone that stood alone in the middle of the chamber. Its surface was scorched, the entire rock illuminated by a circle of light from overhead. Kubar leaned over the stone and looked straight up into the dim light of the sun, which seemed to float at the top of the chimney directly above. The stone had been pushed aside, revealing a circular hole that seemed to drop like a well.

There was a smell of death in the room. The half a hundred dead who had occupied this place, unable to be cremated because of the shortage of wood, had been dragged back out and laid in the streets and in various apartments throughout the fortress. They had been denied the right of final rest upon the cremation stone and the rising of their ashes to the Unseen Light above.

They could still serve in death, Kubar had explained. Their bodies would serve to deceive the enemy as to the numbers who had survived to the end.

Each of them bowed to the altar, then following Wirgth's lead, they started down.

Two of the guards stayed behind and Kubar suddenly realized that Wirgth had not told him about one final detail regarding their retreat.

"Wait!"

But it was too late. Even as he cried out the guards leaned into the stone, and with a shuddering grind it slid over the hole, closing off those who were looking up. With a *boom* the altar dropped back into place.

He had to brace himself, to give the example, but his mind could not tear away from the thought of those two warriors who would soon die, trading their lives so that his deception and stratagems could be played out.

He had to set the example, and cursing silently, he followed Wirgth down the ladder. Far below he could hear a rising murmur of voices. The rest of the garrison was waiting for their arrival. He set his face, and reaching the last rung, Kubar let go and landed on his feet in the middle of a broad corridor.

* * *

For a moment he was stunned, and he knew that his amazement and fear showed.

The corridor was so wide that half a dozen mounted Gavarnians could have ridden abreast. From overhead a soft yellow light radiated from translucent panels, flooding the corridor with a comfortable warm glow. It was dry and held a comfortable cool scent. When Wirgth had said that he knew of a tunnel that stretched for nearly three days' march, Kubar had imagined groping in a dank, fetid darkness.

He was disoriented and looked over to Wirgth, who motioned for him to follow.

After several minutes Kubar gained the head of the column. The warriors were quiet, fearful of the strange spotless surroundings.

Ahead of them the corridor was in darkness. Kubar was about to call for a torch when Wirgth, as if sensing his command, stepped forward a dozen paces and suddenly a battery of overhead panels lit up.

Those who had yet to see this phenomenon jumped back with startled shouts and several of them drew their blades, but Wirgth simply motioned for the warriors to be silent.

"Shall we start, Kubar? After all, it is a long march. There was once a hairless one who said something about the first steps of journeys . . . but I can't remember it now."

Again there was that strangeness, as if this old advisor somehow knew too much, but Kubar realized that now was not the time to pursue the mystery.

Following Wirgth's lead, he fell in alongside the bent-over Gavarnian, and behind him there was a stirring rustle as the survivors fell into line.

"Everybody else got out?" Kubar asked, looking over to Paga.

"Yes, everyone but the hundred volunteers who stayed behind. The tools for the forges have been hidden down here, and the material for that project of yours is being pulled along in one of the carts."

"And my clothing and armor, they were used as I requested?"

Wirgth merely nodded. And Kubar did not wish to inquire as to which body was selected to be his substitute.

They walked in silence for a time, until Kubar quietly remarked on the large number of side tunnels.

"The entire Kolbard is honeycombed with these access chambers and service tunnels. They reach right through the shielding of the ring to the other side, out into open space."

"Open space..." Kubar muttered, his words trailing off. It was still hard for him to realize that he was living on the inside of a world, not the outside, and that down was in fact up, and up—the thought was overwhelming.

But if Wirgth's comment was true, then it would be possible to go downward and see the stars. He wondered about that; would they seem the same as they had at home?

"This tunnel, I believe, was once a transportation link for great vehicles that girdled the Kolbard at speeds beyond our imagining."

"And if we followed this tunnel?"

"It would go on forever. We could walk it for a lifetime, and after a hundred generations our ancestors would one day come back here at the starting point. I've heard rumor that there are indeed races that live down here and do just that, moving forever in a great circle."

Kubar involuntarily shuddered at the thought of subterranean beings forever walking beyond sight of light or stars.

"How do you know of these things?"

"Oh, shall we say, it's just bits of old legends passed down through the generations of my family. No one else was ever interested in exploring this part of our world, and there are perhaps reasons why that is best. When that ore carrier crashed during the Great War of the demigods, it revealed a section of the tunnel which my ancestors covered over with the altar, so that as time passed it was all but forgotten."

Kubar was silent. Why was it that such a thing was covered over? Why hadn't they used these tunnels to move quickly from one place to another in comfort? Or was it some sort of primal fear that kept both his race and the Humans out of the subterranean world beneath their feet?

Hours later the column started to straggle, but Kubar wished to push on as long as endurance would hold. It was essential that he return to the fight as quickly as possible. There was a gentle stirring of wind to his right, and turning, he looked into a downward-sloping side tunnel. It was the first such opening that they had encountered, and Kubar hesitated for a moment, his curiosity aroused.

"I wouldn't turn in there if I were you," Wirgth said quietly.

"And why not?"

"You might get lost."

But he could sense something else in Wirgth's tone.

"Call a rest halt," Kubar said quietly. "I'll be back shortly."

The command filtered down the line and the column sank wearily to the floor, mumbling and groaning as soldiers have always done, when a long-anticipated rest is finally called.

Without another word, Kubar turned and started down the side tunnel. Knowing that argument was senseless Wirgth and Paga followed. The panels overhead lit up at their approach, but the coloring was softer and gradually shifted toward red as they moved along.

"My lord Taug, perhaps we ..."

"Why are you trying to stop me?" Kubar asked, turning to look at Wirgth.

"Perhaps it's just that you're not ready for this."

"Let me be the judge of that, please."

Wirgth mumbled something to himself and fell silent.

For nearly a verst they made their way down the sloping corridor until finally the only lighting was a dull, shimmering red. Up ahead Kubar saw that the tunnel was coming to an end.

A room spread out before him, lost in darkness, and he sensed that he was in a chamber of immense length. No panels lit up to illuminate the way.

"By the names of my brothers!" Paga cried, leaping backward even as he grabbed Kubar and tried to pull him along.

Suddenly he felt as if he were falling into endless darkness, and his mind struggled against the panic. But no, he was standing on something after all.

He closed his eyes for a moment and fought for control, while removing Paga's grip. He took another step forward, then opened his eyes again.

Beneath his feet, the heavens were spread out before him. The swirling cloud of the galaxy arched beneath his feet.

"Our home, our long-lost home," Wirgth said softly. "is somewhere in that cloud of stars. For you it was a home you left but yesterday, for me it is a world lost long ago. You are at the bottom of the Kolbard, Kubar Taug. And here, again, you can see the everlasting sea of eternity."

Orientation returned and he could not help but laugh, and his voice echoed in the darkened chamber. How strange to look down and see the stars between your feet.

"Wondrous," he whispered softly, "simply wondrous. Why then the fear in your voice and in your heart when you came to this place?"

Paga's grip returned to his shoulder, and Kubar could feel it tighten in panic. There was something else to this place, and turning, he looked back at Paga and then in the direction his comrade was staring.

The hair on the back of his neck stood straight up.

"Because," Wirgth said softly, "this is the Mausoleum of the First Travelers, the builders of this world. This has been their resting place for a hundred thousand of our lifetimes, and still their attendants who have no flesh see to them, and through those attendants I have learned why you are here."

From out of the darkness a corpse floated into view, and for the first time since his childhood Kubar screamed in fear.

CHAPTER 14

"IT'S UP TO EIGHT POINT EIGHT TO ONE," CORBIN SAID, shaking his head with amazement. "Not even in my wildest dreams did I ever think it'd get this high. Have you pushed the rest of my assets into the game?"

"Right after the capture of the ore carrier and Kubar's disappearance, the odds peaked. I put the remainder of your twenty percent into the game matched straight against Sigma. Nearly sixty percent of his total wealth is tagged into the operation."

"Fabulous," Corbin gloated, "simply fabulous!"

"But all monitoring of Kubar ceased eighteen hours ago," Tia replied. "Corbin, if he's dead, Alexander might pull it off."

"Not to worry, my dear, not to worry. First off, we picked up a wavering in Kubar's signal for several minutes before it shut down; secondly, the body they dragged out into the square, though dressed as Kubar, doesn't match up to the computer analysis. I'm not worried yet; besides, Alexander will be taken care of shortly. The individual to do the job is already in place."

"How, Corbin?"

"Let's just say that if I see any possible threat or shift he'll be taken care of immediately. If I can swing even *higher* action, I'll let him last a bit longer."

Tia leaned forward. "How?"

"There's no need for you to know," Corbin replied guardedly.

"So where the hell is Kubar?" she asked suddenly, realizing that it was safer to change the subject rather than push it.

"Remember, the Kolbard is honeycombed with millions of kilometers of passages. It is possible, after all, that the Gafs know of these. For that matter, why shouldn't they?"

"There is one concern though," Tia replied.

"And what's that?"

"As far as I know, the Xsarn has no monitoring through the bottom of the Kolbard."

Corbin was suddenly silent. Good for her, this girl was certainly on top of the angles. "Any of the Kohs off ship right now?"

"Bukha and Yeshna are on their home worlds. I understand Sigad of Monta is in transit back here. Otherwise all the other Kohs are accounted for."

"All right then, just run a discreet check. If any of them leave, make sure a bug is placed on their personal vessels. What about Aldin and Zergh?"

"They're out deploying a new set of monitor drones."

"All right then, girl." He waved his hand as if to dismiss her, and taking the hint, Tia rose and left the room.

She was doing a good job of looking out for his interests but she was just a little too inquisitive about his contact with Alexander. Getting the contact in place next to Alexander had been the real headache. The problem had been an interesting one, a problem the solution of which he had arranged privately a couple of years earlier, with a number of discreet forays down to the Kolbard long before the project had started. The direct-wire contact from the top of Olympus was secured, as well. There'd be no over-the-air message, therefore no possible way for the Xsarn to find out. Now all he had to do was wait. Turning, he opened the door into his private recreation chamber. It was about time for a little interesting diversion.

As the door closed behind her, Tia heard the door into Corbin's private chamber slip open and a female giggle echoed in the room. Damn that Regina, she thought quietly, and then, smiling, she continued on down the hall.

The endless monsoon of the last two months had finally broken, and with it came a fresh-scented breeze from out of the east. The sun, as always, hung motionless in a perpetual noonday sky, and for a moment Alexander ached for but one clear sunset to reflect its fiery light off the snowcapped pinnacles of the Hindu Kush.

The reports had been filtering up from the south all day. The enemy was giving every indication that they were about to march.

And what had happened to Kubar? That was the disturbing thought. Again he remembered his hunt for Darius. For years he had pursued him across the Persian Empire, across a thousand leagues and two major battlefields, in the end only to discover him murdered by two traitorous Persians. How he had dreamed that in the heat of battle he would step forward from the line, his armor gleaming in the morning sun, and there meet Darius one to one in a fight that would decide the fate of an entire world.

They had shown him the body of the one called the Taug. Though it bothered him to do so, he finally brought Liala to view the body as it lay in state in his own command tent. She had gazed silently upon it, then without a word turned away. She had not spoken since and refused to acknowledge if it was indeed the remains of Kubar.

"Still thinking about the number of casualties?" Yaroslav asked from behind him.

"Just a hundred dead and another fifty scattered around the fortress. Somehow it just doesn't add up."

"Did he take wing then?" Parmenion asked, looking over to Alexander from the brim of his cup.

"I would not be surprised," Alexander said softly. "And yet another thing, the tools for the forges—nothing, it's all gone, even the bellows used for the flame spouters have disappeared. There must have been another way out of here."

"But we have a perimeter several leagues deep completely encircling this place."

"There are other ways," Yaroslav said softly, and Alexander looked at him knowingly, remembering the place of their first meeting.

"Yaroslav, take five hundred men," Alexander commanded. "Start at one end of this ore ship and tear it apart to the other. There must have been another way, and I plan to find it."

Kubar was like him, Alexander knew that. And if all had been lost, his army destroyed, and he surrounded, he would not have met his death huddled in some alleyway. No, he would have donned his finest armor and stood atop the highest place, so that all might see how a king should die.

How a king should die. And his thoughts turned back to the bed of pain he had been taken from in Babylon. What was it from the holy book of the Jews, who called him a liberator? "By the waters of Babylon..." He could not remember the rest. On an impulse he almost turned to Yaroslav to ask if he knew. But no, he wondered too much about that man already. If Yaroslav knew an obscure book from a people most likely forgotten, that knowledge would just compound Alexander's concerns. He pushed the thought aside.

By the waters of Babylon...and he thought of the

strange unseen god that the Jews had worshipped. Were the gods or god truly so remote? Faceless judges who ruled without passion? But even their god had shown anger, and had rained down death upon those who displeased him.

Or were people merely the playthings of the gods after all? Why had he been brought here? Who was this demigod named Aldin, who had a belly like Parmenion and had spoken fearfully of yet higher gods called Overseers?

"Did you ever hear of a god named Aldin?" Alexander suddenly asked, looking over his shoulder at Yaroslav. Parmenion stopped what he was doing and looked over at the aged philosopher, as well.

Yaroslav was motionless. Almost too perfectly so, Alexander thought.

"What god was that, my lord?"

Alexander smiled his knowing smile and looked away. Was this all some elaborate plaything of the gods? He had often wondered that when he lay alone at night, as they crossed the vastness of Persia. Did the gods of Olympus watch his actions, did they care? In his heart of hearts he had dreamed of being their equal, of one day holding all the world in his sway so that even the gods would look upon this one of mortal flesh with envy and admiration. For a god could be worshipped only from afar, and his voice was never heard, while he, Alexander, could arrange the world to his vision. Arrange the world.

He looked to the southward plains. From what appeared to be but a short march away rose another tower, then beyond that, across the shimmer of the sea, rose yet another and then another. Mountains made by gods, an entire world made by gods, and he was merely an actor upon their stage. Were they watching now? And almost by instinct he looked back to the tower that he had called

Olympus. If you are watching, he thought, then watch carefully. For beyond all else, I am still Alexander.

"Prepare the rest of the army to march once the dimming has come," Alexander said, turning to face his staff. "We'll have to go into battle with the weapons we have."

"Why not stay here and let them come to us?" Parmenion ventured.

"We can't let them gain our left flank and cut the approaches to the Anvil. If so, we'll be pinned against the bay, and in spite of our ships, I'll not risk a supply and retreat line across water. I wish to face the enemy as close to his city as possible, so when we beat him he'll have no time to reorganize before we have already gained the gates. Get the men organized. We march within the hour."

The men saluted even as he turned away and strode out of his command tent.

The real reasons for his advance he would not share. In their first battle he had allowed himself, in fact had sought, a position from which there was no retreat. Knowing how the enemy fought, he was confident of success as long as his men were forced to stand.

But this time he was uneasy about it all, and he had no desire to be pushed back into a fortress from which there was no retreat. The ore citadel had fallen far too easily. It was as if the enemy had read his own mind, for he had already resolved that if the ore carrier did not fall before the reinforcements marched from the Gaf capital, he would pull back across the Anvil. Otherwise he'd be forced to fight an army of unknown quality, with yet another enemy force entrenched to his rear.

Not only did this one know what I was thinking, Alexander thought, but he had also studied how I fought, as well. Desperation could breed desperate actions, or at times it can create a whole new way of thinking. If

Kubar was alive, Alexander knew that there would be no desperation in the coming battle.

Bowing low to the single urn that contained the ashes of his three brothers, Hina touched the talisman around his neck. Within its leather casing was a miniature of the urn upon the family altar, and like its larger counterpart, this miniature urn carried the ashes of his three brothers, as well. The tradition of the last surviving brother carrying the ashes of his three male siblings was old even in the time of Kubar. It served as an everpresent reminder of the bond that united four souls who came into creation together and who would one day face the judgment before the Light together, where the brothers would be judged as one for all their deeds. It was the last survivor who could continue the line, but it was the last survivor, as well, who carried the heaviest burden. For it was his actions more than any other that weighed the heaviest in the final judgment.

His three brothers lingered in Binda, the Hall of Waiting Rest, and their ashes about his neck were a reminder. For they could see his every action and know his every thought, and if he failed, they would know even before he rejoined them that his actions had condemned them all.

"It is time." He felt a light touch upon his shoulder.

Turning, he saw Kaveta standing in the doorway to the family temple. She was part of the inheritance from Kalin, as well, for if the oldest had married before his death, the last surviving brother took his wife. But for Hina that was no burden; he had loved Kaveta from afar even as Kalin claimed her, and in his heart he knew that she had preferred him, in spite of her clan obligations to Kalin. She drew closer and brushed her hands over his shoulders, and his hands gently touched her on the abdomen.

The day before she had told him that she was pregnant, and that the children would be his. To him that had been more a proof of her love than anything else, for no children had been born between her and Kalin. It was believed by many that a Gavarnian female could control her breeding cycle. If that were so, she had allowed the cycle to begin the first night they had been together, after the twenty-dimming mourning for Kalin had ended.

So there would be five lives soon—the four sons and a single daughter that came to all of the Gavarnian race. Three of the sons would be named after his brothers, and the fourth would be named after their father, for so it had always been. And the daughter would be named after Kaveta's mother, honoring her line, as well.

She looked so like Liala. The damnable fool, sneaking aboard a supply ship to reach Kubar. At least this Iskander had again shown that he understood chivalry when he informed him that his sister was safe in his care. The damn fool, and he could not help but wonder what could have so strongly motivated her to go to Kubar, who had not even noticed her during the brief time he had stayed at the court. As long as she was safe, though, then his thoughts turned back to his brothers.

Would he already be with his brothers when Kaveta came due, when the next quarter had passed and the rains came again?

"I love you more than my own life," he whispered. "If I should fall, tell my sons and daughter that I love them as I love the memory of my own brothers."

She smiled gently, and taking his hand, they left the temple and stepped into the glaring light of the palace courtyard.

It was empty except for a single horse, and beyond the sight of all others he hugged her close one last time then swung into the saddle.

Beyond the city wall the ranks were drawn up in thirty-five columns of a thousand, each of the thousand broken into ten separate groups of a hundred. And at the sight of their commander a wild roar rose up, terrible and proud. These warriors who had been landless and title-less could sense a new change and power in their lives.

Hina galloped down the road, and his staff of signal-bearers and officers fell in behind him. His first regi-ment, the veterans of the first battle at the ore carrier, lined the road on either side. Each man held a short spear in his right hand. The wooden shaft, as long as a Human was tall, measured as thick around as a warrior's fist. The top of the spear was capped by an iron shaft, to which was affixed a barbed iron point. Each warrior car-ried two more of these ugly-looking weapons mounted to a harness on his back, and by his side he carried the long, curved sword.

Getting the swords for his new army had nearly caused an open rebellion at one point. Since it had been impossible to make the number that were needed in the short time available, he had been forced to requisition them from the noble families. But swords had histories and lineages the same as any Gavarnian, and the nobles had come near to rebellion when the supply staffs had shown up at their individual estates to take the weapons the army so desperately needed.

Still there were only enough for half the warriors to be thusly armed, and as a result a fair percentage of war-riors were merely armed with the three short pikes and somewhat shorter imitations of the Human phalanx spears.

All of this was desperation; the plans that arrived nightly by messenger hawk from Kubar's position had laid it out step by step, but there had been no message for three dimmings. Hina was on his own.

Without looking back, Hina continued down the road. As the cheering died, the thirty-five thousand warriors of his army fell into marching formation then spread out across a broad arc to either side of the road. The army moved north to the final confrontation.

* * *

"So you think it will come within the next three days?"

Aldin looked up from the data board and nodded to Zergh, who fell into the cushioned chair alongside him. The Gavarnian vasba held up an uncorked bottle of brandy; in his other hand were two goblets. Aldin nodded in agreement, both to the question and the offer, and Zergh poured half a snifter out and handed it to Aldin, who took a long gulp without any of the usual effete rituals practiced by the Kohs.

"I'll be glad when this damned game is over with," Zergh said wearily. "I haven't had a decent night's rest for the last bloody month. The betting from my half is pouring in faster than can be handled by the computers. Damn my eyes, Aldin, it was for a total worth over a *trillion* katars. One bet came in right after the taking of the ore carrier for over twenty billion. Just one bet, specified against some of Sigma's holdings."

"That bet must be some sort of record," Aldin muttered absently.

"It is. I already checked."

"Who placed it?"

"It came out of some code-name accounts from the Eldarnian banking system, no identification; somebody is trying to keep his placings quiet. I don't like that, the game's supposed to be limited to those with Koh status.

"Yeah, well Xsarnfood on that. Half the damn Cloud must know about this thing by now. Hell, I'm changing my private contact number twice a day now to keep away from the damned calls for tips, bribes, and long-lost relatives looking for a deal.

"Twenty billion... By the way," Aldin continued, "did Sigma make any inquiries as to who was betting against him?"

"Not a word. I contacted him personally to confirm it, and he just smiled and agreed. That's not like him, he's usually more cautious than that."

"Then why have you bothered to tell me?"

"Oh, no reason, no reason at all," Zergh responded, looking meditatively into his drink. "By the way, do you have one of those awful cigars of yours?"

"Need you ask?" Aldin fished around in his jacket pocket and pulled out two slightly bent brown cylinders, one of them already half smoked. After putting both in his mouth at the same time, he picked up a lighter from the desk and quickly had both of them pumping out twin plumes of curling smoke. He offered the longer of the two to Zergh and watched as his old mentor leaned back, took a pull, and then doubled over with a coughing spasm.

"At your age, you should take better care," Aldin ventured.

"I doubt if *these* things will take me, it's what's in my food that I tend to watch more of late. I tell you, Aldin, this profession isn't what it used to be. When I first brought you into it, it was still a sport of gentlemen. That's when nobles knew how to be nobles. There was a breeding to them then, and I admired their dignity. But these games have become like a drug, each one having to be just a little bit bigger than the last. Each one having to be more elaborate, with more variations and side bets to satiate their appetite for amusement. I don't see a gentleman in the lot, except maybe for Bukha and of course old Sigma. But I daresay he's the last of a dying breed. Why do we serve these thieves, Aldin?"

"It's what we're in business for."

"This is my last one," Zergh said softly as he pulled on the cigar again, and this time managed to inhale the smoke without choking.

"Retiring then?" Aldin asked quietly.

"Call it what you will. But this game has taken something out of me. Before this we merely watched a fight on a primitive world. We'd sneak in, set up the monitoring unit, evaluate the odds, then manage the bets. There was no way we could have stopped the fighting anyhow, since the Overseers control and forbid all contact with the primitive worlds. But now we've become involved, we've taken those two geniuses of destruction from their own worlds and placed them in a situation ripe for mayhem."

"You didn't voice these scruples when we started this venture."

"There was no reason to. My people and yours had been spilling blood down on the Kolbard since they first settled there nearly three millennia ago. I thought, as you did, that Kubar and Alexander would settle the issue once and for all. Besides, it was a question of more than passing interest—the thought of taking two legendary characters and pitting them against each other. I felt, as well, that in the end the victor would set about to raise his people from barbarism."

"Zergh, Zergh, you are starting to sound as if you have succumbed to the philosophy of the Overseers."

Zergh was silent and showed no anger over the gentle insult from Aldin.

"What is it that you really wish to discuss, Zergh? I've not known you to dwell overlong on philosophy and ethics, I've always thought that was more my department."

Zergh looked meditatively at the end of his cigar, and putting it in an ashtray, he tilted his head back and knocked down the rest of the brandy in his snifter.

"An individual becomes a Koh only because his family has consistently bred generation after generation of cunning and sharpness. There was a time when they also bred at least gentlemen with a rough code of ethics, but alas that's gone by the board."

"And that's not your main point, either."

"I'm breaking my ethics, as well, in discussing it."

"Go on," Aldin said softly, "this room was swept not an hour ago for bugs. If there had been any on you, my countersystem would have detected it. This chamber, at least, is clean."

"Just being on a Corbin gaming yacht makes me feel..."

"Damn it all! Say it!"

"All right then. Why would someone field in a twenty-billion katar bet? A sucker bet, at that, especially with Kubar still missing and presumed by more than one to be dead."

"Come now, you know more about Kubar than you'll ever say. And I can tell from your actions he's not dead, and gaming ethics be damned."

Zergh did not respond to the implications in Aldin's words. "Look, Aldin, I think that twenty-billion bet came from Corbin. It had to."

"Why do you say that?"

"I haven't been in this business for a lifetime without learning to smell out a good bet, or also learning how to smell out a game within a game."

"So why are you telling me about it?"

"Because, damn it, man, if he's secretly fielded a twenty-billion katar bet, something is up. Besides that, he's screwing you out of your royalties if that bet pays off; a vasba, as a consultant, is supposed to get a cut of all winnings. Damn it, Aldin, your advice has made that man billions, and you get shit from it.

"Bukha at least has been somewhat honest. Oh, his accountants are creative, but the money finally does trickle down to me nevertheless."

"If only you wouldn't blow it on bad women on some of those pleasure planets, and even worse card games," Aldin replied.

"But at least I have it."

"At least you *had* it."

"Listen, if Corbin is up to something, you should be tracking it down. But what do I find you doing here instead? Playing with old gaming programs on your computer and fiddling around with useless holotapes and replays of Alexander and Kubar. Damn it, man, stop looking at those old tapes and start getting involved with your own survival."

"But I am," Aldin said evenly, "I am."

He looked over at Zergh with a smile, and then, picking up the bugging sensor, he did another quick check of the room before settling back in his chair and offering his companion another drink.

CHAPTER 15

"By the gods," Parmenion whispered, "look at them. When will they stop coming?"

For hours the Gaf army had been deploying on the opposite ridgeline a verst away. Unit after unit had swung out of column and filed out to either flank. What was occurring in the valley beyond the opposite ridge-line, they could only imagine, since the last of the Human scouts had been driven in hours ago.

Alexander could only assume at this point that what was being revealed on the opposite ridgeline was only a minor portion of the total enemy forces. Since it was an obvious goal of the Gafs to cut the Humans off from the Anvil, Alexander assumed that most of the hidden forces were shifting to threaten that end of his line. Out on the edge of the Anvil a majority of the cavalry from both armies was positioned and already engaged in a swift series of raids and counterraids, but neither side was willing yet to commit to a full-scale engagement.

Alexander studied each move carefully from the command post in the center of the line. He had chosen his position carefully. It was a third of the way up toward the enemy capital, with a defensive line that followed a ridge just slightly higher than the one opposite them. The far left was anchored on a rounded hill that dominated the rest of the line and looked out over the flatness of the Anvil, which came up to the very base of the hill. The right curved back gently and was anchored in a low out-cropping of bared subsurface, surrounded lower down by a thick tangle of woods.

To match his position, the Gafs would be forced to deploy on the outer side of the curving line, thus occupying a longer front, which meant their positions would be more lightly held if both sides were equal. It also meant that he had the advantage of being able to shift reserves across the inside of the curving position, rather than the outside, as the Gafs would be forced to do.

He had weighed the advantage of the position against the possibility of advancing forward rapidly and trying to catch the Gaf army while it was still in column. But their numerical edge in cavalry prevented such a bold stroke and might have forced a confrontation on a field that did not offer superior advantages. The other problem with a swift attack was the simple fact that the closer he came to the capital, the farther he would have had to extend his flank to the left in order to prevent the enemy from turning his line. It was not in his nature to assume a defensive stance, but in his heart there had been a warn-ing to not press his luck any further. In spite of his vic-tories, most of his troops had yet to face the Gafs in an open encounter, and for that he wanted the advantage of position to place the odds in his favor.

The last column of a thousand had swung to the left, and after some minutes no more troops had appeared.

"Have you noticed," Alexander said, looking at the regiment commanders around him, "that their units seem to march and maneuver in groups of a thousand? While we operate in units of five hundred. I think they plan to mass them in depth and use their superior size and weight to crash through our lines."

The commanders were silent and looked nervously one to the other.

"When we go at them, it will be in the formations we drilled with—fronts of a hundred by ten deep. The first wave will have ten regiments across, a front of a thousand paces. Field catapults will deploy behind the advance and move in with it. But remember, we want the Gafs to come to us, and you'll withdraw before contact is made. They'll be expecting the main blow to come on the left, but, gentlemen, there'll be twenty regiments in a column five regiments deep on the right, concealed there." He pointed down to where the men were already deployed behind the clump of trees.

"Once we gain their flank, we'll be between them and their line of supply and retreat."

"But what if they anticipate that?" the Avar commander asked.

"I doubt that, since they know that if they can turn our left the battle is theirs. These Gafs seem to think only in terms of the offensive. But I plan to be with you on the right, and there is where the battle shall be decided."

The men were silent and Alexander smiled in an attempt to encourage them. "Don't worry, that's where I'll be. And wherever I am, that is where the battle is decided."

Alexander looked at Parmenion, who would be responsible for the left, and smiled. But his second in command had a look of worry in his eyes.

"What is it, Parmenion?"

"Just remembering what you've always said, my lord."

"And that is?"

"That this Kubar was their version of you. Even though he is missing and there are no indications that he rides with that army, still I worry that his spirit might be guiding those warriors over there. Otherwise they would not have come to us with such confidence."

Is Kubar dead? For a moment the thought chilled him. He had wanted to meet the legendary Gaf, to replay his hunt of Darius, only this time to a conclusion worthy of a king. Until this day he had never lost a major battle, and the words of Parmenion lingered with him.

But he was Alexander, and with a smile of confidence he turned away to look out across the field that would soon decide the fate of an entire realm. To either side the Kolbard arched up into a distant cloud-studded blue, and he dreamed the dreams that only he could understand.

"Let's just say I wish to make sure my bet is perfect," Corbin said smoothly.

"You know something, I can't help but think that you want him dead simply because over the months he has come to symbolize something superior to you and your damned Kohs. He's a man with integrity and honor."

"Come now, my dear Tia," Corbin replied smoothly, "integrity and honor are for fools. Too much of my wealth has been pulled into this game already. Remember, the technical wording of all bets centers on the final victory of the armies, not on the actual presence of the commanders. The life or death of Alexander and Kubar were secondary bets that only fools would play. There are too many random factors involved when betting on individual lives; it's the overall scope, which is more predictable, that interests me."

"Which you can control better, as well."

"Precisely. Just remember that one percent you're taking, and let the death of Alexander to insure that percent be my concern. The Gaf armies still have Hina, and after all, they're fighting now for the survival of their kingdom and this new social order that Kubar has brought about. Really distasteful, that, allowing the rabble to gain political control. But the Humans have only Alexander: with him gone the army will collapse, be driven into the hills, and the Xsarn will declare the game finished. Anyhow, the arrangements have already been made, as you well know, and shall be carried out shortly."

"As I well know," Tia said softly.

"Prepare to advance," Hina roared. Checking the strap on his helmet one last time, he nodded to the signal drummers. The deep, rolling thunder of a half a hundred kettle drums started, to be picked up by the regimental signalers up and down the line.

"Remember," Hina cried, "the center only, unless I give personal orders otherwise. We don't know where their real strength is! Remember, on my order only."

He knew his proper place was to stay on the hill, that's what Kubar would have done. But he could not order his warriors in and not go with them. He had to set the example. It was foolish Gaf honor, he knew, but regardless of what was foolish or not, he could not live any other way, in spite of Kubar's admonishings. And where was Kubar now? Was he dead in the fall of the ore carrier as a Human prisoner had claimed?

"Sire, there's no need for you—"

"Forward!"

The pipers started up and down the line and the five vustas, the elite regiments personally trained by Hina, stood up in position.

"They're starting to deploy," Parmenion cried. "See? There, in the center."

Alexander merely nodded. "They're meeting our center with their center. Now the trick is to get them to deploy the rest of the formation once the center is engaged."

With a steady measured pace the ten regiments of his own line started forward at a slow walk. Alexander kicked Bucephalas into a gallop and swung down toward the extreme right flank of the advancing line. They'd meet right in the middle of the valley, but so far the enemy had given no indication that it would commit either flank to the assault. The Gaf leader was holding the rest in concealment, the same way he would, and he was not happy with the thought.

All up and down the line the pipers were now in full play, blowing a shrill, dissonant cry that literally set the hair on edge. This made Gaf warriors look even more ominous. The range was down to only several hundred paces, and the slope of the hill was shallowing out into slightly marshy ground. Ahead, skirmishers from both sides were engaged at long distance, and showers of rocks and arrows arched up, passing each other in mid-flight to rain on the opposite lines.

The Human line started to pick up its pace, and the quiet thunder of wood striking wood rolled along the ranks as thousands of spears were lowered into attack position. The majority of weapons were still wooden tipped, but here and there along the line the cold burnish of tempered steel shone in the light of the never-moving sun.

"Spears up!" Hina cried, but the command had already been given for most of the regiments, which had suddenly come to a stop.

The Humans picked up their pace, drawing closer. Hina looked over his shoulder and saw that the regiments were reacting as planned, the formations suddenly breaking open into a checkerboard pattern of a hundred warrior units, three ranks deep and thirty-three wide.

Less than a hundred paces away, the Humans were out onto the flat, open space. A wild thundering cheer broke from their lines, drowning out all other sounds.

"Now!" Hina screamed, "Now!"

His command went unheard, but the training had not been forgotten. Thousands of spears arched skyward, and such was their mass that a visible shadow raced across the ground beneath them. But it was too soon.

Most of the spears fell short, sticking in the ground in front of the Human ranks like a forest that had suddenly sprouted unlooked-for in the middle of the plain. However, this new form of attack had its effect nevertheless. Stunned by the awe-inspiring sight, the Human line slowed to a walk; the back lines, unable to see what had happened, still pressed forward. Hina saw that it was the moment.

Directly before him rode a single warrior, his armor shining in the sunlight.

It was he, it had to be he. And suddenly all that he had been taught by Kubar was forgotten. It was as if the old days had returned, if only for a moment. The honored warrior of the most westward position riding to face the most honored of the other side. The memory of his brothers could not be denied, not now.

Calling the name of his father, and his father's father before him, Hina unsheathed his sword and started forward. The warrior saw him, and unsheathing his own sword, he stood in his stirrups, his arms outstretched as if to gain his attention. But the fates that guided Hina's clan had decreed otherwise, and he never saw the arrow from the Human footman. He never saw the face or heard the family name of the man that drove a meter-long shaft into his body.

"I think this is it," Bukha said sadly. "Our army is breaking up and retreating to the rear."

The other Kohs had turned away from the monitor units. The high-resolution cameras could pick out individuals and had followed Alexander and Hina as they had rushed toward each other, and several hurried bets had been placed. But there had been a universal groan of disappointment when the arrow had slammed into Hina's body, lifting him out of the saddle.

The Gaf assault had broken the moment their commander fell. All along the front, the Gafs had pulled back, abandoning their positions to stream to the rear. It was only the age-old character of them that had saved the army as here and there units had suddenly swung around without order and plunged into the Human line, slamming it to a standstill, until finally the action had broken off as the Human host fell behind and the Gaf retreat was covered by their own cavalry pulled in from the right flank. Nearly an hour had passed and the dimming had set in, cutting down on the clarity of the images. Several of the cameras had shifted over to infra to provide a clearer view of the two armies, which were still deployed on the reverse of the two hills.

Betting for Alexander had climbed to nearly eleven to one, and Corbin had sat to one side, smiling quietly to himself. He had placed, over his secret wire down to the surface, the order to eliminate Alexander. But he saw no indications that Alexander was anywhere near his operative. He had assumed that his target would pay his usual visit the night before the battle, but that had not been the case. And suddenly it looked as if Corbin's fortune might be in the balance. There was a chance that Alexander would rout the enemy forces after all. Corbin had felt a moment of fear when Hina fell and it looked as if the Gafs would break, but Alexander had held his assault.

All the monitors but one had been reporting clearly. It had taken a good bit of manipulation to scramble that particular line, but then again, after all, this ship had been of his design, just for use in this game. A discreet check in his private quarters had confirmed what the others didn't know. Kubar Taug was only minutes away from the front, bringing up a small reserve and his leadership skills which would help to tip the scale. The betting was at an all-time peak, he realized, and he almost regretted not having held back some capital through Tia as a reserve.

Corbin was surprised when Bukha, who had been watching him from one side, suddenly stood up and motioned for him to follow him back to Corbin's own chambers. Leaving the other Kohs, he followed the Gaf down a narrow corridor into his private wing of the ship.

Corbin felt the static field click on, and a quick check showed that Bukha was clean.

"I'll get straight to the point," Bukha said evenly.

For a moment Corbin felt a sense of panic. Had Bukha somehow detected the jammed transmission, or was it worse than that?

"How about a drink first? That last action was a little unnerving. I think your army's had it and will be beaten without much more of a fight. Do you mind?" Corbin pointed over to the liquor cabinet, and without waiting for Bukha's reply, he went over to the sideboard and pulled out a bottle of brandy, uncorked it, and poured out half a snifter.

"Little early in the day for that?" Bukha ventured, but Corbin ignored the tone of insult in his voice.

"What is it that you want then?" Corbin asked coldly, looking straight at the head Gavarnian.

"Just that I was wondering if you would care to make a personal bet on all of this."

Was this merely a scam? Corbin wondered, or had the runaway gambling bitten Bukha, as well?

"Whatever for?" Corbin replied. "Don't tell me you still think your side can win."

"I don't," Bukha said evenly. "In fact, I think it's all up for my side."

"Surely you're not suggesting that I bet for the Gavarnians to win in all of this?" Corbin asked. "I mean, somehow that would strike me as being, how should I say, disloyal, to bet against Alexander."

"Come now, Corbin, I've called you many things, but I never thought of attaching the word loyal to your name. No insult intended, of course."

Corbin was silent.

"It's just with odds of eleven to one, I thought you might be interested."

"But why would you be willing to bet against your own people?"

"Just call it a hedge against the other side, since I've already sunk a tidy sum into this. I wouldn't mind picking up some money on Alexander's win to cover my losses should the followers of Kubar lose."

"This is absurd." Corbin finished his drink and made as if to leave. There had to be a trap in this somehow. "I think we should return to the others. After all, as host of this ship I do have certain duties."

"All right then, let me get straight to the point. Let's just say I represent a little consortium of financial interests. We know your assets, and we were wondering if you would be at all interested in placing 100 billion katars against 931 billion? I realize that's slightly below the current printouts, but that's all we've agreed to front."

By the gods! Was this Gaf crazy?

"What is it that you know that I don't?" Corbin asked suspiciously.

"Let's just say a gut feeling that Alexander has a sure thing and we want to recoup. If I bet with anyone else, word would spread, and I would lose honor for having gone against my own kind. This secret would be between us, since both of us would lose face if the others knew. Call it greed if you want, but I wish to win back at least some of my losses. Now, I realize that a hundred billion is damn near sixty percent of your total assets, and why should you bet on a sucker bet like this? Let's just say I think you're a gaming man, and in one swoop this could make you the richest being—Human, Gaf, or Xsarn—in the entire Cloud."

"But why should I bet against my own?" Corbin asked, only half listening now. Bukha's comments had hit the mark. Bukha was only doing precisely the same thing that he would do under the circumstances.

"I think you'd be interested in taking it because you, too, wish to hedge your bets against any unforeseen events. If you've bet anything at all on Alexander, especially early on before the first fight, then you got favorable odds. So this little bet could be a match up, balancing one side against the other."

"Ah, yes, of course, of course," Corbin said absently. "Quite a bit, as a matter of fact."

"Then look at it this way. Alexander wins, you'll most likely still come out about even, but if not . . ." The Gaf shrugged his shoulders.

Richer than I ever dreamed, Corbin thought. I'll be the richest single being in the entire Cloud.

"I have the papers here," Bukha continued, "already bonded by Zergh in private and cross-registered through memory systems. Just remember that this is private, and if I win, the transfers will take place through an intricate series of holding companies as outlined in the contracts."

Corbin snatched up the papers and examined them briefly. They were straightforward and clearly bonded and registered. After removing a pen from his pocket, Corbin signed the papers then pressed his thumbprint down next to Bukha's and Zergh's. Taking the document, Corbin inserted it into the banking register of the computer, where it would be officially logged and become indisputable fact.

"Very good," Bukha said smoothly, "now I can sleep better." And without another word he strode from the room.

Corbin could feel a cold sweat breaking out. He had just laid well over half his total holdings on the line. But still, the thought of what he was about to win . . . With a wild laugh of delight he poured another drink.

In the distance he suddenly heard a number of Gafs break into cheers, but he already knew what had happened. The odds would shift downward again, the peak had been passed. So now the others knew, and he was already chuckling to himself since Bukha had taken the bet at higher odds, which even now were dropping.

Then the battle alarm sounded. So Alexander was

moving again. By this time tomorrow, Corbin gloated, he'd be the richest Human in history.

"The Taug!" Kubar struggled to make his way through the swirling host of cheering Gavarnians and up to the command post situated atop the crest.

He had met the lead elements of the army a half hour before. They were already withdrawing in good order down the road. There had been no sign of disorder or rout, it was simply that the warriors had started to disengage and withdraw. Why Alexander had not taken advantage was beyond him, and then he had heard the word that Hina was dying. Ordering that his strange baggage be unpacked and a fire to be built on the left flank, he pushed forward, rallying the troops as he went.

The guards by the command tent parted at his passage through their ranks, and the worried staff gathered around the bedside moved aside quietly as he approached the bed.

He could see that it was almost over, but at the sight of him Hina struggled to rise up on his elbows. As the blanket fell off him Kubar saw the scarlet bandage wrapped around Hina's chest.

"I knew you were not dead," Hina whispered. "I knew you'd come back to save us all. I'm sorry, sorry that I failed."

Why, why did they always look at him that way, even as they died because of him? And Kubar fought with his emotions. How many countless times had he come like this to the tent of a dying warrior, only to have an old comrade apologize for dying and leaving the task undone?

Kubar took Hina's hand.

"You did not fail," he said softly, looking into Hina's eyes. "I've seen what you've done. You've made them equals and you've made them proud. They'll win with your name on their lips."

"You are my Taug," Hina said, his voice starting to

slur. "Honor me by lighting the pyre. Tell me, O Taug, did I do my duty?"

"Yes," Kubar said, his voice breaking, "you did your duty well. Now go to sleep."

Suddenly Hina forced himself upright, as if struggling against an unseen force.

"He is the Taug, the one true Taug!" Hina cried. Desperately he fumbled for the small satchel about his neck, and a gentle smile crossed his face. His eyes shifted away as if gazing unto the face, or three faces, of those who had gone before him. He slumped forward into Kubar's arms and died.

Sobbing, Kubar held the body close, until finally unseen hands gently took the burden from him. For long moments he sat in silence until he finally became aware that there were others in the tent with him.

He stood and saw in their eyes the acknowledgment. They were united now—perhaps it had been his miraculous return, or that final cry of Hina's, but now they believed that he was who he had claimed all along. And he knew the word would spread; it was said that the last cry of one who was dying were always words of truth, for at such a moment the knowledge of the Unseen Light was so often revealed. It was not the placing of steel circlet that had anointed him, it was instead the cry of a dying friend that united the people under his command. He looked at Arn who stood outside the tent, and even he bowed his head.

"Paga!" And his second came up to him.

"You know how to prepare what it is that I made."

"But of course, remember I was with you when the great Ulseva made one."

"You'll use it then. I shall stay here in the center. The rest of you prepare for the assault. Our right flank shall open, then the center, and finally we commit our reserves after we see how the enemy is deployed."

He walked from the tent out into the dim light of the middle dimming; from down in the valley came a continual roar of conflict as thousands of skirmishers from both sides maneuvered for position.

He looked back over his shoulder at the mountain he had just come from. So now he understood why this war was happening, and his rage knew no bounds. And there was the darker memory just below the surface; the metallic image of the thing Wirgth had called a First Traveler. He had seen the servant machines on Zergh's ship, but they were small, innocuous. What he had seen in the passage beneath the Kolbard was no servant—it was a machine that was a master.

It had towered over him to twice his height, a thing of a hundred arms that snaked out in every direction, appearing and disappearing from hidden recesses within its body. Its form was covered with curving metal armor that shimmered in the starlight, having the vague outline of humanoid or Gavarnian form. The multitude of arms made him think of some mythical god that could strike at will in any and all directions.

It floated past, as if drifting upon unseen legs, smelling of oil and the sharp pungent odor after lightning has struck from the sky, and Wirgth had bowed at its passage. The First Traveler had taken no notice of them, as if they were beyond its realm or its caring. So those were the creators—things not of flesh. They had created the world for their amusement, but the war being fought upon it was not of their doing or concern.

Then Wirgth had told him what he knew of the gods who were of flesh, who at this very moment were watching them from above, for Wirgth knew the language of the First Travelers and they told him of all that they saw.

Kubar looked toward the east, to the mount the Humans had come to call Olympus, and he cursed silently.

CHAPTER 16

"MACEDONS, FORWARD!"

At last they were turning again to face him. Just the simple fact that the Gafs had a longer stride had been telling in the retreat, that and the organized cavalry that was pulled in to cover the withdrawing army. In order to cover what at first appeared to be a rout, the Gafs had pulled in their right flank, breaking off all contact with the Anvil and forcing Alexander to pull in, as well, to strengthen the center. But now they had turned, and after a brief flurry of orders he shifted his men out of columns and back into attack formation. Fortunately his massive reserve on his right flank was intact and not yet detected, concealed just on the other side of the slope. When the moment came, they would charge at the double and smash right through to the capital road, thus cutting all retreat.

All along the line the spears were leveled once again, and he pushed forward into the assault. The cloud of javelins had given him pause. It was a new tactic of the enemy, and if they had held for but another twenty paces before throwing, his ranks would have been over-whelmed by the sheer volume of heavy bolts. That more than anything else had caused him to pause for several hours as he reconsidered how to approach the Gafs and then communicate that information out to the phalanxes.

He had faced javelins against the army of Porus, but those were light things of bamboo, dangerous only to an unarmored man. But these Gafs were strong, and the spears had hit like an avalanche, punching right through the leather armor and wooden shields of his men. There was only one way around it, and that was to send a lighter line forward to lure the enemy into throwing early and quickly charge in with the main van before another volley could stop them.

And what of their commander who had been struck down? For a fleeting instant Alexander thought that he faced Kubar, but when the Gaf went down he could clearly hear the warriors crying the name of Hina. He could not help but think of Hina's sister, and he resolved that once the action was decided he would go to her personally and tell her what had happened.

But the most important question was where was Kubar? That thought was predominant in his mind.

All these doubts were wearing at him. However, there was no time now for such distractions—the battle was about to be joined, and he could not let other things cloud his judgment.

The Gaf army poured down the slope and again they broke into the strange formations he had noticed last time, a checkered pattern in units of a hundred. Curious, he thought, they would have no weight against a pha-lanx.

"Just hold the left, Parmenion. Simply hold the left and don't let them turn you."

Parmenion nodded and, with his staff falling in behind him, the overweight general galloped off. Damn him, that old one-eyed Macedon was as good as any of the original Companions.

The Gafs continued down the slope. He could see no hesitation, and the shrieking of their pipers was maddening as the enemy drew closer. They were not silent this time, their howls of rage and anger thundered over the field like a cataract. Something had happened to them to renew their spirits. Troops who had been retreating only hours before did not come in to an assault like this.

The pace of his own advance slowed, as up and down the line the men suddenly realized that this time they were facing Gafs who would stop at nothing, unless it was the razor point of a lowered spear.

The skirmishers started to pull back, but the Gafs held their javelins. All up and down the line the front ranks of the attacking host drew blades that shimmered in the pale light of the dimming.

Alexander positioned himself in the center of the line, directly behind the company of Ris, his own guard regiment.

"Brace your spears," Alexander roared. The men directly to his front heard the command, and kneeling down on one knee, they braced the butts of their spears into the ground and leaned back on the weapons in preparation for the shock of impact.

There could be no fancy tactics now, Alexander realized, he could only hope the line would hold. The Gafs up forward came on and broke into a full run while the checkered pattern of units behind suddenly slowed.

Even as the front ranks of the enemy line hit the picket wall of spears, a shadow arched up over the line. With a thundering impact, thousands of twenty-pound spears rained down on the line along a front of nearly half a kilometer. Seconds later a second shadow rose up, and then a third. It seemed as if thousands of Gafs and Humans disappeared in an exploding sea of blood. The enemy hacked through the openings carved by the javelins.

Now he could see why the Gafs used the small formations of a hundred. Wherever an opening had been cut

the Gaf unit would break out of the checkered formation
from the rear and rush to exploit the opening.

From behind his own line the hundred-odd field catapults slammed out a steady fire of two-meter-long spears
that slammed into the opposite slope, sometimes pinning
two or three warriors with a single bolt.

The Human line started to surge back a meter at a
time as the superior weight of the Gafs pushed doggedly
up the slope.

Alexander nodded to the signaler next to him, and
above the roar of battle half a dozen horns cut through
the cacophonous thunder while other signalers waved
the red flags atop the signal pennants carried by Alexander's side.

From the far side of the ridge, the second wave of five
thousand men appeared charging down the slope at the
double. The slowly retreating line was suddenly pushed
from the rear by the onset of ten more heavy regiments,
and the flow of battle started to reverse. The Gaf line
slowly started to fall back as thousands of men pushed
up over the mounds of dead and wounded who covered
the field.

The Gafs, as always, had the advantage of size and
weight, but the Humans still were better able to hold
formation and had the advantage of agility against their
larger foes.

The fighting raged across the bottom of the valley and
then slowly started to push up the Gaf slope. Another
wave of reinforcements came down from the Gaf center,
and as they hit the rear of the battle line, three more
clouds of spears arched up and into the Human line,
slamming the assault to a halt.

In the front, it was as if the pent-up hatred both sides
held for the other across three thousand years was finally
unleashed. Men whose spears had been smashed leaped
barehanded against their enemies, viciously stabbing
with the small daggers that most of them carried. Gafs
down on the ground and dying would still slash out, cut-

ting at anything in their way. In places the casualties piled up two and three deep. The fighting would pause for a moment while the warriors from both sides struggled to push the bodies aside so that they could get at their foes.

Nowhere was quarter asked or expected. It was a fight unparalleled in the history of the Kolbard. The slow minutes dragged by inexorably as the two sides remained locked in a bloody duel. Here and there the line would start to shift, suddenly stabilize, and then shift back yet again. All up and down the front Alexander rode at the rear of his men, watching in amazement as both sides drove at each other with a fury beyond his wildest nightmares. His Macedons had fought coldly, with a dark, fierce professionalism, but these men...They had suddenly learned what they could be if united, and they fought with a savagery he did not imagine was in them. But still the Gafs held.

He had to push this assault, and he nodded to his signalers and barked a command.

After several minutes a column of troops came over the slope from the left flank and deployed down the line. He had committed his reserve to the left, but his main knockout punch was still intact on the right. But that he would not commit until they had gained the top of the slope, to see the deployment of the rest of the Gaf army.

With the additional weight thrown in, the Gaf line started to buckle dangerously in the center, while the left and right flanks still held. The center of the line surged forward. The crest was only half an arrow's flight away, and suddenly the assault stopped up and down the line as a wild cry of panic filled the air.

"Release the hold-downs."

The Gavarnian warriors were awestruck, but since their Taug showed no fear, but rather a look of delight, they fought with their own emotions and said nothing.

"Just write it down and drop the messages," Kubar roared as Paga slowly lifted up beside him.

He stepped back from the crackling heat of the fire, and Paga quickly scurried up the rope ladder and alighted on the dangling makeshift basket.

The hot-air balloon lifted slowly into the sky. Fearful that panic might seize his own army, Kubar made it a point to climb up onto the makeshift command platform next to the moorings so that all up and down the line his warriors could see that he stood beneath the fearful object without hesitation.

The balloon continued its rapid ascent, while the ground crew played out the lengths of guide rope that prevented the silken bubble from floating away with the wind.

Paga felt as if his stomach were dropping away, to be left on the ground. For a moment he thought the contents of his last meal was begging for release, but such a thing would be a disgrace, so he fought the urge until it passed.

The battle was raging just on the other side of the ridge, and already a light stream of catapult bolts came skimming over the top of the hill to hit into the concealed formations waiting to be sent forward. Looking down the length of his own line, he could see the massive column of reserves deployed to the center.

The ridgeline dropped away and suddenly the entire panorama of the battle was beneath him. But even as he looked down upon them, the sound of strife changed in its tone. The Human formations looked like a long coiling snake that undulated slowly down its verst-long length. The balloon was starting to slow in its ascent. Kubar had explained to Paga how it would ride up on the column of smoke from the fire but as the smoke cooled the balloon's ascent would slowly be checked, and then it would start to come down again.

He strained for a view over the opposite ridge. In the far distance he could clearly see the ore carrier atop its high hill. But closer up, the next valley over was still blocked from view.

There, he could see something! Even above the cries down below he could hear them from the opposite slope. The balloon shifted and jolted with the wind but he barely noticed it as he grabbed hold of the rope ladder that curved up the balloon's side. He tried to scurry up it, but the giant bag of silk started to roll with the shifting of his weight.

The opposite ridge dropped away. They were all on the right! Alexander had stripped his reserves from his own left in order to reinforce the center! Their right was extremely powerful, but the left—there was next to nothing there!

Picking up a piece of charcoal, Paga quickly sketched a map showing the deployment of Alexander's line. After tying it to a rock, he looked down to the ground over thirty meters below him.

Even as he had worked, the balloon had reached its maximum height and was already starting to descend. But there was no time to wait. He spotted where Kubar was standing and tossed the rock in his direction. His task completed, he turned his attention back to the fight.

It had all changed! The Humans were starting to break! For a moment he was confused, since there was no visible reason why such a thing should happen. Not when they had only moments before been pushing the Gaf line back.

And then he understood. The eyes of a nearly hundred thousand beings had been turned to him. For half, it was a symbol of the strange power of their Taug, and they had taken hope and courage from that. But for the other half, it must appear to have been a new weapon of terror, and their fear had cut the courage from their bodies.

There was a wild shout to his right, and pouring downward like a freshet burst from its dam, twenty thousand Gafs started their charge—driving straight toward the enemy right—and Kubar rode at their head.

"Hold them, you've got to hold them!" Alexander screamed, but even as he shouted a wave of fugitives swept past him, taking half the command staff along with them in a wild panic-stricken run.

Reining Bucephalas around, he galloped up the hill, riding just ahead of the panic-stricken army. From his left flank he could see a knot of horsemen approaching —it was Parmenion and his staff.

Reaching the crest of the hill, he turned quickly to survey the field of strife. Half his army was on the run, casting aside their cumbersome spears, crying in panic as the Gaf host bore down relentlessly. There was no chance to rally the shattered line; men ran past him blindly, as if he did not exist. He had harbored a hope that by standing alone, exposed on the ridgeline, his shattered regiments would see his example and rally. But these were not veterans of a dozen campaigns, and they ran past with unseeing eyes.

Parmenion came galloping up, and Alexander could see the fear in his eyes, as well.

"What in the name of the gods was that?" Parmenion cried, pointing back to the opposite ridgeline where the balloon was slowly sinking from view.

"There was a Gaf riding it," Alexander shouted. "It was some device to see where our own troops were hidden. If only Aristotle were here."

But he was not, Alexander realized. Even the location of his dust had already been forgotten for five thousand years.

"Commit the reserves," Parmenion screamed, "you've got to commit the reserves!"

Alexander looked to his right. The twenty thousand men were still in formation. He knew that he was breaking an age-old rule of war, that one should never reinforce a failure. But he realized, as well, that if the men behind the ridge in reserve were ever turned around in retreat, they would not stop running. Already the Gaf assault was gaining the crest of the hill a league away. Within minutes they'd cut the road back to the ore carrier and the Anvil beyond. He'd have to meet it here and now.

"Parmenion, go to the right. Lead them in, try to strike that assault on the flank and smash it. Do you understand? Smash it!"

"Where are you going?" Parmenion cried.

"We still have the reserve cavalry regiment back at the command tent on the next ridge. The Ris and Kievant regiments might be rallied back there. Those men are tough, they'll know they need to stand! I'll try to hold the center till you come up. Now move!"

Parmenion looked into his commander's eyes and saw something there that drove a cold tingle of fear into his heart. Reaching over, he grabbed Alexander by the shoulders and hugged him close, then turning, he galloped back down the slope.

"We're driving them!" Arn roared. "Look at them run."

At the head of the advancing column Kubar and his staff crested the ridge. Before them they could see thousands of Humans running off in every direction. The entire enemy to the right had disintegrated, but that was only half the army. Looking down the length of the enemy line, he saw the dark masses of Alexander's reserves. There was a leakage of men from the rear of the line, but the sheer mass prevented those to the forward and in the middle from breaking. A column of horsemen were galloping down the length of the line, and as they passed, the men behind them started to ripple forward. The assault would be joined in a matter of minutes.

Kubar realized that if he could keep driving the broken enemy wing, they could cut right through to the outer edge of the Human fortifications. If they could reach the lines and punch through before the Humans had a chance to rally, the war would be won. He was torn. Should he turn and meet the Humans on his left or push on? There was the chance of a partial victory in smashing the reserves, or pushing straight in, exposing his flank by taking the ore carrier back and thus cutting off all hope of retreat. Directly ahead, not a verst away, a thin line of infantry backed by all the Human cavalry was forming up as a blocking force to phalanx formations that were advancing forward. A line of cavalry was deploying next to what he assumed was the command tent. Alexander had to be there, he had to reach Alexander!

"Forward!"

"But, Kubar, that flanking force!"

"We've got to hold them here," Alexander cried, "until the flanking force can close in."

The single regiment of cavalry swung into attack formation, flanking either side of the two exhausted phalanxes.

"They're still in column," Alexander roared. "Hit them at the head of the column and slow them up. We can still win this if Parmenion hits them hard enough in the flank!"

Looking over his shoulder, he saw the second regiment of cavalry swinging into position on the left flank.

His staff crowded around the command tent, snatching up the rolls of paperwork that followed behind any army and working frantically to load them into a cart, so that the information could be taken to safety.

He saw Yaroslav pushing his way through the disorganized troops still streaming to the rear, holding Neva by his side. Through the swirling crowd of men, Alexander pushed up to their side.

Neva was looking up at him silently, while Yaroslav held her arms by her side, as if to restrain her from doing something foolish.

"Everything's all right now," Yaroslav yelled.

It was a strange way of putting it, but there was no

time now. With a nod of farewell Alexander turned and started back to the front.

The enemy column was spreading out, deploying from column into line of attack. It was the moment when an army is at its weakest, when it is changing a formation, knocked off balance, and there could be hope, some precious minutes till Parmenion came up.

"Faster!" Alexander screamed. The foot regiments were left behind as the cavalry slowly picked up speed. But were they really moving faster? He felt as if it were all going far too slow, as if time were winding down, with each heartbeat passing twice again as slow as the last.

There was the Taug—yes, it was he, riding to the forward of the column. At last, at last the dream of a lifetime would be played out against desperate odds. He was somewhat to the right, and Alexander started to shift himself in the direction of the Taug even as he charged forward.

They were going to catch the column in midturn. Some of the Gafs, in their eagerness to engage, broke from the ranks and came charging individually down the hill, shouting their family chants. The first javelins arched up, then more, and finally a virtual blizzard of iron and wood lifted into the sky. Alexander held his shield up high. A shaft slammed into it, hanging fast, and he cast it aside. He dropped his spear low and braced for the impact.

The line of horsemen crashed into the enemy line.

Screaming with terror and pain, hundreds of horses went down, caught by the javelins or the Gaf swords. But their sheer size alone devastated the front of the enemy line. Alexander suddenly felt Bucephalas give way, rolling over onto his side. Leaping from the saddle, Alexander crashed into the side of a Gaf, knocking him off balance. Coming in low, he drove his spear clear through the enemy's body, dropping the warrior to the ground.

All around him was a nightmare confusion of scream-

ing Humans, terrified horses, and enraged Gafs pushing
forward into the line of death. Men and Gafs fell over
each other in the confusion. None could pick his target
as the battle line heaved back and forth, as if the thousands engaged had suddenly become a single living serpent, twisting and coiling upon the ground.

Alexander could see him. The Taug was not a dozen
paces away.

"Kubar!" Alexander roared, and he struggled to meet
the one who he knew was an alien mirror of himself. He
felt as if he were pushing forward against a flood. Everything seemed to be locked in slow motion; each thundering beat of his heart seemed to shake his body. But the
crush of bodies pushed him back and away, no matter
how desperately he struggled to reach the Gavarnian
commander, whom he knew did not see him.

He was fighting for his life now as he never imagined
possible. All around him, by the dozens, the Ris and
Kievant warriors were swept away. The defensive line
stumbled back, driven like a wood chip on the foaming
crest of a blood-red wave. But still they held.

Alexander stumbled, tripping on a body. An armor-
clad Gaf loomed above him, his sword raised high for the
killing blow. A spear suddenly drove through his chest,
sending the Gaf over backward, while eager hands
grasped at Alexander and pulled him back into the momentary safety of the phalanx line.

It was nearly impossible to think. The roar of battle
had become so loud and constant that it caused a sense
of deafness, as if there were no sound at all. A warrior
turned to him, trying to scream something, but he could
not hear the words. Then, as if in silence, the warrior
collapsed—his head smashed in by an enemy spear.

He noticed that they were at the crest of the hill, the
command tent was suddenly alongside him, the Human
warriors pulling in to surround this, the highest point of
land for their desperate stand.

A wave of javelins arced up, darkening the sun, and then came thundering down. There was no pain, only a ringing, stunning blow to his head, and he was down again.

Though he would not have believed it possible, the roar of battle increased yet again, so that he feared the very earth beneath him would split asunder from the sound.

A wave of Gafs surged over him, and then seconds later was pushed back. Desperately Alexander tried to regain his footing.

Several warriors gathered around, screaming hysterically, but he could not hear their words. And he feared that either he was going mad or that the blow to his head had destroyed his ability to hear.

He looked at them uncomprehendingly. The warriors dragged him to his feet and pointed, yet still he did not understand. They dragged him back toward the tent, where, to his amazement, he saw Bucephalas streaming blood from half a dozen wounds, yet still alive. How he had managed to get through the action and, as if by instinct, return to the command tent was beyond Alexander's understanding. He was so overcome that for the moment he broke and started to weep.

The warriors pushed him over and grabbed hold of his body, helping him back into the saddle. He looked down into their faces, and as if for the first time realized that most of them were still just boys, terrified, yet caught up in the wild delirium of battle. One of them handed him his sword, and then another shower of spears rained down, and most of them were swept away.

The knot of men around him had shrunk to just a small remnant of the once-proud phalanxes that had first marched with him so long ago. He saw a tall gangly youth, whom Parmenion had taken special delight in berating because the boy could not tell his left from his right, standing to the fore holding the dirty strip of cloth that was the standard of the Ris. In his right hand he held one of the massive scimitars of the Gafs and fought with the fury of despair, while clustered around him were a mere score of men—the last survivors of the regiment.

And now, at last, he saw why his men had been shouting to him and pointing off to the right. The sacrifice of the cavalry and the Ris and Kievant regiments had not been in vain. Parmenion's attack had come at last.

Along a front of nearly half a verst, they came at the double, their spears held low. The Gafs swung out to meet them. Their dark volley of javelins filled the air, and it seemed as if the entire front rank of men went down, but the army surged forward, climbing over the bodies of the fallen. And then the shock of battle hit as thousands came crashing together.

With that impact, the pressure on his own front suddenly stopped, as the Gaf army turned to face the new threat. He noticed now that the men around him were looking back over their shoulders, and turning, he saw to his amazement that the regiments which had broken earlier were starting to stream back into the fight. The majority of their men were missing, the weaker hearts having lost all stomach for the fight. But at least a dozen units, some with only fifty men, others with two or three hundred, were straggling back into the fight. His desperate stand had given them time to reform on the next ridgeline, and seeing that the battle was still not lost, they had come back in.

His gaze returned to the ground around him. It was carpeted with the dead and dying.

"My Macedons," Alexander whispered. He felt a warm trickle running down his face and absently he tried to brush it away. His hands were sticky and he looked at the blood, not sure if it was his or from someone that he had fought, for Gaf blood looked just the same.

Gavarnians. Where was Kubar? He must meet Kubar

and decide this thing once and for all. As if in a dream, he tried to urge Bucephalas forward. He suddenly felt as if he were riding up the side of a mountain toward a scorching sun of hot white fire that spun and spun before him . . . and then darkness came.

CHAPTER 17

THERE WAS SOMBER CONSTERNATION IN THE MONITOR-ing room. Entire empires were on the point of changing hands at this, the climax of the game. The scene displayed was one of absolute carnage. Estimates were that close to one-third of both armies were casualties. It was exhaustion, not victory, that finally ended the struggle; both sides collapsing on the ground that they held, not willing to withdraw from their hard-fought gains. In the end, neither side possessed the advantage; they had fought each other to a standstill there on the plains between the ore carrier and the Gaf capital.

There had been cold tension and silence in the gaming room as the desperate struggle finally wound down, if only for a brief rest, before the carnage began again. Both Gavarnian and Human Kohs had never expected this. No one had ever thought that this game would come to such a bloody final encounter, where neither side would finally admit defeat and graciously withdraw, thus ending the war.

For that matter, they had all expected that Alexander

or Kubar would be proven the superior general. But in the terms of Zola, who was an old racing fan, the battle was "a dead heat." Both armies, though fighting in different ways, were equally matched, and both generals were matched, as well.

It was now or never, Corbin realized. He had been in a near panic when he realized that the nerve agent most likely had not yet been introduced. It would be a simple thing, merely a drink, and within minutes a mild hallucinogenic agent would take effect, slowly reacting, distorting judgment and vision.

Merely a drink, that's all she had to do. Both armies had fought to a standstill, but all that was needed now was for Alexander to be struck down, and it would be over with. For, knowing Alexander, Corbin expected that the moment had come for the grand gesture.

The dimming had passed and the exhausted armies rose from their numbed sleep. Across the open fields fifty thousand Humans and Gafs slowly formed into ranks. From behind the lines came a steady nightmarish sound as thousands upon thousands of wounded cried in anguish while waiting for the attention of the healers. The dead were silent. Their only form of witness to what had happened was the sickly sweet smell that now rose with the heat of the sun.

Silently Alexander walked the length of his line, stopping to speak to the battle-shocked men; kneeling occasionally to hold the hand of a dying warrior or to comfort a hoplite pushed to the edge of reason by what he had seen and done only hours before.

"They're veterans now," Parmenion whispered, as they walked away from the four score of men who were all that were left of the once-proud Ris and Kievant regiments.

"But at what a price," Alexander replied. "They've been pushed to the edge—in fact, beyond it. These men aren't Macedons born to warfare, imbued with the glory of dying for me."

He spoke the last sentence with a tone of infinite sadness, and Parmenion was shocked to see tears in his commander's eyes. He had seen Alexander cry at the death of a friend, or horse, but this was somehow different.

Alexander turned toward his second and smiled. "Did you ever wonder why the gods have allowed all of this to happen?" And as he spoke his arms swept out, pointing across the field of battle.

"Which gods? Our gods, or the gods of this world?"

"Any of the gods, all of them. I'm sick of them all and curse them." He thought again of Darius and for the first time Alexander felt that at last he knew how that tragic king of the Persians must have felt—when abandoned, he turned his face to the sky and died.

"But I shall play my part for them all," Alexander said softly, looking at Parmenion.

"What do you mean, sire?"

But Alexander had turned away even as Parmenion spoke, and looked back at the exhausted assembled ranks.

"Do you think they see any glory in all of this?"

Parmenion turned and surveyed the warriors drawing up behind him.

He could remember so clearly the fields of another world. But the memory was not one clouded by drink in a tavern hall, while spinning tales that would bring another free mug or the attention of a wide-eyed girl. No, he could suddenly remember it as it had actually been. The crossing of the Issus, against the leveled spears of the Persian host. Or the taking of Tyre, and the boy, his nephew with an arm hacked off, bleeding to death while he fumbled blindly to somehow stop the torrent of blood. Or the smashing blow of a Bactrian arrow plunging half his world into night.

He could remember it all as he looked into the faces

of the men behind him, and the terror, the gut-tearing fear that would scream through his worst nightmares, returned.

Parmenion looked at his king, a man whose father he had first served and who he now had followed across two thousand leagues of Earth and then across the heavens themselves.

"They see the same glory in it that I now see," Parmenion replied. "It'll be the glory in a history book or in the tales of aging men before a warm fire. But you are Alexander the Great, and for you the world is different."

Alexander looked toward Yaroslav, who was now standing behind them. But the old philosopher could only smile and shake his head.

Alexander nodded and looked back at his soldiers smilingly.

"They've had enough," he said evenly. "This is my fight now. It's time that I became the actor upon the stage. Parmenion, send a herald over to the Gafs. Inform Kubar Taug that I shall meet him alone, upon foot in the valley between our two lines. There let the fight be decided once and for all."

"Sire, are you mad," Parmenion cried. "You're wounded already, it knocked you clean out. And that's a Gaf you'll be facing alone. We've managed to hold them, and you've said it time and again: we beat them by fighting together, but one to one we're doomed."

"Just do as I command," Alexander said with a strange and distant smile upon his features. "It shall be the plains of Ilium." He looked back toward Olympus and smiled.

"My lord Taug, don't accept. Not now!" Arn shouted. "We've backed them into a corner. One more assault and we have them."

"Have them for what?" Kubar responded. "A third of our army is down, do you want to spend another third to finish this? Think of the price, just think of it. Those

Humans over there have done nothing less than prove their worth. For a hundred lifetimes you and your nobles have hunted them with contempt, and finally they've stood up and shown us all that they have the courage of a Gavarnian in their blood. In my mind, it is already settled."

"What do you mean?"

But Kubar turned away from Arn and gazed at the single Human warrior before him.

"Tell your lord Alexander that I shall meet him."

"It'll soon be time," Yaroslav said softly.

"I know, but there is something I have to do first." And turning, he walked back up the slope to the command tent, which had been the scene of such bitter fighting only hours before.

After entering the tent, he went into the back chamber. He knew he should have sent her back to the ore carrier, but there was something in his heart that had told him not to.

Liala rose to her feet when he entered.

"I think you know what I am about to do," he said softly.

"I know, Iskander. You are like him and he is like you, therefore I know."

"I just wanted to say. . ." And he fell silent.

She drew closer to him. "It is your fate, O Taug of the Humans. You know my wish, of course, that Kubar should live. But still my heart breaks for you, as well. For if you win, you shall understand all that he now is. And yet if he wins, he will yet again feel what he never wanted to face, ever again.

"There is an old Gavarnian custom," she said softly, and turning, she reached for a goblet of wine resting on a table.

"I knew you would come to see me before this thing you must do. For a woman of my race to offer a drink to a male is an act that she may do only for her spouse, for the one she loves, or for her brothers. In some strange way I sense that even across our races you are like my brother and also in a way, like the one I love. So drink, Iskander."

He took the cup from her hand and raised it to his lips.

She smiled knowingly at him as he drained the goblet.

"Now, Iskander," she whispered, "no matter who wins, I shall mourn. For I have in a sense betrayed the honor of being a Gavarnian, by being the first to thus pledge myself to a Human."

"I've already made Parmenion and Yaroslav pledge that if this thing should go against us, you are to be released at once. Tell Kubar..."

And again he could not find the words.

"I think I know what I should tell him," she said quietly. "Now leave me, Iskander." Turning away, she covered her face and sobbed.

Alexander stepped back out into the glaring light of day.

"If I should die," Alexander said calmly to the men drawn up in front of him, "that is to be an end to it all. Hold the men in check, Parmenion, and under signal of truce meet with Kubar. Try for the best terms you can and then evacuate. Even if we lose here today, the shape of this world shall never be the same. The Humans will have the hills and, I daresay, no Gaf shall ever trespass there again. There'll be more wars, to be sure, in the future, but never again shall they treat us with contempt. Do you understand me?"

Alexander looked over at Yaroslav and smiled.

"I don't care what you say or think in this, but it will be to the death. The things you told me earlier this morning..." He fell silent.

"If only I had realized earlier what I had truly been facing. But that is past now, and I must face Kubar."

"It doesn't have to be," Yaroslav said evenly.

"But it must be, if only for my own honor and his.

That's what it has been about since the beginning. Thus it shall be ended here, once and for all."

"My lord."

Alexander turned and noticed Neva standing to one side. Guards on either side of her, as Yaroslav had ordered. Now was not the time, he did not want that type of scene before the assembled troops. Without another word he turned away from her, and her wild sobs filled the air until Yaroslav finally ordered her to be taken away.

For the first time since the game had started, Corbin felt a cold rush of fear. Suppose something should go wrong even now? But no, that was impossible. Only minutes before his personal paging implant had given three short beeps. She had finished her task for him at last; the agent had been administered and even now should be taking effect.

"They're doing it. They're actually doing it!" Zola screamed excitedly, pounding the armrests of his chair.

"Look, it's going to be a one on one."

Corbin's fears were forgotten as all eyes turned back to the battery of screens. The room grew quiet, as if any sound that they made might affect what was happening on the surface of the Kolbard a hundred leagues below. At maximum magnification the cameras planted on Olympus and on hovering drones zoomed in, while the remote and shield drones hovered directly above the field.

"If only Aldin and Zergh could see this," Yeshna said softly.

"They're being paid to monitor the equipment, not to watch a fight," Corbin replied coldly. "They're out there hovering above the playing area. Now shut up, they're closing in."

Kubar was already in the middle of the valley and he slowed his pace; in his right hand was one of the throw-

ing spears, and a similar weapon, taken from a dead Gavarnian, was in the hands of Alexander.

The two of them stopped, not a dozen paces separating them.

"At last we meet each other, Kubar Taug," Alexander
said, the speech of the Gafs coming with difficulty.

All the Humans were small to Kubar, but even in the
stature of Humans, this one was smaller still. But that
was merely in physical size. Here at last was his Human
equivalent, the one who if he had lived long enough back
on Earth would have united all their western world two
thousand years before it actually did unite.

"I can somehow sense that you understand what is
happening now, as well."

Alexander nodded sadly in reply.

"Can you see no other way then?" Kubar asked.

"No, there is no other way—it must be to the death.
For your people and mine have suffered too long against
each other, and we are the blood debt, in spite of what
others think or do concerning this. Yesterday ten thousand died at our command, and now one of us will die at
their command."

"My people have a belief," Kubar replied, "that in
war one must seek out an opponent who will make one's
death worthy. We have found that with each other, Iskander.

"Then to the death?"

Alexander nodded. He hefted the spear in his hand
and Kubar responded in kind.

Not a sound was heard; the last snatches of idle chat-
ter died away. The two toylike images circled on the
screen.

The Human feigned a rush, Kubar swung back bringing his shield in low while holding his spear high. Alexander backed up.

Again Alexander came in low, and Kubar jumped to

one side, slashing out with the point of his spear. They backed off again.

Suddenly the Xsarn turned in its chair and started to punch up a stream of data on one of the side boards. The Kohs ignored it. To turn away for a second might mean the missing of the kill.

"Ah, gentlemen," the Xsarn shouted, "there's a problem."

The others roared for it to be quiet.

"Gentlemen, it's Aldin calling in, there's a problem!"

The monitor screens started to flicker, and like sports watchers throughout history who were interrupted during the climax of the game, the Kohs reacted with near hysteria.

But their shouts were drowned out by a warning alarm, and the screens suddenly flicked off, to be replaced with Aldin's image.

"This is a warning, this is a warning," Aldin was shouting, "an Overseer patrol is closing in on approach three seven oh two. I think—"

His words were cut off as the Overseer vessel started to jam.

"The battle!" Corbin screamed. "We've still got time. The battle, damn it!"

The monitors showed only static. The room was a scene of wild pandemonium as some of the Kohs were already rushing to the exits for their personal vessels, while others screamed at the Xsarn to pull the signal from the drone monitors back in.

All six appendages of the Xsarn were working furiously punching up the different control boards and bypass channels.

"I can't get it, the Overseers are jamming it. Just a minute, just a minute, it's opening up."

A picture suddenly snapped into soft focus. Alexander was down on one knee, and all in the room froze. Kubar was standing back, his spear raised on high for the killing blow.

The spear snapped from his hand and Alexander fell to the ground, his shield upraised. The spear drove right through the metal.

A wild cheer went up from the Gafs in spite of their other concern. But no, the Human was still alive, as he cast his shattered shield aside.

Drawing his scimitar, Kubar rushed in for the kill. Alexander rolled to one side and came up, his own spear braced low.

The two came together and for a moment it seemed as if the image had frozen, the Gaf and Human commanders locked together in a deadly embrace.

Kubar rose up to his full height and stepped backward. A cry went up from the assembled Kohs.

Ever so slowly the Gavarnian chieftain crumpled to his knees, clutching the spear that was driven into his chest. He rolled to one side and then was still.

The camera swung up and panned across the field— the Gaf army was breaking, running. The camera quickly swung to the other side, and as if moved by a single hand, the entire Human army came sweeping down the hill waving their weapons on high. Alexander had won.

The image suddenly distorted. For several seconds Aldin's picture filled the screen, but there was no sound and then it snapped to another image.

Overseer!

The only thing visible was his head, and most of that was cloaked by a veil. But the disquieting array of eyes and breathing apertures was still enough to fill the Humans and Gafs with terror.

"This is an Overseer patrol," the voice said quietly, as if admonishing a wayward child. "We've suspected for some time that there was an illegal interaction with primitives in progress. Your foolish efforts to conceal the economic disruptions caused by this game were soon traced by our agents. All of you will stay exactly where you are. Boarding shall occur shortly. All assets involved will be confiscated and organizers shall be sent to reeducation sessions.

"This is an Overseer patrol . . ."

The Xsarn snapped the screen off.

"I declare the game as finished," the Xsarn roared, spraying everyone with the contents of its last three meals. "Decision to Alexander. All bets are logged in my personal computer. Let's get the hell out of here!"

"What!" Corbin screamed hysterically. "This is impossible. It's damned impossible, Alexander was losing!"

The others ignored him in their wild panic to get away. Chairs were upset, bottles of brandy spilled, and burning cigars dumped on the pile carpeting as the high nobles of the Cloud rushed for the single exit. All of them were screaming into their communicators calling for the servobots aboard their personal vessels to power up for an evasive jump out.

"If you don't get out of here now," Sigma yelled, "they'll have you for reeducation!"

His sense of survival finally took hold, and Corbin followed his rival out the door. There was no way that he could possibly get the massive pleasure yacht undocked from the tower in time, but he could still punch out through his personal life vessel and abandon the yacht to the Overseers. Of course, they'd know it was his and eventually they'd catch up, but in the meantime he could get his legal people working on it and come up with the necessary alibis.

Turning the corner to his escape craft, he saw Tia standing by the entryway.

"Not enough room, girl. It only takes two, and Regina's one of them," Corbin roared.

"That's why I smashed the control panel," she said coldly. "I knew, dear uncle, that you'd leave me behind, so I figured I could use some company."

"You damned bitch!" he roared, and pushing up the access hatch, he saw that she wasn't lying—the control panel was in ruins.

"I'll kill you for this!" he screamed.

"Cheating on the games is one thing," she shouted back, "but killing your mistress and third cousin, now how would you explain that to the Overseers? It'd be life in a reeducation camp."

With a wild roar he rushed past her into his private chamber. Seconds later he reemerged dragging a half-naked Regina behind him, her hair still in the perma-former, and the two of them disappeared up the next corridor.

Tia stood alone and listened as a series of vibrations rumbled through the ship as one after another the Kohs punched out to make good their escapes.

Several minutes later the vessel was quiet, the only sound the occasional whirring as a servobot rolled by picking up the refuse left by the fleeing Kohs.

The sound of footsteps approached from a side corridor and Sigma stepped into view.

"So he took your ship."

"At knifepoint, no less."

They looked at each other and smiled, as if this betrayal by Corbin was some sort of secret bond.

"Shall we go forward and see what's happened?" Sigma asked.

"Nothing else to do," Tia replied evenly, and together they returned back to the forward deck.

Returning to the empty room, Sigma walked over to the sideboard and pulled out a fresh bottle of brandy.

"No, not brandy, let's have some Mium Champagne for a change."

"Ah, but that's Corbin's private stock. He doesn't even share it with his brother Kohs."

"The hell with him, we deserve it after this."

Together they settled into the extra-large seat formerly occupied by the Xsarn, but not before a servobot had scrubbed the area down.

"Shall we take a look?"

Sigma leaned back and broke into near-hysterical

laughter. "It was precious, absolutely precious. Why, you and Aldin had that planned down right to his hijacking my ship!"

Tia smiled.

"Everything, just everything, you two set up was remarkable. That fake holotape of Alexander killing Kubar, the warning signals Aldin patched into the Xsarn's board, why, even that phony Overseer. By the way, where the hell did you get that?"

"I'll explain that twist later, it is an interesting story. That will teach that son of a bitch Corbin to offer me one percent and to cheat my uncle besides. With our split of the take from Corbin, I'll make forty times that amount."

Sigma looked over at his coconspirator and smiled.

"But anyhow," he said quickly, changing the subject, "it was simply marvelous. To think that Corbin felt he was cheating us and arranging the game right from the beginning, when in fact you and Aldin had him outfoxed at every turn. Did you see the panic in his eyes? By the heavens, I don't know if he was more distressed about losing his shirt or his fear of the Overseers. You stung that old bastard good and proper. It's a shame no one but you and I will ever know."

"Well, there are Aldin and Zergh, but they'll keep quiet."

"And there're two others, as well, who now know what the gods have been doing."

"Alexander and Kubar," Tia said, and Sigma could not help but notice a strange touch of emotion in the girl's voice. Something he had not expected from someone who was now one of the ten richest Kohs in the Cloud.

"They're still fighting down there," Sigma said quietly, as he leaned over and called up the genuine signal from the battle. The fake holotape had kicked in the moment the first one raised a weapon. "To those two, this is all on an entirely different level. It's not money for them, it's their lives, God help them."

Tia could not help but notice the sadness and guilt in his voice.

Exhaustion had drained both of them. The spears had been smashed long ago and now the two circled each other wearily, swords in hand.

Kubar fought to keep Alexander at a distance, hoping to bring him down with a wide sweeping blow, while Alexander fought to duck in under Kubar's guard for a finishing cut.

Not a word had been spoken between the two and each was locked in his own thoughts. For Kubar it was the memory of the Plains of Oler, where alone and with one blow of the sword the Unification Wars, and Cliarn's life, were ended.

Cliarn had been his own brother, so that even as he drove his blade home, he cut out of his own heart forever any hope for joy or happiness. Where was Cliarn now? The brother who in the end had fought against him for what he in his own wisdom believed was right—the preservation of the old order of nobility. Where was the shadow of the very brother he had slain in order to unite a world? Why had the Unseen Light exacted such a price from him? And in his weariness he looked at Alexander who wondered that same thought, even as Kubar raised his sword up high.

There was Darius, at last. The hunt across the high plateau, the hunt across the Issus and the plains of Guagamela come now to its end. There was Darius, the man whose own mother had turned away from her natural-born son to proclaim Alexander as the son she should have borne. There was Darius, whose own wife had come to Alexander's bed, willingly asking that he father a son that would be more worthy to be a king.

But no, they were dust. Five thousand years of dust behind him, and this was the Taug, and they were on the plains of Ilium. Was Hector watching? And what would

Achilles now say as they battled before the gaze of the gods?

The gods . . .

Kubar's sword came down—he ducked to one side, coming in low.

The opening, Kubar was open and Alexander looked into the eyes of Darius even as he cut in. His eyes . . .

Kubar staggered back, the sword dropping from his hand, numbed by the slashing blow that laid his side open.

The sword came back poised for the drive to the throat that would end it all. He could hear tens of thousands of voices rise up—some in triumph, some in pained fear—as the fate of all hung on the edge of a razor-sharp blade.

Where was Cliarn, was he laughing now? No, not Cliarn, not his beloved brother, he was weeping for the pain of his beloved brother about to die.

The eyes of Darius.

The sword pulled back further, as if coiling like a serpent ready to drive into flesh. And there it hung, suspended in time.

"Darius!"

The blade flashed but there was no cold searing, no flash of light that beckoned into the night.

Alexander drove his sword into the ground with such terrible force that the handle snapped from the blade.

He bent low for a moment as if gasping for breath, then Kubar realized that he was sobbing. The cries of all those around them died away to silence.

"It's finished," Alexander said, looking up. "I once said that only a king may kill a king. But I now say, as well, that only a king may spare a king."

Kubar looked at the Human before him. This one had reached at last the understanding of the Gavarnians, and at that moment Kubar suddenly understood the Humans, as well.

"The war then?" Kubar asked.

"Over."

"The terms?"

"The lands we now occupy are ours. That which you have is yours."

Kubar looked over Alexander's shoulder back to the ore carrier in the distance and Alexander turned to follow his gaze.

"That's the only supply of metal on this whole continent," Kubar said softly. "Do you plan to hold that, as well?"

"Your people did for two thousand years. But there's something called trade."

He could see the justice in it. "Tell me, Alexander, did you know about these gods who had created all of this?"

Alexander nodded. "No better than the gods of my own time. Those gods I had worshipped, wishing to be like them. But these..." He looked back toward Olympus. "Their messenger Aldin and his accomplice on this planet are in my camp right now. He told me all, just before I came to meet you. It seems my own mistress was set to poison me just before this fight, but Aldin stopped it, and then tricked the gods into believing that the poison had been administered.

"Somehow I don't think the gods involved in this will be all that amused."

"You Humans have a phrase: 'They can go screw themselves.' I like that."

Alexander smiled, looking at a king who he knew understood. Finally there was another who was his equal.

"We'll talk again," Alexander said quietly. "There are legends across five thousand years to be shared. Come to me tonight, there is someone there whom I hope you will find pleasure in meeting."

Turning away, they started back up from the valley to tell their people the war was over.

CHAPTER 18

"So you were in on it, as well?" Alexander asked.

Yaroslav shook his head, smiling. "Well, let's put it this way. I just so happened to have written a little paper on this ring-structure years ago when I was a teacher. Aldin and I go way back, back to when I even thought he'd wind up being a professor himself, before he got into this damnable vasba business. Aldin here's been planning this thing for years, and he made sure a copy of my paper got into Corbin's hands. Corbin took the hook, and Aldin snuck me out and dropped me off down here. Oh, it was good fun suddenly being an oracle and all that."

"But why didn't you say anything?"

"We knew that Corbin had managed to plant someone here with the intent of killing you, we simply couldn't risk it."

"Why not?" Kubar asked, leaning across the table. "Just bring it out in the open or, for that matter, settle it once and for all." As he spoke he looked accusingly at Zergh and Aldin who sat in the far corner of the room.

"Let's put it this way," Aldin responded. "Your two races were both locked in stagnation. The Humans were nothing more than lawless brigands degenerated to the lowest form, while the Gavarnians were atrophied by a feudal system that showed no possibility of ever ending. The synthesis of this war was the radical transformation of both societies. Granted, there was a price, but view it as payment on the future. Already, in just the last thirty days, trade has started between your two societies. And each of your races has learned respect for the other.

"Yaroslav was nothing more than a little insurance to make sure that, how shall I say, the Olympian gods did not interfere beyond setting this situation."

"But didn't you interfere?" Liala asked softly from the back of the room.

Aldin could only spread his hands and smile. "Would you have rather had our interference, or the nerve agent that Neva would have provided?"

Kubar could only shake his head. Granted, more than one Gaf would rather have had a total victory, the same as the Humans. Arn was still proving to be a problem. He would give Arn time.

"This Neva, whatever happened?"

"Did you kill her?" Paga asked. "After all, that would be only justice."

Alexander shrugged his shoulders. "Aldin dropped her off on the next continent beyond the wall."

"Humans are there?" Paga asked.

"Ah, yes, and you should see what they're fighting against," Aldin replied. "Lizard things that practice Human sacrifice! Now, if ever creatures needed stopping..."

Already Alexander and Kubar were looking toward each other.

"Marlowe," Yaroslav whispered.

Alexander turned to Yaroslav and smiled.

And even Kubar nodded in agreement as Yaroslav called for his parchment roll to be fetched from the command tent.

Then Aldin and Zergh rose to leave, and the two kings looked up at them.

"We'll never know all the reasons why," Alexander said softly, a trace of a smile on his lips. "Yaroslav told me enough the evening of the great battle. I do not hold a grudge toward the two of you or toward your gods, for if anything, you've given me life and an entire world to unite, and thus begin the dream again."

Kubar came up to Alexander's side and nodded silently as the two vasbas left the room. Aldin turned to look one last time—the two were already back at the table, gazing at the map spread before them. Liala had shifted around the table to stand behind the two, and Aldin noticed that her hand was in Kubar's.

Leaving the two kings behind, Aldin and Zergh started through the ore carrier toward the underground corridors that would lead to the docking bay on the outside of the Kolbard.

As they turned into the main corridor they ran into Parmenion, who was calling for someone to follow.

Even though he had been used to seeing the god-messengers, he still stepped back for a moment.

With a grumbled curse the old one-eyed warrior pushed on, and from around the corner behind him a slender female appeared.

"Who's that?" Aldin asked as the girl hurriedly slipped past him.

Parmenion stopped for a moment and a smile crossed his face. "I found her this morning over at the Avar camp. She's the daughter of their commander. Her name's Roxana. Can you imagine that? So I couldn't help but think a little introduction... Well, you know." Cursing softly, the overweight general pushed on.

"May your gods watch over you, Parmenion," Zergh called.

"Some gods." Parmenion snorted. "I'll put my trust in Alexander." And then he was gone.

Several hours later Aldin and Zergh finally reached the docking bay that Kubar had discovered in his long underground march. After punching in the security code, the ship's entry lock opened and the two clambered aboard. There were no signs of the First Travelers that Wirgth had reported. That in itself fascinated Aldin. It was something definitely worth looking into. After all, there were always interesting possibilities.

That was one point of the puzzle he still couldn't figure out. How did Wirgth know about them? Let alone be able to communicate with them and thus find out about the Kohs' locations and what they were up to.

He had asked Zergh, but his old friend was stumped, as well. In the end he could only suspect that though he had been playing an elaborate game within a game, perhaps Bukha Taug had been doing the same, even before he was pulled in at the last stage of the scam.

At least Corbin had been wiped out. They still had no idea where he was hiding—in fact, most of the Kohs had taken off to parts unknown. So now it was simply a question of getting control of his assets and then enjoying the comfortable retirement he had been planning for years. And this time there would be no worry about royalties.

Zergh finished with the access code and together they stepped into the main salon of the ship that had been their secret command post for the last stage of the game.

"Damn it, Aldin, will you please stash that dummy Overseer?" Zergh cried, stepping back from the three-meter-long android lying deactivated in the far corner of the ship.

"I kind of like it. You never know when we might need it again."

"Damn thing gives me the creeps."

"All right, all right." He called a series of commands, and the droid came to life and crawled through a hatchway into the aft storage area, whining all the time about not being treated with respect.

"So, you pulled it off," Zergh said, uncorking a bottle of Mium Champagne.

"Yeah, not bad. No one's caught on yet, they're still shaking in their boots, hiding from one end of the Cloud to the other. It will be a couple of years, at least, before anyone realizes that Tia has controlling interest in any of the corporations that changed hands. And I get control of half a hundred worlds in payoff. Finally I can retire."

"And you finally got even with that bastard Corbin."

"Yeah." Aldin leaned back in his chair inhaling deeply on one of Corbin's prized cigars.

Zergh started to punch in the exit commands to the ship's nav comp. "You serious about retiring?"

Aldin looked over at his old friend and smiled. "Just about the same as you are."

"You know, Sigma was talking about a little private arrangement."

"I'm all ears."

"Later, later." He typed in the activation command, and the ship dropped away from the bottom of the Kolbard, cutting a straight line out, as the dark underside of the structure filled the heavens above them.

Accelerating, they cleared the edge of the structure and the sun above them flooded the cabin with light. Several million kilometers in diameter, the Kolbard floated above them—a gleaming circle of blue green studded with white, floating in the vastness of black and endless night.

"What was that thing about Marlowe?" Zergh asked,

as he leaned back to admire the most spectacular view in the Cloud.

"Earth author—Marlowe." Aldin could not help but smile as Alexander and Kubar's ring floated above him.

"Bring me a map and let me see how much is left to conquer all the world."

ABOUT THE AUTHOR

William R. Forstchen, who makes his home in Oakland, Maine, was born in 1950. Educated by Benedictine monks, he considered the calling of the priesthood but decided instead to pursue a career in history. Completing his B.A. in education at Rider College, he went on to do graduate work in the field of counseling psychology.

William was a history teacher for eight years and currently devotes his time to writing, educational affairs, and the promotion of the peaceful exploration of space. William lives with his wife, Marilyn, their dog, Ilya Murometz, and Tanya the cat.

He recently led a group of fifty high school students to the Soviet Union which presented a resolution passed by the Maine State Legislature calling for a Soviet/American manned mission to Mars.

William's interests include iceboating, Hobie Cat racing, sailing, skiing, pinball machines, Zen philosophy, and participation in Civil War battle reenactments as a private in the 20th Maine Volunteer Infantry.